THE VILLAGE CAFÉ IN THE LOIRE

GILLIAN HARVEY

B
Boldwood

First published in Great Britain in 2025 by Boldwood Books Ltd.

Copyright © Gillian Harvey, 2025

Cover Design by Alice Moore Design

Cover Images: Shutterstock

The moral right of Gillian Harvey to be identified as the author of this work has been asserted in accordance with the Copyright, Designs and Patents Act 1988.

All rights reserved. No part of this book may be reproduced in any form or by any electronic or mechanical means, including information storage and retrieval systems, without written permission from the author, except for the use of brief quotations in a book review. This book is a work of fiction and, except in the case of historical fact, any resemblance to actual persons, living or dead, is purely coincidental.

Every effort has been made to obtain the necessary permissions with reference to copyright material, both illustrative and quoted. We apologise for any omissions in this respect and will be pleased to make the appropriate acknowledgements in any future edition.

A CIP catalogue record for this book is available from the British Library.

Paperback ISBN 978-1-80549-988-6

Large Print ISBN 978-1-80549-989-3

Hardback ISBN 978-1-80549-987-9

Ebook ISBN 978-1-80549-991-6

Kindle ISBN 978-1-80549-990-9

Audio CD ISBN 978-1-80549-982-4

MP3 CD ISBN 978-1-80549-983-1

Digital audio download ISBN 978-1-80549-985-5

This book is printed on certified sustainable paper. Boldwood Books is dedicated to putting sustainability at the heart of our business. For more information please visit https://www.boldwoodbooks.com/about-us/sustainability/

Boldwood Books Ltd, 23 Bowerdean Street, London, SW6 3TN

www.boldwoodbooks.com

for Vicky

1

Her reaction was physical, as if she'd been punched in the chest.

'I'm sorry,' she said, her head spinning slightly. 'What did you just say?'

'I'm recommending a month off work.' The doctor handed her a piece of paper.

'But... there's nothing wrong with me.'

The doctor rested her blue, serious eyes on Becky until she reluctantly raised her own to meet them. 'Rebecca,' she said. 'You have severe burnout.'

'What? Oh, come on! This is completely ridiculous! I don't have burnout. If anything, I'm thriving.' Becky brushed away some strands of hair that had escaped from her normally perfectly coiffed ponytail and tried to appear relaxed. 'Yes, I work hard. Yes, sometimes I get a little... stressed. But who doesn't? I'll take up yoga or something.'

The doctor resumed her steady gaze. She looked mid-thirties or thereabouts. Just a few years older than Becky. Probably charging Becky's firm hundreds an hour. 'Rebecca,' she said calmly, interlocking her fingers on her desk. 'You threw a laptop across the office.'

In the cold light of day, in this white painted office with its shiny tiles and bright lights, chucking a HP EliteBook did sound quite extreme. But Doctor Fuller didn't know what it was like to perform in the kind of fast-paced environment Becky had worked in for the past decade; didn't understand the stakes, the fact that tensions often ran high.

This wasn't a time for comparisons though. She needed damage limitation. 'Well,' she said carefully, 'yes, I did. But in my defence, I'd just come off a pretty frustrating call.'

'It says here, the laptop almost hit Stuart, the intern.' Doctor Fuller checked her notes, her forehead creasing.

Becky sighed. This again. 'Yes, but it didn't hit him, did it? Plus, you know... He's an intern – he was probably glad of the attention!' She looked at the doctor for a reciprocal eye roll and smile.

None were forthcoming.

'I'm not sure it's a laughing matter.' The doctor's brow furrowed with concern. 'Someone could have been hurt. Not to mention the matter of damaging company property. A lot of firms would have classed this as grounds for instant termination.'

The word 'termination' made Becky's heart lurch. She'd been trying not to think about how close she'd come to losing it all.

'Look, OK, I was stressed. But the call wasn't even about work. It was—'

'So it was a personal call?' The doctor made a note in her file.

'Oh. Well, not personal. An official call. It wasn't as if I was having a relationship drama or...'

'Do you often have relationship dramas?' The doctor's eyebrow raised slightly.

'No! I don't have relationship dramas! I don't even have a relationship! I haven't had sex since 2023. I... Not that that's relevant. I mean, I *could* have sex. If I wanted to. It's not that I never... I do have a sex drive. I'm just... I've been busy and...' she trailed off, sensing she was not onto a winner here.

'So, as I was saying. A month will...'

'OK, OK,' Becky said, sitting up straighter, fixing the doctor with what she hoped was a calm, thoughtful look. The look of a sane person who wasn't about to lose her cool. Someone who'd had a blip, but was far from having any sort of breakdown. 'I'll admit, it wasn't my finest hour. But you know, all's well that ends well. Come on, look at me. I'm fine.'

'Your eyelid appears to be twitching.'

Becky felt the familiar flicker in the corner of her right eye. Why? Why now? She put her finger against her eye. 'Well, that's never happened before,' she lied.

'And your leg has been trembling for the last five minutes.'

It was a bad habit. Whenever she was under pressure, Becky seemed to consign all her excess energy and adrenaline to her limbs. 'Oh, that!' she said, trying to laugh it off.

'Burnout can be serious, Becky. Living under that level of stress can—'

'Well... say I do have a little bit of – let's call it "excess stress",' said Becky making finger quotes. 'I'll deal with it. I'll get some therapy, start doing some stretches. Whatever. Can we move past it?'

The doctor shook her head. 'That's all very... admirable. But I'm going to insist on a proper leave of absence, say a month. Just to get your head straight. I'm signing you off.'

She was properly, properly serious. Becky felt her breathing quicken. 'No, listen. You've got this all wrong. I can't take a month off!' she said, realising her voice had somehow gone up an octave, and trying desperately to bring it back to normal levels.

'I think if you don't, you could become seriously ill,' the doctor said gravely. 'Think of it this way, Becky. A month off now could save you a few months off in the future if things continue down the same path.' Her earnest eyes were full of empathy. It made Becky want to scream. 'Also, you're on a final warning from HR over this. Better to make sure you're fully well in case something happens again?'

'Look, it won't, I swear,' Becky said desperately. 'I'll... look, I'll do anything. Want me to take up jogging? Meditation? Book a therapy session or two?'

'Well, yes, all of those things will undoubtedly be helpful. But I'm sorry, I'm still signing you off.' The doctor looked at her kindly. 'It would be unprofessional of me to—'

'Surely there's something we can do?' Becky asked desperately. 'I'm fine! I'll prove it!' She got to her feet, thoughts racing. 'Ask me anything about my job. Anything! I promise you I am nailing it!'

The doctor gave a sympathetic head tilt. 'Sit down, Becky,' she said, using the kind of weary voice a teacher might use with a wayward pupil.

Becky sat, chastened. 'It's just... there must be something I can do to convince you.'

'I'm so sorry. If it helps, I can see how committed you are to your job. It's admirable. But Becky, high-flying types like yourself, the way you *care* about your job... it just makes you more prone to burnout.'

'I promise I don't need time off though.'

'You'll thank me eventually.'

Becky felt a sudden urge to reach for the doctor's possessions – the cute family photo, the neat stack of folders, the laptop, a tiny plushie in the shape of a frog – and dramatically sweep them from the desk.

Instead, she clenched her fists, smiled thinly, got to her feet, picked up her bag and made her way to the door, past the rows and rows of diplomas and silver-framed photos of the doctor shaking hands with various important-looking people. I bet, she thought, nobody's ever forced *her* to have a month off.

Stepping out of the office into the waiting room, she saw Amber flicking through last month's *Good Housekeeping*, her head nodding as she took in whatever wisdom was being imparted. It was only when Becky stood right in front of her that her best friend raised her eyes, her expression turning from thoughtful to concerned. 'How did it go?' she asked, making a face.

'Not good.' Becky looked at the other patients in the waiting room. Just two – one reading a book on meditation, the other sitting, glancing at a phone screen from time to time. Nobody appeared to be listening in. Still, she inclined her head towards the exit and, understanding, Amber folded her magazine and stood up.

'They've signed me off,' she said as they waited for the lift, trying to keep her voice steady. She didn't want to cry, not before they were at least in the car. But it was going to be a close thing.

'Oh! Well, that's OK,' Amber said, putting a hand on Becky's back. 'You'll be OK. If I'm honest, I wouldn't mind a bit of time off myself! Did you know that Rufus—'

'It's *not* OK,' Becky said. 'Amber, they've signed me off for a *month!*'

'Wow. Long time.'

'Yeah. A month *is* a long time, with Stevie in the office.'

Stevie, graduate extraordinaire, had been snapping at Becky's heels for a while, clearly vying for a place on the management team. Now, there would be no holding her back.

They were silent for a moment. The lift slid into position and the doors opened. Thankfully it was empty. Becky avoided looking at herself in the mirrored wall, not wanting to see her no-doubt reddening eyes, instead turning to face the buttons and pressing the 'G' emphatically. Amber gave herself a brief once-over, tucking a strand of curly hair behind her ear. Her battle with her curls was constant; and she knew they would always win. But it didn't stop her trying.

'Come on,' Amber said, turning back to her once the lift started to descend. 'It could be fun. I mean, I know it's not ideal, career-wise.'

'The understatement of the year.'

'But once you... accept it... it'll do you good, Becks. God. Maybe I'll ditch *my* job. We can travel the world together. Relive our wild youth!'

Becky raised an amused eyebrow. 'Wild youth? What, staying out past eleven in the pub? Sneaking cigarettes in the park in our teens? The time we lied to our mums about having a sleepover and tried to get into a nightclub?'

'That's about the sum of it.'

They smiled at each other, momentarily transported back to being the teenage conspirators of fourteen years ago. But Becky's face soon fell again. She covered it with her hands and let out a groan. 'But seriously, it's just insane! I'm at the top of my game. Yes, I occasionally get a bit stressed. But you can hardly call it burnout.' She thought again of the office – its sleek windowed wall looking out over London, her wardrobe stuffed with designer work wear. The flat – the flat she'd set her heart on owning. All of these things required money, maintenance.

The Village Café in the Loire

Losing her job could literally lose her everything. Why had she taken the call at that moment? And why hadn't she held in her emotions? Or done something less dramatic and kicked over a wastepaper basket or something?

Amber remained silent as the doors slid open again. A man with a leather satchel over his shoulder stepped in before they could step out.

'Excuse *us*!' Becky said loudly, half-barging into the man with her shoulder as they passed.

'Becky!' Amber said as the doors slid closed behind them.

'What? He was rude. It's not good elevator etiquette!'

'Elevator etiquette?!'

'You know what I mean.'

They walked in tandem through the glass doors and out onto the street, turning the corner and walking towards the Tube. 'You know,' Amber said carefully as they approached the entrance, 'I have been worried about you.'

'About me?'

'Well, yeah. I'm not saying the doctor's right as such, but you have been... well, a bit stressed the last little while. Not yourself. Even that man just now. He was a prick, right? But you were... well. Rude.'

'You think?'

Amber nodded, tapping her Oyster card and entering the station. 'I do,' she answered at last. 'I'm sorry Becky, but maybe it's good you... reset. If you went back too soon... well. You might not have a job if something else happened.'

Minutes later they got onto a Tube and by some miracle, managed to find two seats next to each other. Amber looked at Becky as if weighing something up. 'I know you've got a lot on your plate. But... you know, maybe this is a good thing. Perhaps you're not in burnout yet. But you're getting there, hon.'

Becky shook her head vehemently. 'No. I've been stressed. But that's it. No more than you are most of the time these days.'

'Yes, well, Rufus is always—'

'What I'm saying is maybe that's normal for our early thirties. We're trying to get up the career ladder and it is stressful. It's meant to be stressful. It's just how it is. Do you know my mum didn't take a day off for a decade? Except for Dad's funeral. And even then, she was back at her desk within days.'

Amber nodded. 'Maybe,' she said.

Becky turned away slightly, shaken by thoughts of her father. What would he do if he were here? Give her one of his enormous Old Spice hugs, let her cry into the wool of his familiar jumper. And make her feel better somehow. Not adrift. Not a loser.

'But you know, you've always said you don't want to turn out like your mum?' Amber rubbed her left shoulder where her bag strap sat against her jacket.

'Still giving you gyp?'

'Yeah. I'll go to the physio eventually. Just... no time.'

Becky nodded. 'Anyway, you're right. I don't want to end up like Mum, not personality-wise. But her career trajectory...?'

'And her salary...' Amber said, raising an eyebrow. Both of them were on a good wage, but Cynthia's yearly pay cheque had at least seven figures.

'And she's got a great lifestyle now. But she didn't back then. That's what I mean. A bit of self-neglect is normal at our age.'

'It shouldn't be though, should it?'

'We're strong, independent women! We can take it.' Becky grinned.

Exiting the Tube, they made their way along the familiar streets, towards the apartment they shared, seeing shoppers, tourists, mums and dads with buggies; the people they never usually saw who populated the city centre during working hours. 'Thanks for taking the time off,' Becky said quietly.

'Of course.'

'You know the worst thing about it?'

'What? Telling your mum?'

'Yeah – trying not to think about that yet,' Becky grimaced. 'No, it's the fact that the call... you know, the one that tipped me over the edge?'

'The one that put paid to the poor laptop?'

'Yeah. That one. It wasn't even a work call. It was about the bloody café.'

'I know. Typical, eh?'

The café had dominated their conversations for the last few months since Becky had received a letter out of the blue to say that her great-aunt had left her the café she'd owned in the Loire region of France. Becky had immediately decided to sell, assuming it would be straightforward. But nothing seemed to be going to plan. Information was sparse, phone calls were confusing. Emails were difficult to understand even with an online translation app. Then, just when she was hoping she'd made progress, she'd been told, as if it were an afterthought, that there was *'un locataire en place'* – a tenant who refused to shift.

'I know. I mean they barely contact me for three months, then casually leave a message telling me there's a sitting tenant so if I do want to sell, I'll take a big hit on the price.'

Yes, perhaps she'd been foolish to rush into signing up for the London flat she'd seen. But in her defence, she was currently throwing away £1,500 a month in rental and the flat she'd earmarked was bloody gorgeous. She'd paid a reservation fee there and then, assuming she'd be able to sell the café and would get the money in time to pay the deposit. Now she'd passed the deadline and despite negotiating an extension, it was looking less and less likely she'd be able to complete in time.

Surely anyone in that situation would be tempted to chuck something across a room?

'And you told the doc it was a personal matter that made you feel... frustrated?' Amber asked.

'Burnout is burnout apparently. And I reckon she probably just thinks of me as some entitled rich girl now, too.'

'To be fair, you *are* an entitled rich girl. At least compared to some.'

Becky gave her friend a little shove. 'Hardly!'

'*Oh, I inherited a café in a French village from a distant great-aunt. And I want to buy a really posh flat for myself with the money. But I can't sell it and release thousands of euros because there's a sitting tenant!*' Amber teased, putting on a posh voice.

'Amber!' Becky laughed. 'If anything, it's a poisoned chalice. Mum said Great-Aunt Maud used to be a bit manipulative. Reckons I should just sell it as is and take the hit.'

'That does NOT sound like your mum.'

'I know. She's all for squeezing every last penny out of investments, usually.'

'But maybe you should?'

Becky shook her head. 'No. I'm not a quitter. I'll get rid of that stupid tenant.'

'If anyone can, you can.' Amber unlocked the front door and they both walked instinctively to the kitchen where Becky got out some mugs as Amber boiled the kettle. 'You know I wanted to talk to you about my work, if you've got a—'

'Do you mind if we save it? I don't think I can face talking about work stuff right now.' Becky made a face. 'I've got to call Mum yet, and she is going to go insane.'

Amber nodded, filling the cups. 'Sure. Later maybe?'

'OK. And film night?'

'Definitely.'

It had become a tradition a few years ago: Thursday nights were old movie nights where they'd slip a favourite, battered DVD from a sleeve and rewatch. The DVDs had been theirs since their teens and were for the most part romcoms of the sort they'd never admit to watching. Using the DVDs despite their ability to stream almost anything was part of the tradition – the cases and their contents were as comforting as old friends.

'Jerry Maguire?'

'You mean the film about a guy who's fired? Who flips out in the office and has a breakdown?'

'Ah. Yeah. Maybe not this time.'

'Four Weddings?'

'Sounds splendid!' Becky said, putting on a posh English accent in place of her usual sub-posh Hertfordshire one.

'Yes, I agree, splendid.'

'Well, then, splendid!'

'Splendid.'

Becky took her mug into her bedroom and slumped on her bed, scrolling through her phone. Six months ago, she'd felt on top of the world. Now she was signed off work, had an eye that had taken on a life of its own, and hadn't slept properly for as long as she could remember. It was amazing how quickly things could change. Sighing, she found her mother in her contacts and pressed *Call*.

'Mum? Yeah, I've got something to tell you.'

2

Her mother's voice was as artificially gushing as always on answering. She must have been in earshot of some colleagues. 'Hello, darling!'

'Hi, Mum.'

'Just a moment, I just need to step back into my office. Right.' There was the click of heels, then the creak of leather as her mum sank into her expensive seat. 'So, how did it go? I hope you told that silly doctor what nonsense it all was. Sending you to a psychiatrist indeed.'

'She was more of a workplace specialist.'

'Well, whatever. Load of opportunists, if you ask me. Stress is what drives us! And that laptop wasn't even a decent model. Probably did it good to chuck it against the wall.'

Becky laughed in spite of herself. 'Mum! It was a top of the range – probably cost a couple of thousand. And it's totally ruined.'

There was a snort. 'Complete waste of time and money,' her mum said, although Becky wasn't sure whether she was talking about the PC or the appointment.

She took a breath. 'Well, the doctor seems to think I'm approaching burnout,' she said, scrunching up her face as if to ward off a blow. She held the handset a little distance from her ear.

'Burnout? Whatever's that?' Her mum's voice sounded outraged, as if the doctor had invented a new illness just to mess with her. 'Absolute codswallop.'

'It's... well, being so stressed that your body sort of gives up,' Becky explained. 'And honestly I don't think—'

'Of all the nonsense, Rebecca! I've never heard of anything so silly! All this modern woke terminology.'

'Mum! It's an established medical condition!' Becky had googled it before the call to ensure she was completely informed. 'And I mean, I've known people who've got really ill with it. But—'

'Claptrap.'

'Richard Branson had it? Hillary Clinton?'

'Yes, but darling, these are CEOs, presidential candidates! You work in advertising. It's not... well, quite the same.'

'It's very stressful at work though, Mum. We're working on a—'

'Oh, pish posh!'

Becky's mum had a habit of using outdated but non-offensive expletives that usually secretly tickled her. She'd often repeat them to Amber later on. In her current state, she was less than amused, but still chalked 'pish posh' to her in-brain memo board to use on Amber at a future date.

'Well, you're not burnt out! The very idea! A hard-working young woman like you.'

'That's what I've been trying to say. I don't agree.' Becky drummed her fingers on her bedside table. She was not looking forward to telling Mum the next bit. 'It's just... she was adamant that I take some time off.'

She'd done it. She'd delivered the blow. Now for the fallout.

There was a brief pause, and Becky could almost hear her mother's nostrils flaring down the line. 'Horse feathers! Time off indeed! I take it you told her you're the account manager for Tudors?'

'Yes. Of course.' Securing an account for the hotel chain had been her biggest achievement thus far and, Becky silently suspected, the first career win she'd had that Mum had actually been impressed by.

'Well! Did you remind her that they're the largest boutique hotel chain in the region? You are needed!'

'Mum, she's a doctor. I'm hardly going to argue with her. Not when I'm in there for... getting a bit angry in the office. I did try to explain but she was adamant.'

'I suppose you told her the call you'd been on was about that ridiculous café.'

'Yes, of course!'

Her mum harrumphed. 'Maud has a lot to answer for, leaving you that... that sugar-coated Trojan horse.'

'Mum, come on! Maud isn't trying to derail my career from beyond the grave. It's not her fault I got signed off.'

'So the time off isn't just a suggestion?' Her mother's voice went up an octave in alarm. 'You let her sign you off? Oh, Rebecca. That's going to be on your work record.'

'I didn't *let* her. It wasn't up to me. And anyway, work can't discriminate against—'

'Well, OK. Take a breath, darling. It's a disaster, but we can get you back on track. Don't panic. We'll get through this like we get through everything. By hard work and determination.

Pushing through. Give your boss a call, remonstrate. I'm sure she—'

'They're the ones who employed the doctor. They're hardly going to get her to rescind a medical note, Mum.' Becky massaged her forehead, reminding herself that she'd actually considered most of these strategies herself and that her mum only had her best interests at heart.

A silence.

'Well, how long do they think you need? A week?'

'Two weeks,' Becky lied. She would build up to the month in later conversations, once her mum had digested the idea. Anything else would be far too exhausting.

'Two weeks! Balderdash!' Becky had already moved the receiver away from her ear in readiness, so luckily didn't suffer a burst eardrum. But it was pretty clear that Mum wasn't happy.

'Yes. Look, Mum, I know how extreme this must seem to you. It does to me really, but it is what it is. I can maybe do some training, meet up with some contacts for a friendly coffee. It doesn't have to be a wasted fortnight.'

'No. Well, I just hope that company appreciates the hard work you've put in so far, enough to overlook this… unfortunate situation. It's hard work climbing the career ladder as a woman, Rebecca, I've drummed it into you enough. Let alone allowing emotions to rule the day. We've got to be harder, stronger, better than every man in the building, just to get our dues.'

Mum launched into one of her habitual speeches on the patriarchy – more familiar to Becky's childhood than fairytales or kids' TV. The best thing to do was to let it run its course.

'OK,' Becky said at the end. 'Anyway, that's where we are. And you know I haven't been feeling great. Perhaps I have let my mental health—'

'Mental health? You don't have mental health!'

'Mum. I just mean I need to look after—'

'Enough. You're beginning to sound like mad Maud.'

'Mum. That's not very nice...' But it was no use. Now she was getting the story of Mum's aunt who embraced all things 'new age', had dropped her job as a top lawyer and disappeared to live a life of reckless freedom. A story Becky had heard many, many times.

Ten minutes later, Becky ended the call with a promise that she'd look into whether it would be possible to get a second opinion.

Lying back on the bed, she wondered whether everyone felt so depleted after speaking to their mothers. But then again, not everyone's mother was Cynthia Thorne, CEO of Thorne Asset Management – the original hard-hitting career woman who stood for no nonsense and took no prisoners. Mum had worked her way up from rather lowly beginnings to CEO of a FTSE 100 company, bearing her share of knock-backs and setbacks over the years, and had always assumed Becky would follow in her footsteps.

The minute Becky had left university, she'd helped her write a five-year plan, finessing it each year so that Becky knew at any one moment what she was meant to be doing and the impact it was likely to have on her life.

Burnout was not on the plan.

Becky and Amber would laugh a little at Cynthia's pushiness sometimes; but Becky knew deep down that without her mother's support and borderline pressure, she'd probably still be working as a junior, rather than a director.

'She's forceful. It's what makes her who she is,' her dad had told Becky once, and she hadn't been sure whether he'd meant for better or worse. Mum was brilliant, but she also expected brilliance of those around her, meaning Becky got the best education shoehorned into her, whether she liked it or not, had her career mapped out by the time she left for university, and had had to get used to a mum who asked her how her job was going before she enquired after her health. After Dad had died unexpectedly fifteen years ago, if anything, it had become more intense – Mum and her ambition had become one entity.

Mostly, Becky was grateful. She saw how some of her contemporaries were faring on the job market and felt proud of how far she'd already come. But sometimes – just sometimes – it would be nice to have a mum who would be concerned about a daughter's potential burnout and come around with a flask of chicken soup and an even deeper well of sympathy.

There was a tentative knock on her bedroom door. Amber stuck her head around and grimaced. 'Everything OK?' she asked.

'Yeah. Job's done.' Becky sat up and smiled at her friend.

'How did she take it?'

'About as well as you'd expect.'

'That bad, eh!' Amber moved over to the bed and sat down next to her friend, wrapping an arm around her. 'Well, remember, she does love you. It's just her way of showing concern.'

'So I keep telling myself!'

Amber shrugged. 'It's not always great the other way, either. I mean, my mum worries about me so much I daren't always tell her everything, just to keep her from getting anxious.'

'Ah, I know. Your poor mum. What do you think she'd do if you got signed off for burnout?'

'You mean, if I dared tell her about it?'

'Yeah.'

'Probably force me to move back home, sleep in my childhood bedroom and eat hearty soups until she felt I was back to full health. Which, knowing Mum, would take about two years.'

'That actually sounds quite nice.'

'That's because you've never tasted one of my mum's soups!'

'Anyway, I think I need to take my mind off it all,' Becky said. 'Distract me. What were you going to tell me earlier?'

'It's just a work—'

'That reminds me! I have to write an email to work – promised Mum. Doubt it'll do any good but worth a shot. Do you want to watch the film after?'

Amber nodded. 'OK. Well, good luck.'

'Thanks. Think I'm going to need it.'

3

In the end, after a restless and wakeful night, Becky awoke with a solution.

It was a quarter to six, but Amber was going to be getting up for work in fifteen minutes anyway, and Becky was sure she wouldn't mind being woken. She walked into her friend's room and gave her a nudge.

Amber snorted, turned over, her eyes opening slightly and then more widely in alarm. Finally awake, she sat up with a little cry. 'Becky, what the hell?'

'I've had a brilliant idea,' Becky said, sitting on the edge of the bed and grinning.

Amber groaned. 'And this brilliant idea couldn't have held off for, say, another twenty minutes?'

'It really couldn't. Sorry,' Becky grimaced.

'You know it's not Christmas morning, don't you? And you're not seven?'

'I am aware.' Becky smiled at her friend and, after a moment, the smile was returned.

'Go on then, you idiot, what did you realise? Have you found that elusive cure for all diseases? Discovered a way to save the planet?'

'Better. I know what I'm going to do with my month.' Becky's eyelid twitched and she held it in place for a second. Luckily it settled down.

'You do?' Amber's eyes widened; clearly she was genuinely interested now.

'Yeah. I'm going to France!'

'What, like on a retreat or something?'

'No! Retreats are for people who actually *have* burnout, not those who are misdiagnosed by a vindictive doctor. I'm going to Vaudrelle.'

'To the café?'

'To the café. And I'm going to get that tenant to leave, if it's the last thing I do!'

'Hang on. Hasn't he got the legal right to be there? What are you going to do? Smoke him out? Attack him with a laptop?'

Becky laughed. 'No. Believe it or not, I'm going to go reason with him. Get difficult if I have to. Get him out so the place can finally sell. And you know what that means?'

'You'll have thousands in the bank? Buy this dream property you keep going on about?'

'No! It means I won't have any more stress! Think about it, Amber. I've had this job for years. It's only since Maud left me the café that I've felt... twitchy.'

'Twitchy, what, the eyelid?'

'Especially the eyelid. I'm serious, Amber. I think I've actually solved it! The café will sell, I'll get another extension on the flat reservation – sure I can pay another fee if necessary – I'll get the deposit in time and my burnout will be a distant memory!' Becky looked at her friend, delighted, but was slightly perturbed that her wide, enthusiastic smile wasn't being shared. 'That'll sort everything, right?'

'So you're going to cure your burnout by buying a luxury apartment?' Amber said slowly.

'No. Keep up! The burnout doesn't exist. Stress over the café does. I get rid of that place and *voilà!* The road to happiness is cleared of debris!'

'*Voilà?*'

'What can I say? I'm practically bilingual.'

'Ha.'

'So, what do you think?'

'Honestly?'

'Honestly.'

'Listen, I know the idea of a month at home sounds a bit... impossible for you,' said Amber gently. 'But if it were me, I'd give it a few more days to really sink in. Don't go rushing off trying to change the world. You'll end up worse off, if you aren't careful.'

'You're seriously not supporting me in this?'

'No, idiot. I'll support you in anything. Who was it that took the blame when we were caught forging a "get out of PE" letter at school?'

Becky rolled her eyes. 'You did.'

'And who lied to her mum so that her best friend could sneak away with her boyfriend overnight?'

'You, again. I get it.' Becky smiled at the shared memories. 'But I've got this time. It seems like a sign... and you know how much easier things are to handle in person.'

'Even if the people you'll be dealing with only speak French, and operate under a completely different legal system to the one you're used to?' Amber asked, eyebrow raised.

'I can speak a bit of French. Not a lot, admittedly...'

'Becky! You had to use Google translate just to understand

that solicitor's letter! And you let all his calls go to voicemail so you could listen twenty times if necessary.'

'I know. But that's on the phone. I feel like if I can see people in person, they'll see how important it is – even if my French is awful.'

'At least hire a translator?'

'Seriously, I've got this. I'll talk to this guy. Maybe even find him somewhere else to live. He's probably just an old guy who needs a bit of help to resettle.'

'So you're swooping in like Florence Nightingale?'

'If Florence Nightingale is secretly trying to evict an old man from his forever home, then yes.'

Amber shook her head. 'This is a lot to take in before coffee,' she said. 'But how about this. My annual leave renews in a few months. I could book a couple of weeks off. We could go together. Rather than rushing to France, you could use this time to chill, maybe Marie Kondo the flat or do something useful. It's June – summer will kick in any moment. You could go to the park, read a book. Get some sun on your face. And then, later, we'll go.'

'I couldn't ask you to waste your holiday on me!'

'In all honesty, I could do with the escape.'

'Well, it's really appreciated...'

'But?' Amber prompted.

'Honey, you know what I'm like when I get the bit between my teeth.'

'Then stay for me? I'm pretty stressed at work myself. Not feeling great. I could do with the company.'

'Ah, poor baby,' Becky said, scrunching up her face. 'Nice try. But I've already booked my flights.'

'Oh. OK,' Amber looked a little downcast, then shook herself slightly.

'Plus, I'm against the clock what with the flat and the deposit...'

'What about your mum? What are you going to tell her?'

Becky lay herself fully on the bed – a gesture of mock surrender. 'Haven't said anything about France yet. Thought I might give her a call once I'm there...'

They'd been friends long enough for Amber to know exactly what Becky's mother would think about the trip. For some reason, any talk about France had always been shut down in the past, especially if it involved Maud. Becky had vague memories of summer holidays with her great-aunt, but they were hazy and ended abruptly when she was ten. She'd been too young to know why they'd stopped going back so had just accepted it when their four weeks in Vaudrelle had morphed into package holidays to Greece or Spain.

They'd always received Christmas cards from Maud, then over the past two years, they'd dried up. The next thing they'd received had been a letter telling them about Maud's legacy and how she wanted to gift Becky her beloved café, with its living space above.

'Typical,' Becky's mum had muttered. 'She was always determined to get you back under her thrall. As if you're going to up sticks and move to France and run her crummy little café.'

'Mum!' Becky had been quite shocked. 'She wasn't a witch, you know! She was nice, as far as I remember.'

'She was nice enough,' Mum had sighed. 'Just had her funny ways. Began to try to convince you of all sorts of silly things when we last went.'

'Oh.' Becky had looked at the letter, perplexed. 'Well, anyway, I'm far too busy to go to France, don't worry. I'll just sell up.'

'Good idea.'

Once she'd emailed the solicitor to tell of her intentions, she hadn't paid it much thought; had naively believed she'd get something to sign and that would be it. But then, instead of news on the sale, a tax bill had arrived – clearly owning a home in France as a non-resident didn't come cheap. And despite her emails, it seemed nobody was in any hurry to move things forward.

Finally she'd found the reason for the hold-up. The sitting tenant, Pascal.

'Can't I just evict him?' she'd asked in a furious email.

'It's very complicated, *madame*,' she'd been told. 'He does have the right to stay in the property. Plus your aunt has given him permission to stay as long as he wants...'

She'd sent back what she'd hoped was a strongly worded reply (using a free translator, you could never quite be sure) asking him to start eviction proceedings, but her solicitor had rung her mobile and left a voicemail saying it was impossible. Hence the sudden frustrated fury and the laptop chucking. And hence her month of enforced leave.

Sure, there were other work stresses. Long hours. A new member of the team who seemed suddenly to be vying for the same promotion; there were a few problems with her main account and rivals were always sniffing around hoping to poach. But most of her stress had been about the café. She was sure once she rid herself of it, things would be better.

'Perhaps she won't mind you going now that Maud's... you know. Not likely to take you under her wing now, is that what she said?'

'Under her "thrall", whatever that means.'

'Your mum has an amazing vocabulary.'

'I think her dictionary is from the 1800s. She'll probably tell me it's all codswallop or something.' Becky sat up and grinned. 'Oh God, look at the time. Want me to make you a coffee?'

Amber groaned. 'Why can't *I* get a month off work?'

'Take a sabbatical?'

'Can't afford it.'

'Then maybe try slinging a company laptop across the room?' Becky suggested wickedly.

They both laughed.

'I can't change your mind? About going?'

Becky shook her head. 'Afraid not.'

'Even if I really feel I need you right now?' Amber looked at her with large, pleading eyes. She was actually a pretty good actor.

'Even so. Just think of the new, improved Becky you'll get back in a couple of weeks.'

'I suppose she'll just have to do.'

Instinctively, Becky leant across the bed and gave Amber a squeeze. 'I'll miss you though,' she said.

'Me too.'

4

Becky had always liked the buzz of being in an airport. The sense of momentum, the way everything was organised and followed a set of rules. In the taxi en route, she'd thought about what Amber had said and wondered whether she was doing the right thing. Perhaps it would have been nice not to strike it out alone – after all, she had no idea exactly how she was going to achieve what she was setting out to achieve – but once she'd stepped through the sliding glass doors of London Stansted, she'd fallen automatically into the airport routine.

Checked in, she wandered the shops, buying a few treats – some perfume and make-up, a book for the journey – then made her way to the gate once her flight was called. Finally, she settled into her seat and tried to clear the niggling thoughts of work that continued to stalk her. Somewhere, someone was taking a meeting instead of her this morning. She wasn't sure whether she wanted them to succeed or fail on her behalf. She wanted to prove in her absence that she was indispensable, but at the same time, not lose her hard-won clients.

She tried to focus on the view out of the window. Down on

The Village Café in the Loire

the tarmac, workers were removing the staircase after the plane had been boarded. Soon the pilot gave his spiel on the loudspeaker and they were trundling along the runway, picking up speed. Becky opened her book and began to try to lose herself in a story of someone who was clearly going to be murdered in a few chapters, but her mind kept snapping back to the café, the sale of the flat, the imminent financial disaster she had to solve.

She only had vague memories of Vaudrelle and Great-Aunt Maud. Childish snapshots of moments that had meant a lot to her back then. Ice creams and sunny swimming pools. Sitting in the back of their hire car, head resting against the window, spotting distant chateaux against lush green backdrops, scattered stone houses and sparkling lakes. The way the car bumped sometimes on cobbled streets as they made their way towards Vaudrelle. She didn't remember Maud really – just the idea of her. An older lady who used to pick her up and swing her round when she was tiny, who made the best macarons she'd ever tasted. Someone benign and smiley who seemed to love spending time with her.

It was odd that this woman, whom she hadn't felt she'd known well enough to grieve, had changed Becky's life in this way. No doubt with the best of intentions. She'd probably thought the café and its premises above would set Becky up in life, give her an adventure. Instead, she'd given her the promise of cash wrapped in a logistical and administrative nightmare.

Poor Maud. From what Becky could ascertain, she'd led quite a lonely life by the end. Mum and Dad had become estranged from her and she didn't have any other living family that Becky knew of. Yet she'd had quite the career in her younger years – been a lawyer living in London back in the seventies. Suddenly giving it all up.

'She lost her mind, poor soul,' was all that Mum would say

about it. 'Lost her drive. Wanted to live a simple life. Her parents tried to talk her out of it, but she was adamant.'

'She seemed happy though?' Becky had ventured. 'From what I remember.'

Mum had shaken her head. 'No, I can't imagine she was,' she'd said. 'But she was a stubborn woman, never did admit her mistake. We stayed in touch for a while but…' She'd waved her hand as if to mime the idea of their eventual fallout.

'Didn't you ever write back to her? When she wrote?'

'Oh, we sent cards, that sort of thing,' Mum said. 'But you know what life can be like.'

Becky did indeed.

Still, perhaps she should have made an effort to go see Maud while she was still alive. Just to be kind, if nothing else. That was the trouble with a full-time job – the hours around the edge of every day were so stretched, the days so busy, that time seemed to fly past. All her good intentions each year – about being a better friend to Amber, a better daughter, a better advertising executive, losing the couple of pounds she was always regaining – would fall away as she struggled to keep up with the pace of everything.

It would all be worth it though when she'd made something of herself and could afford to take her foot off the pedal. At least once she'd adjusted her five-year plan to take this little hiccup into account.

The book was failing to hold her attention, so she shut it and looked out of the window at the light blue sky, the dotted clouds, which seemed so substantial from a distance but turned into nothing but mist when the plane cut through them. Below, the sea sparkled and riffled in the sunshine. She closed her eyes and tried to relax enough to sleep.

'Oh my God, are you all right?' the voice, and its proximity to her ear, made her jump.

'What happened?' she said blearily, her eyes focusing on the face of the flight attendant, so close to her own, his brow creased with concern.

'Oh, nothing.' He straightened and she noticed for the first time that several of the other passengers were looking at her. A child was pointing. 'I think you may have had a nightmare. Nothing to worry about.'

'Did I...'

'You screamed.'

'Oh.' She felt her cheeks get hot. 'Sorry,' she said.

'Something about a laptop?' he added helpfully.

'Right.' She straightened up. 'Well, I'm fine. Thank you.'

The nightmares were nothing new. She'd been having them for the past year or so, but this was the first time she'd had one so publicly. She was relieved when they landed and she was able to push her way off the plane, grab her luggage and find a ride to Vaudrelle.

The area around the airport was a little shabby, but as they drove farther out and into the countryside, the buildings fell away and she found herself looking over wide fields full of sunflowers, grassy meadows peppered with brown cows; the cars on the road thinned and the sleeker cars of the city gave way to older, clapped out rust buckets, some of which would have been consigned to the scrapheap back home.

They got caught behind tractors that looked flimsy, paint-chipped and old; a couple – neither of whom looked like seasoned cyclists – on a tandem bike of all things; at one point the driver had to stop because a couple of cows had made it through the pathetic wire fence and were chewing on grass at the side of the road. The driver got out and flapped his arms alongside the farmer to get them back into the field.

The whole time, Becky's eyelid was doing its stress-dance. And she didn't blame it, actually. Taxis were meant to take you from A to B with minimal fuss and while Jean-Luc, her driver, couldn't be held responsible for the various hold-ups, she didn't like his smiling acceptance of each delay, his nonchalant shrug when she reminded him she was on a tight schedule.

'Ah, well you might need to loosen this schedule,' he'd said, seemingly amused. 'I think you will find that things do not always go very fast here.'

'You're not kidding,' she said to herself, leaning on her hand and trying to relax as she took in the countryside. In reality she wasn't on any sort of schedule, certainly not a tight one, but she was hard-wired to hate wasting time in taxis and on transport when she could be Doing Something of more value.

Still, once she surrendered to the fact she had little or no control about the speed or efficiency of her journey, she felt something inside her relax. Leaning her head on the edge of the headrest, she looked out over the scenery, feeling a little as she had as a child, sitting in the back seat and watching the open, grassy fields undulate towards the horizon, wondering at the odd tower or half-concealed building en route. And for a second she allowed herself to believe that she was ten again, that her father was alive and driving them to Maud's, her mother – a slightly more relaxed version of her current self – sitting alongside him, sometimes putting a hand on his arm, or passing him a toffee.

The next thing she knew they were passing a sign reading *'Vaudrelle'* and she had to snap back to reality. The one in which she was alone. And thirty. And on enforced sick leave.

The village was both strange and familiar at once. The stone buildings, the little back streets, the tiny fountain; the small town looked like many they'd passed through, but something stirred in her as she took in the surroundings, all bathed in warm sunlight which bleached the stonework and threw dark cool shadows onto the road. She wound down the window and fresh air flooded into the interior, bringing with it the scent of pollen and cut grass – and possibly the whiff of croissants, although that was probably wishful thinking, she thought, as her stomach growled.

Yes, she could handle a week or two here. Hopefully after she'd sorted the house stuff she could take a bit of a break, maybe reminisce about the old days. Perhaps learn to relax, take in a bit of French culture?

Plus, she thought, she could probably make a fortune on the café once she'd turfed out the unwelcome lodger. She was willing to bet nobody in this little backwater knew anything about marketing; properties were probably advertised locally, sold by word of mouth. She could get a great agent on this and really open up to some people with money who wanted to embrace a little authentic French living. Soon her brain was ticking over numbers and she was fantasising about her new flat. And she felt, at last, more like herself again.

The taxi slowed and turned left along a small road with a few shops dotted here and there – the *boucherie*, the florist, some kind of tiny nursery or crèche. And yes, there it was, *La Petite Pause*, its sign slightly paint-chipped and faded, but instantly familiar in its purples and whites. She had a flash of memory – her great-aunt smiling, welcoming them, ushering them inside. Holding out her hand for Becky's and taking her through the flag-stoned café and up a staircase to the living quarters above.

Her own bedroom, the small, neat box room with its painted cladding and the Blu-Tacked drawings she'd created on former holidays. Mum and Dad's smarter guest room next door. And Maud's room which she'd sometimes entered in the morning, cradling a cup of tea made by Dad as carefully as if it were made of crystal.

'Are you OK, *madame*?' the driver said softly, and Becky realised she'd been sitting entranced, lost for a moment in the past. She shook her head as if to dismiss the memory – this kind of nostalgia didn't help anyone – and smiled thinly.

'Yes. Sorry,' she said, opening the door and stepping out into the warm, sunlit air.

It was the work of a moment for the driver to get her small, wheeled case from the boot and then he was gone, meandering back to the airport with seemingly not a care in the world.

It was quiet on the street, but she could see even from outside that there were a few patrons in the café, that an '*Ouvert*' sign was hanging in the glass of the purple-edged doors. She felt a shiver of unease – she'd had no idea the café was open, and no idea what this meant. Was there a manager she'd have to befriend or dismiss? Was the lodger responsible for running the café? Would the spare room – that she'd assumed would be left empty – actually be occupied, forcing her to stay in the tiny box room or pay for a hotel? Where were the profits going? Who was responsible for it all?

She pushed open the door, meaning to walk past the few populated tables and ask to speak to someone, but the minute she stepped inside the buzz of conversation dropped to nothing. Each and every head swivelled to take in her high heels, smart black trousers, neatly buckled coat. Beret. She'd known on some level the beret was a bad idea – a bit too *Emily in Paris* probably.

Well, Becky, she thought, *I have a feeling we aren't in London any more.*

Before she could ask them what they all thought they were looking at, the people turned and resumed their conversation, having decided clearly that although she was a stranger, she really wasn't worth pausing a coffee break for.

5

Rather than let the intimidating atmosphere of *La Petite Pause* get to her, Becky put back her shoulders and walked up to the coffee shop counter, behind which a man was preparing an espresso for a customer. As she waited, feeling both impatient and nervous, she took in the dull decor, the old, worn wood, original floor tiles. The tables that didn't match and the individual chairs made in a variety of woods and finishes that definitely hadn't been bought as a set. It was quaint, but more than a little run-down.

The air was thick with the smell of roasted coffee beans and the rumble of conversation. An occasional exclamation pierced the air as confidences were exchanged or anecdotes relayed. It had a homely feel, but other than that wasn't a patch on the light, bright, modern coffee shops she was used to. Even the ones which purported to be years old, or traditional, or even French, opted for a more polished look.

Many of the customers wore boots – either of the wellington or thick walking variety. There were a couple of women with pushchairs sipping espresso. But they didn't look like the coiffed 'yummy mummies' who populated the café around the corner from Becky's flat – they looked pretty and young and energised, but without make-up or heels.

At last, the man finished serving the customer before her and Becky had his full attention. '*Bonjour,*' she said, trying not to smile at his beaming face. This was no time to be friendly, she was on a mission.

'*Bonjour, madame.*' He smiled, then rattled something off in such rapid French it was impossible to keep up. His dark hair was neatly combed, but the neatness was jeopardized by an untamed curl at the front that stuck slightly in the air. His eyes were dark and warm, and she found herself smiling back in spite of her determination to be ruthless.

'Can you speak any English?' she asked him. It put her on a back foot, having to ask this. Although she'd mugged up on some of her schoolgirl French on the plane, hearing it fired at her with conversational rapidity, instead of being written clearly on a screen, threw her completely. But it was what it was, she decided. She had no need to speak French in her real life. Anyway, she'd managed so far thanks to Google and a bit of paraphrasing.

'*Oui*, a little,' he said. 'Would you like a coffee?'

'Yes please,' she said. 'Cappuccino, if that's OK?'

He made a face. 'I can do a *café long* with a little milk?' he suggested.

'That will do.' It seemed bizarre that a coffee shop didn't serve one of the most popular types of coffee, but then again it seemed bizarre that the café was open at all four months after Maud's death. She took a breath as he began to prepare her drink. 'Actually,' she said. 'I'm looking for the manager.'

'*Oui*, that's me,' he said, barely glancing up. 'Is something the matter?' He put the coffee and a little side-jug of milk in front of her and she took a rather dubious-looking sugar lump from a silver pot to add to it.

'Well, it's complicated,' she said. 'But I think I need to talk to you in private, if that's OK?'

'René!' The man yelled, making her jump. One of the farmer-looking chaps at a far table looked over. A conversation ensued that sounded close to an argument, but eventually René got to his feet and came up to the counter.

'*Merci*,' the server said. Then, 'Come, we will go to the back where it is quiet.'

It occurred to her that she was going into a private space with a man she didn't know, which she would never usually do. But he seemed friendly and the café was well populated – if he decided to murder her, she'd probably be able to raise the alarm, she decided, and followed him through the door that led to Maud's former kitchen.

He closed the door and the noise of the café was shut off, reduced to a murmur. 'Pascal,' he said, holding out his hand.

'You're *Pascal?*'

'*Oui*. Why?'

'Nothing. I just... nothing. You live here?' Someone must have got it wrong. This youngish man couldn't be a sitting tenant, surely.

'*Oui*. What is this about?' his eyes narrowed a little. Perhaps he thought she was from the tax office.

'I'm Becky.' She shook his hand awkwardly and he looked surprised, as if this hadn't been what he'd expected, but said nothing.

'Take a seat, Becky.' Her name – she'd always hated its ordinariness – sounded different on his tongue. Somehow exotic, with his French accent.

'Thank you,' she said.

She perched on a chair and he sat opposite her. 'You wish to speak to me.'

'Yes. It's a little awkward. But I'm Maud's great-niece. She used to run...'

'*Ah, mon Dieu!*' He exclaimed, raising a hand to brush back some of his thick brown hair. The wayward curl sprang forward stubbornly after it was briefly flattened by the manoeuvre. 'But of course you are! You are the image of some of her pictures. I should have recognised you.' He smiled. 'It is wonderful that you have come at last. And you will be running the café now, I expect?'

'No. Not exactly.'

His face dropped like a child's refused an ice cream. '*Non*? Then why are you here?'

'Well,' she explained her predicament; she had no intention of moving to France and becoming a barista, she had a perfectly good job in the UK. But things had become so complicated with the sale, it seemed easier to address the issues first-hand. She didn't mention the burnout or the fact she'd been signed off work but, as if on cue, her eyelid started to twitch as if it were trying to communicate the missing piece of the story to this man via Morse code.

Pascal looked at her, his thick eyebrows knitted together. 'But this is not possible,' he told her.

'Well, certainly not for a good price while it's tenanted,' she said. 'Is it... you're the one living here?'

'Yes! I am your great-aunt's friend and have been looking after everything.' He seemed inordinately pleased with himself at this revelation.

'Sorry, I don't understand,' she said. 'Why do you want to stay here?'

He shrugged. 'It is my home, I suppose.'

'But can't you find, like, another home?'

'*Oui*, of course. When it is time, I will go.'

'Oh,' she said, fiddling with the edge of her coffee cup. 'Well, I'm not sure how much you've been told, but I'm afraid I need you to vacate the property so that I can sell. I know it's possible to sell with you *in situ*, but I'd lose thousands.'

The confused look was back. 'But Maud did not want you to sell immediately! And there is no urgency. I will stay as long as I need to.'

'But,' she said, wondering how well he'd known her great-aunt, 'well, without being indelicate, the café's mine now. And it's not as if Maud will mind.'

He shook his head vehemently. '*Non*. She would mind! It would break her heart! She told me she was gifting the property to you, of course. But I know that she hoped you might spend some time here, perhaps even fall in love with it the way she did.'

'That's very... sweet. But the letter said only that the property was being gifted to me. There was no mention of any terms. Nothing in writing.'

'Ah! Of course! Writing! I have a letter. I will show you.' He moved over to the corner of the room and opened a tin marked *farine*, which seemed to contain a load of disparate papers. 'Ah!' he said, pulling out an envelope. He removed a piece of paper from it and, coming back to the table, laid it out, smoothing the creases where it had been folded.

The paper was lavender in colour and smelt faintly familiar. And the writing too – Maud's scrawl from Christmas cards in years gone by, all the swirls and loops of proper cursive. 'Oh,' she said, feeling her heart shiver slightly in her chest. 'She wrote this to you?'

'Yes. But she wrote it in English, for me to show you when

you came. Because she wondered, when we made this plan, whether you might have some questions.' He turned the paper and passed it to Becky. As she picked it up, she felt a lump rise in her throat, but swallowed it down.

Dear Pascal,

This is to confirm that I would like you to stay in the café and mind the business for me once I am no longer around. I have made plans with my notaire to pass the building to my great-niece Rebecca, when this can be arranged. I realise that she may wish to sell it, but I have a request for her before she does so. Please tell her this when she gets in touch.

Becky, darling. Please try to run the café for a month. Then, if you do not fall in love, you can sell it with my blessing. But spend a little time here first. Remind yourself of the times we spent here together. And see whether it might suit you, even a little.

With much love,
Maud

Becky closed her eyes and remembered the woman she'd known all those years ago. The memory was patchy, made up both of photos she'd seen and her own individual experiences. There were glimpses of happy holidays, of fun times spent together. But the truth was, until recently, she'd rarely thought of her great-aunt. Ever since the falling out with her parents, Maud had barely been mentioned – the odd reference to *Mad Maud in France* would be bandied about, but like many insulting terms, she hadn't thought too deeply about it. It was just a fact: her great-aunt was a bit odd, she lived in France. They didn't have anything to do with her.

It was sad that Maud had been thinking about her so often.

Perhaps she should have taken the time to write, to return the odd Christmas card. Poor woman.

'So?' Pascal said.

'So what?'

'Well, you see it is your aunt's wish for you to do this; it is a *condition.*'

'But come on, Pascal, you know what old people are like! It's all very well her having had this fantasy about me running the café, but it won't make any difference to her whether I do or don't, will it, in reality? And I'm so busy at work, and I need this place to sell. Because...' To her horror, she realised that tears were welling in her eyes. 'Can't we just find a way to work this out?'

Pascal's hand approached hers over the wood of the table, but he drew it back before it made contact, probably thinking better of it. 'I am so sorry that you are sad,' he said. 'And if it were in my power to help, then I would. But this promise...' He sighed. 'Maud has been very important to me. She took me in when I had nothing. And I owe her this. I am sorry, Becky. But perhaps it will not be so bad?'

'No! You don't understand!' Becky's voice sounded a little screechy even to her. He sat back in his chair abruptly, eyes wide. 'Sorry,' she continued. 'I'm just... I don't know what I'm going to do.' The tears came then, and she had no way of stopping them.

Becky wasn't a crier. Her mother was always eager to tell anyone who'd listen that she hadn't even cried when she'd broken her arm aged twelve. Just come into the house with the arm at a strange angle, looking pale and asking whether her mother had time to drive her to A & E.

But whatever she'd repressed in her younger years seemed to be coming to bite her now. It was too much. The work thing.

The situation she'd put herself in by committing to the new flat purchase. The fact that unless she could sell the café, she could never afford it. A few months ago, everything had seemed rosy. Now it was falling apart about her ears. Plus, seeing Maud's handwriting seemed to have awakened something in her.

'Ah, *madame*, do not cry,' Pascal said, standing up and hovering behind her, clearly not quite sure what to do. 'I realise this is not your dream. But it is not a bad life here. And a month, it will pass very quickly. Then, if you want, you can sell. I won't stand in your way. And your aunt will be so very happy. It is not worth your tears.'

* * *

'Then I blew my nose on a napkin,' Becky said, relaying the whole sorry situation to Amber an hour later from the small room she'd last inhabited twenty years ago.

'A proper napkin?'

'Yep. Fresh-pressed linen.'

'Well, not any more.'

Becky laughed, in spite of herself.

'So,' said Amber, 'other than that, what's the place like?'

'It's a bit run-down. But it's so cute too. And upstairs, it's just as I remember: Maud's room; another that this guy, Pascal, is living in. I'm in the little room I used to sleep in as a child.'

'Oh, that must be weird. Has it changed much?'

'No,' said Becky, walking to the wall where a few yellowed pictures were still hanging. 'Nothing has.'

'Wow. I think I'd feel... kind of strange.'

'I do, a bit. I keep expecting Mum to come in. Or... well, or Dad obviously.'

'Oh, Becky. That's tough. I wish I could go out there with you.'

'Me too. Oh God, Amber, what am I going to do?'

'You could come back home? Forget the café for a bit? Wait for this Pascal bloke to move on naturally?'

'I'll lose the flat.'

'There will be other flats. Or you could borrow the rest of the deposit from your mum?'

'And never hear the last of it? No thanks.'

'Well, maybe put your flat dreams on hold. No one owns anything any more anyway. I doubt I'll ever get a deposit together.'

'I know. I just kind of set my heart on it.'

'OK, but think of it this way. I know it sounds harsh but if this café was as important to Maud as it seems, well, maybe she deserves to have some say in what happens to it.'

'But I can't work in a café!'

'Well, maybe not forever. But you don't have to rush to sell it. Spend a little time there, get some sun. Take a moment to consider all your options.'

'Do you think if I employed my own French solicitor, I could force things...?'

'Maybe, but it's very complicated by the sound of things.'

'Just a bit.'

'How's the eyelid?'

'Doing the bloody "Macarena".'

'Ouch.' Amber was quiet. 'I know I've said this before, but we could go together later in the year? I'd help you.'

'Thanks... just... it would be too late for the flat. And...'

'It's really that good? The flat? I mean, it's beautiful from what you showed me. But is it worth... this?'

Becky thought. The flat with its smooth, clean lines, newly

installed kitchen. 'I think so. But it's more than that. I don't like being pushed around, forced to do things. I shouldn't let this Pascal guy win.'

'It's not a competition, hon.'

'It feels a bit like one. Like I'm being made to stay against my will.'

'Well, maybe reframe that. Do it for Maud. They're her wishes after all. He's just trying to honour them, by the sounds of it.'

Becky was silent for a moment. She imagined herself staying, getting some sun. Convincing Pascal to leave somehow despite the letter. Or returning home, cancelling her flat purchase. Sitting in her rental, twiddling her thumbs. Neither option felt particularly appealing. But neither did fulfilling Maud's wishes and running the café.

'Are you OK?' Amber asked into the silence.

'Yeah. Just thinking…'

'Well, if you need something to get your mind off it, I was meaning to ask—' Amber began.

'I'll sleep on it.' Becky said decisively.

'What?'

'That's what Mum always says. Sleep on it. It'll feel better in the morning.'

'But I—'

'I know. You think I should give it up. And maybe I will.'

'No, I—'

'Speak tomorrow!' she said, feeling suddenly exhausted and ending the call.

She lay down on the tiny bed, feeling strangely enormous, and gazed at the pictures on the wall in the half-light until her eyes grew heavy and she finally slept.

6

The next day, when Becky woke, it took her a minute to work out where she was. The wall behind her bed was wallpapered in an outdated, floral pattern, the cladded walls just visible where slivers of daylight peeked in from gaps in the wooden shutters. She raised herself on her elbows and let her brain update with the events of yesterday. She was in France – stuck, potentially for a month. She didn't feel much clearer on things, but at least she'd slept. Now, as her mum would say, was the time for action.

Sitting up, she picked up her phone and discovered that it was already nine o'clock. Already she was slipping. Back in England she'd have been up for a couple of hours already. Downstairs she could hear the hum of a coffee machine, the noise of people talking. The café was open.

She pulled her laptop onto her bed from the side table, opened up a notes page on her screen and wrote down her options:

Clarify legal situation.

Becky was no lawyer, but the whole situation around Maud's conditions felt a little left field. Was everything strictly legal? She'd find out. If there was no legal basis for them, she could go ahead and sell, return to London and resume life as planned.

Cancel flat reservation.

The flat, the opportunity to buy something without involving Mum or too much of a mortgage, was a chance in a lifetime. But she could still withdraw from the transaction if she couldn't find another way to force the sale. Then she'd just have to leave Pascal in perpetuity to run the café until he got bored and finally vacated.

Stay and see it through.

Fate had given her a café, and had also somehow given her a month in which to fulfil her great-aunt's wishes. She didn't have anything else she had to do. But the thought of taking over the café, even for that short window of time, seemed exhausting. Surely she was meant to be having a break, not taking on a whole new enterprise?

The list, at least, clarified her thinking. Out of the three possibilities, she decided, the best situation would be if someone spoke to Pascal on her behalf, explained that Maud's letter wasn't legally binding, and sent him on his way. Then she could finally get the café on the market for a fair price and get on with her life.

With a new burst of energy that came from having a plan, she slipped off the bed and made her way to the small bathroom that Pascal had told her was hers to use. There was an unfathomably small tin bath there, with no shower attachment and just enough room to sit with her knees up. With no other options, she popped in the plug and filled the tub with lukewarm water.

Stepping in, she gasped, realising the metal surface had yet to heat, and had the uncomfortable sensation of a cold bottom in a bath of warm water. But she soon adjusted, washed and towel-dried her hair before giving it the best blow-dry she could with her foldable travel hairdryer.

The *notaire* who had sent the letter and presumably dealt with the rest of Maud's estate was in a town twenty kilometres away. But he'd already shown himself to be borderline incompetent. Perhaps it would be better to get some independent advice? An internet search revealed that the local mayor had some say over these matters and might be able to advise her; and seeing as the town hall was in the next street, this seemed like a sensible place to start.

She pulled on a pair of navy jeans and a green, short-sleeved blouse, teamed with the heels from yesterday, then made her way down through the café with a cursory *bonjour* to Pascal, and out into the street.

The freshness was the first thing she noticed. It was as if all her life she'd been breathing in smog, but had suddenly been gifted clear, cool morning air. She found herself gulping it in hungrily as if oxygen-starved. The sun was shining unencumbered by clouds, in a sky that was a deep blue. She felt the warmth on her shoulders and shivered after the coolness of her old-fashioned room.

Right. This was it. She would be confident, self-assured, and channel her inner mum – steely and determined. She would march into that office, request a meeting and outline her problem. Perhaps she could be booking plane tickets back by the end of the week.

Stepping forward, she instantly stumbled on the uneven pavement, her heel catching in a crack in the stone, sending her almost flying. Her bag dropped to the ground and she crouched down to gather her things back into it: purse, phone, tissues, tampons, pens and make-up scattered in her wake.

'Can I help you, *madame*?' A youngish man in beige shorts and a sky-blue T-shirt crouched down opposite her. His face was lightly tanned, and he sported a neatly clipped black beard. But his eyes were what her eyes were drawn to most – sharp and intelligent and almost the same colour as the sky.

'Oh,' she said. 'No, it's fine.' She checked her phone, but luckily the screen wasn't cracked.

'You forgot these!' he said, retrieving a pair of tights that she kept in there in case of in-office snags. They unfurled as he handed them over, waving slightly in the gentle breeze. To her horror, a pair of knickers that must have got caught on them in the wash shook loose and landed at their feet. He looked slightly confused, but said nothing.

'Thanks,' she said, stuffing the tights into her bag and no doubt snagging them in the process, then bending down for the knickers. 'I'd better...' She gestured ahead of her and the man nodded.

'Well, be careful,' he said, looking pointedly at her shoes, clearly judging her choice of footwear.

She felt a surge of familiar short temper. 'What's that supposed to mean?'

He looked taken aback. 'Perhaps these are not the best shoes to be wearing in Vaudrelle? The roads, they are not even.'

'Perhaps,' she said, feeling her eyelid twitch a little, 'it's none of your business.'

His eyes widened but he didn't respond directly. 'Well, sorry. Good day,' he said, with a little upward inflexion of his shoulder.

They began to walk in the same direction, until she hung back a bit and pretended to fiddle with the strap of her shoe to let him get a head start. Then, when he was distant enough that she wouldn't be keeping step with him any more, she straightened and continued her way.

To her annoyance the man went into the small door of the town hall, exactly where she was headed. She pushed open the glass door behind him and stood in a reception area where a board informed her that there were several offices *in situ* – finances, something called CAF, and another with the unfortunate acronym ARS which her brain kept misreading.

Thankfully, the man was nowhere to be seen.

A woman looked up at her from behind a wooden counter and greeted her in French. She had long, brown hair swept up into a bun; her face was make-up free, but had a glow that either suggested expensive facials or excellent genes. Surprisingly for this formal environment, she sported jeans with her more formal, buttoned up blouse.

Having checked a few phrases online before setting off, Becky was ready. '*Bonjour,*' she said. '*Je voudrais parler avec...* um... *le, la, le, la...* the *maire?*'

The woman smiled. 'You can speak English, if you like?' she said, with thinly disguised amusement.

'Oh, thank God. Yes, I'd like to see the *maire* – make an appointment if that's possible?'

At that moment, a door to the woman's left marked '*Bureaux*' opened and the man she'd seen earlier appeared. 'You are here to see me?'

Of course. *Of course,* he was the *maire.*

'Yes,' she said, trying to keep her tone official. 'About the café in town?'

He nodded, picking up a few folders from the desk and

tucking them under his arm. 'Come through,' he said, indicating with his head that she should push open the door next to her.

When she did so, he was standing just inside, at the end of a small, tiled space, in front of a door with a gold plaque. He opened it for her, unsmiling, and gestured her inside.

She felt her eyelid take on a life of its own. She wondered, for a moment, whether eyelid twitching burned off any calories. If so, she'd have the body of her dreams in a few more weeks' time.

He sat behind a desk piled with files and leaned forward. 'So,' he said. 'We have already met. But let us start again. I am Georges Fournier, the mayor.'

'Rebecca Thorne,' she replied. 'I'm sorry about...'

He waved a hand. 'No matter. What can I help you with?'

She explained who she was, why she was there.

'Oh, so you are Maud's niece,' he said, his manner changing, a smile once more stretching across his face. God, his teeth were white.

'Yes,' she said, not bothering to correct him with the 'great-niece' title. It would just confuse things.

'Well then, you are very welcome, *madame*!' he said. 'Maud is a wonderful lady and has been the beating heart of our village for many years.'

The present tense disturbed her slightly – had he not heard of her aunt's death, and was she about to shatter him with the news? Or was it simply that his English wasn't as accomplished as she'd thought at first. Perhaps he was in the wrong tense out of necessity.

'You know... of course that she...' she began.

He nodded, his smile falling slightly. 'Moved on? Yes, it is very sad. She had been running the café for many years. But she is in a good place.'

Becky nodded solemnly, feeling a little like a fraud. She hadn't really grieved her aunt. The first she'd even heard of her death had been when she'd received the letter about the gift in her aunt's Will. This man probably had more right to inherit from her than she did.

'Yes,' she said. 'Anyway, she has given me the café, which I'm so grateful for. But unfortunately, my life is in the UK. I have a great job, good friends, somewhere to live.' An image of the lovely flat flashed into her mind, spurring her on. 'What I'm saying is that I can't adhere to the demands she's made.'

'Demands?' Georges's eyebrows rose half an inch.

'Yes.' Becky explained about the requirement to work for a month. 'Only in a hand-written letter,' she said. 'So it's not really...'

Throughout, he nodded his head as if understanding, sympathising. 'I see, I see,' he said. And 'Oh yes, it is difficult.'

'So, do you think you can help?'

'You want some advice in running the café?' he asked, confused.

'No.' Had he literally not been listening? 'I want to ask whether you can... help Pascal to understand that what Maud wanted, with all the love in the world, doesn't really matter now, does it? And I'm sure...'

Georges's expression clouded. 'Surely you do not mean this? That you would go against your aunt's wishes? She gave you her café, yes, but it is more than a café. It was her life.'

Becky nodded, wishing she'd chosen different words. 'Oh, of course. Of course it *matters*. I didn't mean... In an ideal world I'd love to do what she suggests. But it's not practical.'

The *maire*, she noticed, had stopped nodding. His eyes bore into her. She shifted uncomfortably.

'So you would like me to speak to Pascal and ask him to tear up the letter, *c'est ça?*' He mimed tearing a piece of paper and throwing it away.

'You would?' she asked, leaning forward, eyes wide.

'*Non*,' he said simply.

It was unlikely that she'd misunderstood what he meant by *non*, but she pushed on regardless. 'You won't?'

'*Non*.'

'But you... it can't be legally binding. Should I speak to a *notaire*? Get someone legal on it?'

'*Oui*, you could.' He nodded. Then he leaned forward again, his expression serious. His eyebrows, thick and bushy, were truly something to behold up close. 'But I would not waste your time.'

'Oh.'

'You see, *madame*, there is the law, there is the letter of it. And there is the heart of it.' He tapped a fist to his chest in case she was unaware of where hearts were located. 'And I think perhaps you have the letter of it in your favour. But here in Vaudrelle we have the heart. We loved Maud when she was here. We love the café. We respect people's wishes. And we would prefer to take a little time. Do things right.'

'What about *my* wishes?'

'Your wishes. Well, I think you will get your wish eventually, *madame*. You will sell the café in a little while, I am sure. You will take your money and forget your aunt and do whatever it is you want to do with it.'

'Look, I'm not a bad person or anything, it's just—'

'Of course. But I'm afraid this is how things are.'

She took in his expression, his folded arms. All the friendliness had disappeared from his manner. Clearly he had decided she was the enemy.

'Fine. I'll go to the *notaire*. Get things moving that way!' she said, hotly.

'*Oui*, of course, it is your right.' Georges smiled, rather coldly. 'But I think you will find that if you go to the *notaire*, he may not act very quickly. Perhaps he will think this is not an urgent matter. Maybe he will take many months to help you,' he said, looking at her meaningfully. 'And perhaps if you don't want this terrible delay – ah, the legal profession, they are so slow! – it would be better to do the right thing. And I believe you will find that the right thing is also the quickest thing for you.'

Was he threatening her? It was hard to tell.

'You're saying that he'd delay things on purpose?'

'I am saying,' he said, 'that I think it is in your best interests to honour your aunt's wishes. And perhaps that this will be the quickest way too.'

'But...'

There was a silence as they looked at each other, at an impasse. Then, '*Madame*,' he said. 'I hope you are not suggesting anything improper?'

'Sorry?'

'I see that you are winking at me, giving me the eye? *Madame*, you are very beautiful. But I am sorry, I will not be seduced.'

'Oh! No. It's my eyelid. A stress thing!' she said, putting her hand to her eye, which of course now started behaving itself and acting as if it hadn't literally caused a #MeToo moment.

'OK. Well, *au revoir, madame*,' he said, his tone still questioning.

She eyed his laptop. Her fingers twitched slightly. But she managed to keep control of herself. It definitely would not help to go causing criminal damage in the town hall on her first day. Instead, she stood up, thanked him through gritted teeth and pushed her way out of his office, across the reception area and out into the sunny street.

7

'Hello, Mum!' she said brightly, newly ensconced in her room after her humiliating rendezvous with the mayor. 'How are you?'

'Why is the line crackling, Rebecca? Where *are* you?' Her mum's instincts were wasted in her job; she should have become a detective inspector.

'I'm... well, I'm – look, don't get mad.'

This was a red rag to a bull moment. 'Mad! Piffle! I'll have whatever emotions I choose, young lady. And I'm assuming by your reluctance to tell me that you've gone to France. Am I right?'

'Well, yes, but—'

Her next words were drowned out by a breathy snort. 'Oh, Rebecca! That's the last thing you need.'

'I'm sorry. I just... well, I think it's the best thing, Mum. I want to sort this ridiculous legal business out and it's always easier to do things in person, don't you think?'

'Hmm,' her mother said. And the one syllable expression said more than a thousand words could have. Mother wasn't pleased.

'Well,' Becky stuttered slightly, then regained herself. She was a fully grown woman, and while her mum was a forbidding character, they did still love each other. Mum wanted what was best, that was all – she was just worried. 'I've already had a meeting with the *maire* about the legality of the... situation.'

This seemed to perk her mum up a little. 'Oh really?' she said. 'Well, I'm impressed. And was it productive?'

'Um. He certainly seemed sympathetic.'

'Good. Well, that's a start. And when are you home?'

Becky scrunched up her face. 'Um, not sure yet,' she said.

'Well, don't hang about too long. Best to be in the thick of it. Relaxing is overrated,' her mum said.

'Sorry, what?'

'Relaxing. People seem obsessed with it these days. But really, how does one get anything done?'

'Mum, it's OK to relax a bit sometimes.'

'Yes, of course! At a class, or coffee with a friend. But that place...' Mum paused, selecting the right words. 'Mark my words: it gets into your blood if you're not careful. It did for Maud, and I'd hate you to go the same way.'

'Mum, I am not going to go the same way, whatever way that is. I'm getting out of here as soon as I can.'

'Good. Good.'

The relief over the phone was palpable, but confusing. Why did her mum so desperately want her to leave? It wasn't that she could get back to work; and Maud was no longer here to influence her.

'Is that why you fell out?'

'Sorry?'

'Is that why you argued with Maud all those years ago? You thought she was... relaxing too much?'

'Of course not! Live and let live. It was the effect she was having on you. And your father, actually. You seemed... different when we were there. And she filled your heads with all sorts of thoughts about education. You told me that "school wasn't everything" and being happy was more important than being clever. Which is all very well for people who aren't clever to say. But you? You were bright as a button – still are. And I didn't want you to waste all that potential.'

'You fell out over me?'

'Not solely. If I'm honest, the rift happened years before. When she left. Of course we made our peace, but things weren't perfect after that. There was always... hurt. Then we rowed over some of the things she was filling your mind with, and other things came out... you know how it is. Daddy and I cancelled our trip the following year and I suppose... well, after a while it was just easier not to stay in touch.'

'Poor Maud.'

'Poor Maud indeed. She could have ruined your life, Becky. You'd always been such a motivated girl. Daddy was a bit more forgiving, wanted to make more of an effort with her. Always such a softie, that man. And perhaps if he hadn't... if he were still around, things might have been different.' Her mum's voice faltered a little. 'Your poor father,' she added, her tone more subdued.

'Oh.' The mention of her father brought to mind, as it always did, a vision of the last time she'd seen him. His gentle eyes, the smile. The way he'd wrapped his arms around her when she got home from school; had always had time to hear her prattle on about this and that. Poor Dad.

'Anyway, after Daddy died, things were very difficult for us financially. Precarious even. I never mentioned it, of course, you were so young. The life insurance didn't pay out on a technicality and... we almost lost the house. But it worked out for the best in the end.' Cynthia's voice returned to her normal, direct tone. 'I was driven to push harder, work more. And look where I am today.'

'You did great, Mum.'

'Yes. I did. And it taught me something too. How important it is to be secure – financially. And secure in oneself. The ability to be independent, make money, stand on your own two feet. Especially as a woman. It's the best protection we have.'

Becky leaned against the wall, feeling the uneven texture of the paper against her head. 'Protection against...?'

'Life. Men. Whatever either of those throws at us.'

Becky laughed. 'Oh Mum. But you're OK, aren't you? We both are.'

'Of course. And I couldn't be more proud of you, darling.'

'Thank you.'

'Except for this silly burnout nonsense, but I'm sure that will all be resolved soon.'

'Yes.'

There was a pause.

'Do try to get back soon, Rebecca, won't you?'

'I will.'

'And... stay in touch. I know I can be a bit... pushy. But I only want what's best.'

'I know you do, Mum.'

Ending the call, Becky lay back on her bed and sighed. She often felt exhausted after conversing with her mother – always adapting what she was saying to keep things on an even keel, trying to balance truth-telling with the likely impact of her words. She'd somehow managed to give her mum the impression she was going to sort things out from a legal perspective and that she'd be home soon, when in reality that seemed further than ever from the truth.

The Village Café in the Loire 57

As she often did in these situations, she dialled Amber. The first call went to voicemail but on the second, Amber answered almost immediately. 'Sorry,' she said, her voice hushed. 'Had to pop to the loo to take the call.'

'Seriously? You're sitting on the lav?'

'Yes. I'm not *peeing* or anything, if that's what you're worried about! Just, new rule. No personal calls at work. Apparently, productivity is down.'

'Blimey.'

'Yeah. I told you about Rufus. The new manager guy? Ruthless more like.'

Becky laughed. 'Sounds like a right jobsworth.'

'You have no idea. Anyway, can I help? I'll need to be quick.' Amber's voice sounded unusually on edge.

'Just mother issues. And French café issues. The usual.' She quickly offered her friend a condensed version of the last twenty-four hours. The trip to the *maire*'s office, the call with her mother. 'Now I'm back to square one!' she said. 'I've no idea what I'm going to do!'

'No offense, but we talked about this last night. You know what I think. And I'm at work. It's difficult—'

'Sorry. I know. I just thought—'

Amber sighed, her tone softening. 'Look, I know you're dithering. But like I said last night, the way I see it, you only have two options. You can cut and run, come home and just be a little patient about things. Cancel the flat reservation. There will be other flats.'

'OK.'

'Or, you can stay and jump through these hoops your aunt has set for you. You have the time – and that's not likely to happen again. And what are you going to do if not? At least you won't be bouncing around the flat, stressing out, thinking about work... worrying. It just seems obvious to me. Get on with it and get it done. You'll feel better.'

'You know me too well,' Becky said, imagining how she might spend her days if she did return to London – the free time stretching away in all directions. She shivered. Too much time to think about what she'd got wrong.

'And, if you need more incentive to stay, I was thinking last night that maybe you could, well... work your magic while you're there.'

'What do you mean?'

'Well, you're in advertising, right? So you know a bit about selling. You've already told me that the café isn't being run to its full potential. Maybe the month won't be a complete waste. Maybe if you modernise it a bit, build the business, make it look... snazzy.'

'Snazzy? Have you been talking to my mum?'

Amber laughed. 'OK, modern – is that better? Make it look great. Increase the value, increase the chance of it selling. Stay, but on your own terms.'

Becky was silent for a moment. 'You make it sound so... logical.'

'Well, I am an accountant.'

'True.'

'So?'

'I guess I could try,' she said. 'I like the idea of... adding value.'

'I thought you would.'

'It was just being forced to...'

'I know. Classic Becky!'

'What do you mean?'

'You hate being told what to do. Always have.'

'No! I... OK, well, maybe.'

'It's not a criticism. You like to do things your way. I get that. And with your mum being so...'

'Pushy?'

'I was going to say forceful. Well, I get that you have enough... let's say *direction* in your life.'

'Exactly. I don't need to be pushed around by great-aunts from beyond the grave.' Becky felt a frisson of guilt in describing her aunt that way. Poor Maud.

'But nobody is pushing you, in reality. You have choices. And you know what, they're not too bad. You could be stuck in a job you don't like very much because you can't afford your rent without it.' Something cracked a little in Amber's final words.

'Oh. You don't mean you, do you?'

'Sometimes.'

'I thought you liked your job?'

'It's changed a bit, is all. I still like numbers.'

'Well! Who doesn't! They're just so... so... *numerical!*'

'I just prefer it when my boss doesn't stalk around the office like he owns us outright, rather than just forty hours of our weekdays. And when I don't have to hide in the loo to avoid another dressing down.'

'A dressing down? What happened?'

There was a pause. 'I'll tell you later,' Amber said. 'Honestly, I'd better go. People will get suspicious if I spend any more time in the loo.'

'OK. Well don't let the bastards grind you down.'

'I won't.'

'And Amber?'

'Yes?'

'You still complete me.'

Amber laughed. 'I know.'

Quoting from the movies they loved had become their thing.

An outsider might find it odd, but saying they completed each other had become their way of saying 'I love you.'

Amber really was her missing piece, the person without whom she wouldn't be complete, thought Becky. Without Amber at her side, she'd have struggled at times over the last few years. Or the last couple of decades in fact. Amber with her sage advice, her sense of fun. The way she could look through the complex arguments given by Becky's mother and extract the important bits on her behalf, when she got overwhelmed.

When Dad had had his heart attack, it was Amber who'd come and looked after them both. Staying overnight, making cups of tea. Just being there. She was the sister that Becky had never had. And the soft-sided relative that her mum had never been.

She hoped she'd been the same for Amber over the years. Amber's mum was anxious, not always easy to confide in. So Becky had tried to be there when Amber's mum couldn't.

'Couldn't do it without you,' she whispered into the ether.

Then, 'Right!' she said, stepping into her work persona. She walked over to the mirror and corrected her hair, neatening up her blonde ponytail, checked her teeth and nodded. She marched back down to the café and proprietorially made her way to the kitchen at the back. Pascal was there, a jug of milk in his hand. Their eyes met.

'Right,' she said. 'I've decided to stay for a while after all. There are quite a few inefficiencies here that I'd like to iron out. And a few improvements I'd like to make.'

'So you are fulfilling Maud's wishes!' he said, seemingly only hearing the highlights.

'No,' Becky said. 'I'm fulfilling *my* wishes. Getting this place shipshape for sale. And if that helps move things along for you as well, then so be it.'

'Oh, of course,' Pascal said, with a cheeky wink. 'Of course, these are *your* wishes.'

'No! Seriously! *My* wishes!'

'Yes. I *understand*.' He gave her an even more generous wink.

'Pascal! I'm here because I *want* to be. No other reason,' she said.

'Of *course*! Why would anyone suggest otherwise?'

And then, just when she was about to explain again – more forcefully this time – her eyelid decided to do the talking for her, with a quick trembling wink.

Pascal touched a finger to his nose. 'Your secret is safe with me,' he said. 'I understand completely.'

He didn't. But she was too exhausted with trying to explain. 'Good,' she said. 'So that's settled.'

8

'So, I've written some plans out,' she said, determinedly entering the kitchen that evening. Pascal, who was sitting at the large table in the communal kitchen drinking a glass of red wine, looked up, surprised.

That's right, she thought, *I'm in charge now.*

She opened her laptop and began to list the things she was aiming to improve in the café in her short duration as reluctant manager. 'Paint or replace front door. New matching chairs and tables. A decent coffee machine. Perhaps a glass cabinet on the counter – I was thinking we could sell muffins and doughnuts again? Maud used to years ago, I think. Ideally, I'd like to get a lick of paint throughout the place, just to brighten it up.' Her mouth opened again to form the phrase *What do you think?* But she held it back. She didn't need this man's approval – this was her place and if she was being forced to stay, she was doing it on her terms. Still, she felt annoyingly nervous on the inside.

Pascal shook his head, a flicker of an amused smile on his lips. He leaned slightly back in his chair, and she was tempted to bark at him like a teacher, to keep all four legs on the ground. Luckily, she was able to resist.

'What?' she said, when he hadn't spoken for an unbearable minute.

He shrugged, took a sip of his wine. 'To me, this seems like a lot of work. I think your aunt was just hoping you would learn to use the coffee machine, get a feel for the ambience of the place. Explore Vaudrelle.'

'Yes, I realise that. And I'm sorry, but she was totally misguided. Well-meaning, but misguided,' she corrected. 'I'm a doer. I like to be busy. And I'm not going to slack off because of some letter. I need to get value out of this visit, then get home. My whole life is in the UK.'

He raised an eyebrow. 'Your whole life? You have a big family? A husband?'

'No. My mother is there.'

'Ah, your mother is your whole life,' he raised a glass to her. 'This is a very sweet thing.'

'No!' she almost barked, feeling her face heat up. 'My mother is *not* my whole life. I just mean, she's my... well, I suppose I mean she's my only family.'

'Oh, I see.' Pascal frowned. 'It is just when you said it was your whole life, I thought you must have very many people who are waiting for you back home.'

'No. No one really. But... Just... well, my work – I'm pretty essential in my job,' she said.

'Oh, you have an important job? You are a doctor perhaps?'

'No. I'm... I work in advertising. But I don't just mean my job.'

Pascal nodded as if he were expecting this statement to be the start of a long list of important things she had back home.

'Um, and there's my friend, Amber.' She found herself smiling. 'We've been friends since we were five. She's like a sister to me.'

The nodding continued. Becky found herself racking her brain for more to add to the list. 'And I go to a pretty good spin class on Wednesdays,' she finished weakly.

Pascal's mouth made a brief downward inflection. 'I see,' he said.

'What?'

'Nothing.'

'No, you made a face. What are you suggesting?'

'No, it was not a face.' Pascal seemed confused. 'It was just my face. I am not sure what you mean.'

'You were judging me! OK, so I don't have a partner or children, or a place of my own, or many... many friends when it comes to it. But my life is my life, and I want to get back to it.'

'But of course!' he said, lifting his glass as if in a toast. 'I understand completely.'

'Anyway,' she said, giving up, 'what I'm saying is that, sadly, although I'm sure Maud meant well, there's just no way I'm going to give up everything and come and live here, however full – or empty – my life might be. So yes, I'll do what she wants, practise running this place, if that's what sorts this... this *situation* out.' She looked at him darkly. 'But I'm not going to waste my time waitressing or mopping floors. I'm going to use my skills to give this place a facelift.'

'A facelift?'

'A makeover. Then when it comes to sell...'

Pascal nodded. 'I see.' He seemed to be wrestling with something. 'OK, I understand, but may I offer some advice?'

'What is it?'

'You say that this place needs to be renovated. But you need to understand that this is not London. Before you judge, perhaps it is a good idea to learn a little about what this café needs? Today I served almost thirty people. We made good money. And people come here for the community, not the decor.'

'So?'

'I am just saying, um, *'Ne pas changer une formule gagnante'*. The café is already winning plenty of money. You don't need to make yourself tired. To waste money. So, you do not wish to live this life. I understand. It is not for everybody. But why not find happiness here for your month? Visit the town, find the life. Enjoy yourself. Rest.'

What was it with people telling her to rest all the time?

'Relaxation is overrated,' she found herself saying, almost clapping a hand over her mouth afterwards. Was she actually turning into her mother?

'This is very sad to hear.'

'What I mean is,' she tried to correct, 'I'm more relaxed when I'm busy.'

The downward inflexion again. Pascal nodded. 'OK, as you want.'

'Yes. Precisely,' she said firmly, not quite appreciating the amused smile this provoked in Pascal.

'Well, let me know how I can help,' he said, filling a large wine glass with an inch or two of deep red and pushing it towards her. He grinned, lifting his own to her. 'I suppose this means you are my boss.'

* * *

The next day, she set her alarm for six – an hour and a half before the café opened.

Waking in the room that had been hers for several childhood holidays still felt odd, momentarily disorientating each time she woke. But she couldn't have slept in Maud's room. She'd peeked into it last night, seen the neatly covered bed, the dressing table with an ornate mirror. Maud's things – some brushes, a little make-up – scattered over the top as if she'd simply walked out and would be back any minute. She'd shut the door, feeling the pricking of unwanted tears. She'd leave the room as it was for now.

Pascal was in the middle room, next to hers. The one she'd used to creep into in the night when she was scared, to seek out her dad's reassuring cuddles. She was desperate to see whether it, too, was almost the same as she remembered. But the door had remained closed and she didn't want to snoop. (Well, admittedly, she *did*, but had managed to restrain herself).

And then there was her own room with its tiny bed, chest of drawers and the view out of the back, over the properties that peppered the next road and beyond, to the lush countryside she remembered feeling so excited by when she was younger and more energetic.

Once up and dressed, she made her way quietly downstairs and started by taking an inventory – chairs, tables, cups, spoons. She looked at the range of coffee (exactly one blend), checked the fridge which, despite its outward appearance, was spotlessly clean inside, and the menu – just what was scribbled on the chalkboard. She wrote down a list of the things she'd want to start off by finding. The right colour palette. Someone local who was handy with a paintbrush and needed some work at short notice. Maybe a few paintings.

Last night, she'd taken time to chat to Pascal a little more and, despite her initial misgivings, had decided he was a good

The Village Café in the Loire 67

bloke. A little too attached to the eccentric wishes of her late aunt? Possibly. But nice all the same.

'How long have you worked here?' she'd asked.

'Ah, I do not consider it work,' he'd said. 'Your aunt let me stay in exchange for a little labour. But I also write – that is my passion.' He'd made a fist and lightly tapped his chest twice for emphasis. 'When I am done here, I hope I will have my novel ready too – I am on the final ten thousand words.'

'That's a lot to do.'

'What is it you said?' he'd asked, his head slightly askew. 'Relaxation is overrated?'

It was hard not to warm to him.

She still felt a little annoyed at her enforced break in France, but decided to make the best of her lot. After all, she had been forcibly removed from her workplace, so she might as well be here as somewhere else.

Last night in bed, she'd spent some time online looking up properties for sale in the local area. Most had been purely residential, but there were a few B & Bs and other businesses listed. She'd made a few calculations and very loosely decided that getting the business shipshape might help to net her a few more thousand in the asking price when it came to it.

For now, she'd have to dip into her savings – she didn't have a great deal of money, but it would only be tied up in the café for a short while – to get things moving along quickly.

Now, standing in the empty café, she felt a little strange. It was light outside, despite the early hour, but the street was almost silent. She walked around, pushing back the wooden shutters, imagining the many times her great-aunt must have done the same. Over the past few days, she'd thought about Maud a lot, trying to clutch some of the dusty half-memories that she had of her, thinking more about what she'd been like. Before she came, she hadn't been able to remember much about what they'd done when she'd visited as a child – other than a few trips they'd made. A garden somewhere? Visiting a chateau that looked straight out of a child's picture book, with cream stone walls and grey-topped turrets, and costumed figures depicting a fairy tale within. She had vague memories too of a winery where Mum and Dad had got quite giggly during a tasting, and she'd been allowed a crafty sip of red that had put her off alcohol for another decade.

Now she was here, although actual memories were vague and fleeting, she could remember how being with her aunt had made her feel. Away from the rather strict upbringing at home where Mum was firmly in charge and only the best was good enough, she'd been able to relax. Things that were of the utmost importance back in the UK – not putting feet on the seats, washing sticky fingers, having a bath every night – hadn't seemed to matter so much here. Bedtimes, too, had gone out of the window – she remembered staying up for a meteor shower, lying back on a bench in the dark garden, her head in her mother's lap, waiting for the next brilliant flash in the inky sky.

Perhaps it hadn't been her mother though, who wasn't particularly into sitting, or snuggling, or watching anything going on in the night sky, come to think of it. So it must have been Maud whose floral skirt she'd laid her head on, Maud's hand stroking her hair.

Out of nowhere, she felt a rush of tears and choked them back. This was the problem with not having a job, she realised. Too much thinking time. Perhaps Mum was right about relaxation. It was all very well if you were the sort of person who actually *could* switch off, relax. But someone like her – probably like her mother too – needed to keep moving, stay one step ahead of the introspection and dwelling that came in these silent moments.

The café floor was now flooded with sunlight. Dust particles danced in the air, and she could see how everything – the tables, tiled floor, even the countertop – was in need of a good deep clean. She'd had no intention of starting work yet, but still feeling a little agitated, she made her way to the kitchen and found some cleaning materials, a large plastic bucket, string mop, sponge. She filled the bucket with hot water and detergent and set to work scrubbing surfaces with the sponge, wringing out water, paying attention to detail. Soon the musty, coffee-filled smell was replaced with the sharp tang of lemon.

Then she began on the floor. She'd taken off her jumper by now and it was tied around her waist. Her T-shirt was drenched with a combination of splashed cleaning products and sweat. She changed the water twice, kept going until the tiles began to reveal themselves – bright red and cream, under what must have been weeks of dust and dirt. She wondered when they'd last been properly scrubbed, and couldn't help but wonder whether Maud's had been the last pair of hands to wield the mop.

Once finished, she ignored her aching limbs and dry mouth and climbed the stairs to the funny little bathroom. Washed and dressed half an hour later, she made her way outside where her booked taxi was already waiting. She'd called ahead to secure a van and hoped, with a mixture of English, franglais and French, that she'd managed to book a suitable vehicle. From there, she'd head to Tours and buy everything she needed to make the café her own. After that? Well, the sky was truly the limit.

And it was so beautifully blue, she thought, as she watched the early morning sunlight hit the patchwork of fields that lay beyond the village. The roads were quiet, the taxi driver listening to some music on low. It was a moment of absolute peace. For the first time, she realised how much her body ached, how much the last few days (and probably the months preceding) had taken out of her.

Well, she was in France, she thought. The perfect place to recharge her batteries. Who knew? After her café renovation she might even have time for a little holiday.

9

An hour later she was feeling less confident and definitely less relaxed. She'd never seen the road from this angle. Compared to the small cars she'd driven in the past, the van she'd hired was enormous. Add to this the fact that she had to drive on the wrong side of the road along a route she'd never travelled before, and it made the hour-long journey to the out-of-town retail park she'd earmarked seem both terrifying and precarious.

Then again, she was glad to have been able to hire the van at all. The guy behind the cash desk had looked at her dubiously when she'd handed her UK driving licence to him, as if he doubted it was real.

When she'd finally convinced him that her licence wasn't a fake and that she almost definitely could drive the van safely, she'd been given a set of keys and been walked over to a line of vehicles at the edge of a supermarket car park. Clicking the key fob, she'd been alarmed when, rather than the smaller vehicle she'd been eyeing, one of the larger vans had burst into life. It was truly monstrous, and not the size of vehicle she'd been expecting when she'd scrolled through her list of options at 6 a.m. in bed.

To save face though, she'd smiled as if she'd expected this outcome all along, yanked open the rather stiff door and half climbed, half clambered into the driving seat. She'd even made sure to give the member of staff a cheery wave as she'd departed, before returning her hand to its white-knuckled grip on the steering wheel.

Now on the road and following a satnav that refused to speak English, she felt a little more nervous, mitigating her fear by driving as slowly as she dared and causing a long line of cars to build up in her wake. Ignoring the odd beep of a horn or savage look by a driver who'd finally found a piece of road straight enough to overtake, she tried to focus instead on the shopping expedition ahead. Cups. Coffee maker. Chairs. Small tables. Tablecloths. Paint. Wallpaper. Brushes. Then home.

When she arrived, and after managing to park the van, she finally felt herself relax. And as she took in the variety of large and small stores that populated the retail park, she smiled to herself. Admittedly she was a little out of her depth in the café. But shopping? Shopping she knew.

She took a selfie outside a cute-looking furniture boutique and sent it to Amber:

BECKY

Channelling my inner Carrie Bradshaw: you can never have too many… soft furnishings!

AMBER

I dunno, pretty sure Carrie said that about shoes, not tablecloths…

BECKY

Style is style, my friend (smiling emoji)

AMBER

OK good luck! You still complete me!

BECKY

Me too.

It felt good to be in the bright lights and busier atmosphere of a retail park, even though she had to complete mental gymnastics every time she wanted to work out whether something was affordable. She invested in thirty porcelain mugs with gold rims, ordered some small tables, found a paint in a vibrant, sunshine yellow for the door, and a colourful wallpaper designed to look like blue wooden cladding that would do wonders for the blank back wall. She wasn't entirely sure what she needed in terms of amounts so overbought, if anything, and invested in a range of brushes and rollers to get the job done.

In a large DIY store she found material that could easily be fashioned into tablecloths, and just as she was giving up on finding suitable chairs, she popped into a little furniture boutique and managed to find some gorgeous ones with padded yellow cushions in soft velvet. They were expensive, but she forced herself to think of the bigger picture, buying the ten they had in stock and ordering a further fifteen. She focused on the money she'd make after selling as she typed in the PIN on her credit card once again.

The enormous van was still only half full as she pulled out of the car park onto the busy road, the content sliding around in the back despite her best efforts. But she was pleased with herself. She'd covered a lot of ground – done the hard bit, really. The choosing, considering colour, ambience. Trying to recreate everything she loved about coffee shops back home. She had in mind the type of soft chairs you could sink into with a book, or relax in when meeting with friends. Neat square tables that could seat two, or be pulled together in larger groups by customers when needed. A colourful feature wall, and muted tones for the rest of the café to highlight the space, the light and create a positive atmosphere. Cake and pastry sales seemed to have petered out, but she'd love to reintroduce the kind of fayre that Maud had once served – macarons in colourful piles, fresh croissants, chocolate-dipped madeleines and tiny chouquettes to place on each customer's saucer. The coffee selection could be widened, with special flavours for each season. And something in the decor to make it personal, special. Local art or sculpture. Maybe photographs.

It would take time, but this was at least a start. And perhaps Pascal would begin to see both that she was serious and that she actually did have pretty good taste.

After a couple of wrong turns and a strange encounter with a farmer, she found herself on the main route into Vaudrelle, and minutes later pulled up outside the café, causing the ten or so coffee drinkers inside to pause and stare as she stumbled out of the front seat onto the street.

Stomach rumbling, but with no time to lose as the van needed to be back in two hours, she began to unload, carrying rolls of wallpaper, paint trays and brushes through the café behind the counter and stacking them in the kitchen.

Each time she passed customers, she'd hear them exclaim in French, but had no idea what they were saying. In the little village, everyone would probably already know who she was and why she was here. Perhaps they were excited about the refit? Or impressed that she was getting on with things essentially alone and so rapidly?

'Do you want some help?' Pascal asked when she passed him a second time, carrying two heavy tubs of paint.

'No, I'm fine,' she said, despite being anything but. And actually desperately needing some help. She staggered into the kitchen, deposited the paint and walked back outside, cursing herself for saying what she had, but somehow unable to roll the time back and change her mind.

The chairs finally undid her. They were heavy, solid and she could only manage one at a time. Her plan was to clear a little space at the back, away from the counter, and stack them there as best she could until later; after closure, she could replace some of the ramshackle seating with her new, fancier versions. It was a shame the tables hadn't been available to take away, but it was a start.

Opening the door with her back, she heaved the first chair inside, feeling herself break out in a sweat almost instantly. She dragged it noisily across the floor into the corner and, once deposited, had to fight the urge to fling herself onto it. She had nine more to do. There was no time for a rest.

When she was back in the van, moving the second one towards the exit, with plans to hop down and lift it to the ground when she got there, she saw Pascal exit the café, rubbing his hands as if dusting coffee granules or sugar from them. He looked at her, his enormous smile stretched across his face again.

It was a lovely smile. Pascal was a good-looking guy. But for some reason he seemed to only smile properly when she was struggling in some way, which definitely made it less endearing.

'What?' she said.

'I am here to help.'

'Well, I don't need any help,' she snapped, feeling the prickle of heat in her neck.

'Perhaps,' he said. 'But maybe you will allow me to anyway? It will be quicker.'

This swung it. She really didn't want to have to deal with the fallout if she got the van back late. She'd signed so many forms with very little idea of what they said, and no idea what the penalty might be for any missteps.

'OK, if you want.' She gave a little shrug and just caught his grin before he turned his face quickly away.

'I know you do not need help,' he said. 'But I am worried that if I don't do this, the customers will think I am a terrible person, to allow you to struggle on your own.'

She nodded, intent on getting her chair out of the van. Pascal picked another one up with enviable ease and they staggered and walked respectively into the café, heads turning to watch their progress, then following them out again.

'Let me finish with the chairs?' Pascal suggested. 'Perhaps you can bring in some of those...' he trailed off, looking at the boxed-up mugs, 'enormous cups.'

It was unintentional, but Becky saw him grimace at the sight of the coffee mugs. 'They're porcelain!' she said, as if to defend them. 'Top quality. And they all match.'

'Of course. Of course...' Pascal said carefully, pausing and standing with a chair in his arms by the open van doors. 'It's just... never mind.'

'Just what?'

He shrugged. 'Perhaps most of our customers, they will struggle with such an enormous coffee. We prefer the petite, the little pick-me-up, not... a whole litre.'

'Yes, but I've ordered a machine. We can do lattes, cappuccinos, macchiatos – you wait. People will love it,' she said firmly.

'OK,' he said, nodding.

'No, wait,' Becky said, jumping down next to him, holding a single mug. 'What's the matter? Don't you like them?'

Pascal lifted a shoulder. 'I am a writer, not a businessman,' he said. 'But except for the tourists – and we do not get many in

The Village Café in the Loire 77

Vaudrelle, mainly in the summer months – it is rare that people do not simply order espresso.'

'Yes, because you don't offer anything else!' she said, somewhere between amused and exasperated. 'So they can't.'

Pascal nodded. 'I am sure you are right,' he said, in a voice that suggested he thought anything but.

Eventually the van was emptied, the kitchen stacked high with purchases, chairs teetering in loosely stacked piles in the corner of the café. Becky's muscles ached, her hands were red from carrying so much, her fingers tingling. Her back was wet with sweat and she felt revolting.

She sat in the kitchen for a quick rest before taking the van back to the rental company, sipping a glass of tap water that tasted slightly metallic.

Pascal came in and out, fetching things, putting used crockery in the dishwasher, often whistling to himself. From time to time his eye would graze the pile of decorative items she'd purchased and a judgemental eyebrow would shoot up, she assumed in response to her wallpaper choice, or colour palette. But she decided to not let it bother her.

She didn't know much about Pascal. Perhaps he just wasn't into decor. So what if he thought her coffee mugs were too big, that the chairs were too colourful. Perhaps he hated the idea of the wallpaper or the colour she'd picked to complement it on the opposite wall. He probably didn't want her to paint the rather rustic wooden door, and maybe even felt insulted that she'd invested in a coffee machine and new cups. Yet somehow, for some reason, she really wished he'd show some pleasure in what she was trying to do.

But he simply couldn't visualise it like she could. She worked every day in a world where people talked about vision and appeal – sure, she wasn't an interior designer, but she definitely had good taste. She'd been in a thousand coffee shops and could judge where this one was letting itself down. Besides, although she ached and her bank account had taken a hit, she felt positive and buzzy from the task in hand, and when envisioning what lay ahead. What better way to take the sting out of an incorrect diagnosis and a shattering period of enforced leave?

In a few weeks this place would be transformed. She'd have jumped through her aunt's hoops by working in the café for a period of time. Pascal would agree to go once the property was sold, and she'd put it on the market as soon as everything was organised.

By the time she returned from the rental company, in a taxi she'd had to wait an hour for, Pascal had just finished closing up. As she climbed out of the cab, he was in the process of turning the little cardboard sign in the window to '*Fermé*'. He saw her and smiled, opened the door and bowed a little as she went past. 'Good evening,' he said in quite a good British accent, and she couldn't help but laugh.

A few minutes later, he was taking off his apron in the kitchen when he said, 'I am going to see Maud this evening. I wondered if you wanted to come with me?' His voice was casual, but she felt weight behind his words. An accusation, maybe. And perhaps he was right – she was here because of Maud's gift, but it hadn't occurred to her even once to visit her great-aunt's grave.

'I should,' she said. 'I thought I might today, but I'm just... I'm exhausted, to be honest. But yes, I must do. Soon. Is it far?'

He shook his head. 'Not so far. I have a car, so it is not difficult.'

'Do you go... often?'

'I try. Usually once a week.'

'Wow! that is a lot!' She flushed. 'I mean, I'm sure she'd appreciate it, if she knew,' she added hastily.

'Oh, she knows,' he said confidently. 'She is always pleased, I think. But when you come – she will be delighted.'

'Thank you,' she said. 'Next time?'

'Next time.'

10

The following morning Becky was up early, replacing half of the chairs in the café with her new, plush versions. She stacked the older, ramshackle chairs in the corner, vowing to take them to a charity shop later on. As the day came into itself and the sunshine brightened, she stood back and contemplated her work.

It did look a bit odd at this stage – the chairs' newness and evident luxury made everything else in the café look shabby, highlighting the need for further change. But it was a start.

Pascal appeared behind her, coffee in hand. '*Mon Dieu!*' he said, slopping the coffee a little. 'Sorry, I did not expect to see you there.' His eye cast over the room, taking in the chairs, his mouth crinkling a little.

'What do you think?' she asked. 'I mean, I know they don't match everything yet. But when the tables come – and of course I've got a lot of work to do on the walls – I think they'll be a real asset. The colour pops, don't you think?'

'Yes,' he said, not sounding entirely convinced. 'The colour does, as you say, pop.'

Her eyelid gave a warning twitch as if detecting an untruth. 'Don't you like them?' she pressed.

'Well, perhaps it does not matter what I think. But, if I am entirely honest, perhaps they do not suit this café, this village, the customers we have.'

The fact that he was voicing what she'd secretly been worrying about made it somehow worse. 'Of course they do! People don't always know what they want until they see it!'

'Yes. Perhaps you are right.'

Something in his lacklustre tone, his reluctant agreement made her arms stiffen. 'Half the people who come here probably aren't used to something so comfortable. But if we give it to them, they'll realise how much better things could be. They just don't know any better!'

Pascal raised a quizzical eyebrow.

'What?' she said.

'I'm sorry. But you are making assumptions about the people of Vaudrelle. Yet you don't know them. You make them sound ignorant of the world. It is not true at all.'

'Of course, I know I don't know these people. But I run advertising campaigns for a major corporation. I'm used to thinking about what people want and working out ways to give it to them. Knowing people better than they know themselves.'

Pascal grinned.

'What?' she prompted again, feeling a prickle of anger.

'It is nothing,' he said. 'But it is a great talent to know people so well, so easily.'

'You know what I mean.'

'I am just saying that maybe it would have been better to spend some time here. Talk to people about what they like, what they don't like.'

'Have you *seen* the people who come here? They probably

never leave the village. They probably don't know how nice this place could be. I want to—'

Something in Pascal's expression shifted; darkened.

'*Non*. It is you who doesn't know. I am almost certain that even the backward, rural people who live here will have come across a cushion, *non*? But do they want it when they are stopping in the café for an espresso before looking after their fields, or walking their dog?'

'Well, perhaps they do. How do *you* know?'

Pascal shook his head. 'I do not know for certain. I would not presume to decide for them. But the café has been here for many years, and it is always full. There are always people here, dropping by, coming in. They can come in their boots, with their mud, with their dogs, and it is perfect for them. Maud, she understood this. It is a success. The takings are good. When you come to sell, someone will buy it.'

'There's nothing wrong with trying to make things nicer, better for people,' she snapped, feeling her face get red.

Pascal's nostrils flared. 'Of course not! But there *is* something wrong with deciding you know people, that you know a business, or village – and that you know better what people want. We may be a small village, but people here are intelligent, interesting, they have good jobs. René – he works with film studios in Paris; Clarence, the lady with the tiny dog? She is a poet with two books published. And the others, they have interesting lives. They travel. Do not decide who they are when you know nothing about them.'

Becky's eyelid went into overdrive and she felt tension tighten the muscles in her neck, her shoulders, even her legs. Unconsciously, she balled her hands into fists. 'I'm just trying to make this place nice for people. I'm trying to do the right thing!'

Pascal was shaking his head. 'Perhaps you believe this,' he

said. 'But it is not true. You have looked at the people here and decided who they are.' His voice quietened a little. 'And you have looked at me, too, and decided who I am. But you do not know me. You think I am a nuisance.'

'Hang on, how do you know what I think?'

'It seems to me that you are not interested in working here, fulfilling Maud's wish. Instead, you want to change everything; impose yourself on us when you have no intention to stay. All your aunt wants is for you to spend a little time here. Maud is very special to me. And it matters.'

'Oh, for God's sake, grow up!' she said. 'This is a business, and I'm being... businesslike! And why are you so obsessed with Maud anyway?' Somewhere, deep inside Becky, a smaller version of herself urged her to stop. But she was too far gone.

Besides, Pascal, who'd seemed so kind, so gentle, was being downright mean. What had got into him? They were chairs! How had it come to this? Amber briefly flitted into her mind – her comment about burnout, about anger, but she batted her away.

Pascal's cheeks coloured. 'Maud saw me when I was alone. She took me in, gave me a chance in life, a chance to live somewhere and follow my passion, my writing. And I will always be grateful for that.'

Becky felt suddenly exhausted. 'Well, good for you,' she said. 'Good for you and your... kindness. And I'm sorry. I'm sorry for saying that about Maud. But I don't see why you have to be so mean.'

Pascal stepped towards her, his voice softening. 'I am sorry if you think I have been mean. But you asked me what I think. And I told you.'

'I only wanted to know about the chairs! I didn't want a character assassination. Certainly not from YOU. I mean, what do you know about life? You're, what? Thirty? And you have achieved what, exactly? You run a coffee shop. You write, but you've never been published. You don't even have anywhere to live, not really. Just a room given to you by a pitying old lady. Who are you to judge me?'

Pascal's face was ashen, closed. 'And what have you achieved?' he said, his tone quiet but firm.

'I'm actually very successful.'

'Yes. You have a good job. But what else do you have? As far as I can see you have nothing. You are just someone with a good job. And perhaps not even that. If you are so very important, why is it so easy for you to spend a month here? Why does nobody care? What is happening to your job right now?'

It was like a gut punch. She turned and stormed past Pascal, rushing up the stairs to her room before flinging herself on the bed like an eleven-year-old in a tantrum. Her heart hammered in her chest, and it took a while for her breathing to slow. She propped herself up against a pillow and pulled her phone from her pocket, wiping away yet more tears. Amber. She needed to call Amber.

It took three tries to get hold of her. Each time the answerphone clicked in she'd hang up and call again. Clearly this wasn't a good time for Amber, but this was an emergency – her friend would understand.

Eventually the call was picked up and Amber whispered 'Hello' so quietly that Becky could barely hear her. 'I can't really talk,' she said. 'I've had to come to the loos again and apparently—'

'I'm sorry it's just... oh God, it's so awful,' Becky cut in, her voice still thick with tears.

'Oh no, what's happened?'

Becky took a breath and told her friend about the chairs,

about how she'd got up early to put them out. Pascal's reaction. The argument.

Afterwards, Amber was silent.

'What do I do?' Becky said. 'I mean, he's not right, is he? I don't understand why I have to stay here, why I have to put up with this.'

Amber cleared her throat. 'Well,' she said, carefully, calmly. 'First of all, you don't have to stay, don't have to put up with it. You've chosen to be there and you can choose to leave. You're not trapped.'

'I know, but then...'

'Yes. I know. I know all the reasons why you're there. But have you considered what it's like from Pascal's point of view? This has been his home, his lifeline, for years. And he seems very dedicated to Maud. I know that doesn't suit your plans, but it doesn't make him a bad guy.'

'Well no, but—'

'Nor does him not liking your chairs, Becky. They're chairs, for God's sake!' Amber's voice hardened.

'All right! There's no need to be like that about it.'

Silence again. Then, 'Maybe there is.'

'What?'

'Well, maybe you do need to be told sometimes,' Amber said, her voice still quiet, but firmer, more forceful at the same time. 'Perhaps Pascal does know more about the village, about the clients, what they'll like. He ought to.'

'I've seen the customers! And you should see this place, Amber, it's nothing like the cafés back home.'

'No, probably not. But maybe it's right for the place. Look, I'm not being horrible. I do understand that you're... up against it. Stressed. But they're only chairs. So what if he doesn't think they're right. People will sit on them anyway.'

'Anyway, I've bought them all now.'

'But maybe next time you get something, well, just involve Pascal a little. It can't hurt. Unless you decide to ditch this whole plan, you're stuck with each other for a while.'

'So you're taking his side.'

'For God's sake, Becky. Try to see things from someone else's perspective for once.'

'Pascal's?' she snorted.

'Well, yes. And mine. You've just called me three times at work when you know I'm up against it here, that personal calls are forbidden. You've said it was an emergency but all I can see is that you've had a falling out with Pascal. But you called me anyway, knowing that it would make my life difficult.'

'Amber! I didn't mean—'

'Look, I'm at work. It's... I've got to go.'

'No! I get it. I won't call you at work again. But now you're here, don't go. I need someone to talk to.'

'Don't we all?'

'What's that supposed to mean?'

'Look, you know I've got your back. But maybe Pascal has a point. It wouldn't hurt you to listen sometimes. You're very good at... telling people things. But when's the last time you actually stopped to listen; considered that someone might have had a point?'

'Wait a minu—'

But the line was dead.

11

After her fight with Pascal and subsequent phone call with Amber, Becky didn't feel like coming out of her room. The last thing she wanted to do was face him, or have him see her face all red and streaked with tears. Eventually though, she became so hungry that she thought she might begin to gnaw the woodwork; it was time to take a risk.

She searched 'local restaurants' on her phone, but details were sparse. Nobody seemed to have a website, and the information thrown up didn't include any contact details.

Left with no choice, she went to the bathroom and put on enough make-up to hide her red blotches. Then, wrapping a light coat around her, she crept downstairs as stealthily as a teen sneaking out to see a forbidden boyfriend. Pascal was in the kitchen, so she crept out the back way instead, across the little patch of grass – another underutilised area – behind the café, then over the small wall onto the patchwork pavement.

It was only nine o'clock – still light and still with enough warmth in the air to make her coat unnecessary after five minutes' walking.

The main road through the village was flanked either side by stone houses, of various designs. Some three storeys high, with attic windows open to let the cooler evening air in; others were squat bungalows or renovated barns. There seemed to be no rhyme or reason to the design – as if the town had sprouted up organically according to need, with no real central plan.

One or two businesses were tucked along the way – a hairstylist's bordered by two ordinary houses, then a front for some sort of decorating firm. A small shop, which had closed at 7 p.m., its windows gloomy with no light from within. She put her face to the glass like Charlie from Roald Dahl's famous book – wondering what delights she might glimpse inside. But it looked to be mainly pots of jam and tins of confit, an empty windowed cabinet where perhaps there'd been pastries earlier in the day.

Anyway, what was she going to do? Break in? She'd had enough food with her for her first evening – a sandwich she'd acquired on the plane that had been too enormous to eat, a couple of glasses of Pascal's wine and some bread to mop it up with had felt fine. In Tours, she'd grabbed a few bits and pieces from a small grocery store at the retail park, but now supplies were running low, and she barely had a croissant to her name.

Now she was hungry and too annoyed with Pascal to get off her high horse and ask him where she could get something to eat. Her phone beeped as she walked along and she looked at it keenly, but it was just an overdue text from her phone company welcoming her to France and reminding her about roaming charges. Still nothing from Amber.

Before she could think too much about the argument and torture herself again with her friend's words, a smell hit her nostrils and she sniffed the wind like an animal picking up the scent of a tasty piece of prey. Someone, somewhere, was cooking. *Please be a restaurant*, she thought. *Oh, please be a restaurant.*

She turned down a little road just beyond the tiny church with its mismatched stained-glass windows and enormous wooden door, and could just make out a lit-up window with a sign above the door which read: '*Chez Régine*'. Jack-bloody-pot, she thought, picking up her pace.

The restaurant was tiny, only served one special, and was almost empty, but it was open. And that, by this point, was all that mattered. She walked in and took a seat at one of their small wooden tables, nodding at an elderly couple across the other side of the room. The smell inside was even more delicious and she was horrified to hear her stomach start to growl audibly, certain that everyone within a ten-metre radius must be able to hear the noise of her digestive juices grumbling.

Then, at last, a woman stood at her side, notebook poised. She looked to be about forty, with a long floral dress, apron around her waist, beautiful wavy hair tied back. She smiled. '*Qu'est-ce que je vous sers?*'

And of course, this was where her little bit of French came in handy. They'd done a whole unit on cafés at school and she could just about work out that she was being asked what she wanted. She pointed to the specials board. '*Le plat du jour?*' she said. She wasn't entirely sure what it was, but she knew it would be food. And right now, that was enough. '*Et un verre du vin rouge,*' she added in her imperfect but hopefully understandable French. As long as wine would be served, she didn't much care about her grammar.

Not usually a big drinker, the upset of earlier, the fact she was in a strange place, her eyelid's determination to keep on flickering now and then, whenever she thought it might have stopped, had tied her insides in knots. A glass of red would help her to relax.

The woman nodded, said something rapidly in French –

about the special perhaps? – and disappeared with a smile. She'd eat whatever she'd ended up ordering, Becky decided. She looked at the few other patrons: a couple in their seventies, the man pouring the woman a glass of wine from a carafe; another much younger couple, holding hands across the table. Watching them, it didn't bother Becky that she was alone; she was used to being single, often popped out for a bite on her own during lunchtime or sometimes in the evening.

The final table was occupied by three women who looked to be in their thirties and were a little more dressed up than the rest of the clientele, in fitted trousers and colourful tops. They were laughing at something, one of them leaning on another and all completely lost in the moment. Watching them, Becky felt a sudden longing to call Amber. Or to be at home in their flat, putting the world to rights with her best friend. She turned away, feeling suddenly flooded with emotion, not wanting to embarrass herself in this restaurant, which might well be the only one in Vaudrelle. Without a hire car, she was going to need to come back here frequently if she hung around.

An hour later she made her way a little unsteadily along the dusky road, the light fading and making the houses look more uniform, their colours merging together into an indiscriminate grey. She passed a couple walking their dog, but otherwise the streets were silent and felt rather eerie. Her footsteps echoed on the stones of the pavement and she felt strangely isolated. Lights shone in the windows of houses, the flats above the few shops, but here she was, alone in the shadows.

She shook herself. 'Just get home and sleep it off,' she told herself firmly. 'You'll feel better in the morning.'

When she reached the café, she let herself in the front door, winding her way around the furniture – the old tables and the new chairs clashing even in the half-light – and made her way to the kitchen. Pascal was nowhere to be seen – hopefully he'd gone to his room for the night and she could avoid him until tomorrow. She didn't know whether she was angry or ashamed, but knew she couldn't cope with any more conflict tonight.

She'd overeaten a little and her stomach felt uncomfortable. She'd been so hungry that she'd eaten the rather plain-looking, but actually delicious stew she'd been served in hungry gulps, washed down with red wine and followed by an ill-advised mousse-cake for dessert. She'd never sleep like this.

She helped herself to a glass of water from the dispenser on the fridge door and took a few sips. A little light still came through the window – the last of the daylight mixed with the first light from the moon – and rested on the tins of paint she'd stacked in the corner.

Pascal was wrong, she decided. The café needed a makeover and there was nothing wrong with bringing something up to date. In fact, she'd prove it to him. Suddenly energised, she slipped off her shoes and pulled her hair back with a band she kept on her wrist. Then, before she could overthink it, she lifted one of the paint pots and inspected the colour. It was beautiful, even in this light.

She'd show him. Taking a brush, a palette and the tin, she made her way a little unsteadily through the door to the silent café. There was no way she'd be able to paint the whole thing, but a few metres of colour would be a great way to prove to Pascal when he came down in the morning that Becky meant business.

She switched on a couple of the low lamps rather than go the whole hog and illuminate the café at this late hour, and dipped in her brush, drawing it across the flat, plastered surface, watching it turn from off-white to a gorgeous deep blue. Then again and again.

But soon she was flooded with tiredness and regret: the paint was thin, the paintbrush poor quality, and her body felt heavy and tired as the wine and the adrenaline wore off. She kept having to revisit her work to pick out hairs and work the paint to get it smooth.

Her back began to sweat, her neck prickled and she began to wish she'd never started. But she had to at least leave it in a reasonable state before she went to bed. 'Fuck,' she said to herself as yet another hair came out of the brush and stuck to the badly painted wall.

Bending down to dip the brush in again, she took in the smell of the paint and gagged slightly – it was non-toxic, but still packed quite a heady punch. She was so tired. And so overfull. And probably a little bit drunk. Then, out of nowhere, she felt a strange sensation fizz through her limbs; felt her knees buckle. She grabbed for something, and in her haste upset the tin which spewed its contents across the floor, turning the tiles blue. Just as her vision began to flicker, she heard her name being called.

Strong hands grabbed her waist and helped her move to a chair where she slumped, her head on the table as the dizziness subsided. When she finally raised her head, aware that her hair was sweaty and messy, her face red, her body still not quite sure whether it was going to remain conscious, she saw Pascal, dressed in chequered pyjama bottoms and a white T-shirt, hair dishevelled; his eyes filled with concern. 'Here,' he said, pushing a glass of water towards her on the table. 'Drink.'

She lifted the cool glass and drank, feeling how dry her throat was. Finally, she looked at him.

'What were you doing? It is almost midnight. I thought someone had broken in!' His voice was tense, but his eyes remained fixed on her; kind, gentle. He was worried, she realised.

'I know, I just wanted... Needed really to... This wall – I just thought...' Their eyes met.

'You are rushing,' Pascal said simply, putting up his hand and touching her shoulder lightly. 'First we look after number one. Then we work.'

'Sorry?'

'Like on a plane: the mother must fit her own oxygen mask before she looks after her child. You must take care of yourself before you can take care of the café.'

She felt a slight wave of dizziness and nodded mutely. Then, 'I just want to make this work,' she said. 'This has to work. Otherwise...' Her voice cracked.

'Otherwise what? Otherwise the café will be white instead of blue? The chairs will be slightly less comfortable? It is nice to improve things. But it is not important. Not really. Not worth making ourselves ill over.'

'But I can't fail at this too,' she found herself saying.

'I am sorry if I made you feel like this,' he said. 'Like you are not succeeding. Sorry for my words earlier. I do not think you have nothing. Perhaps I find it hard to understand you. But I should not have said those things.'

'It's not you. I'm just... I feel a bit lost I suppose. Anyway, you were right really. I actually do have nothing. My mum, well, she's... I suppose she's never been quite like you'd imagine a mum would be. Never very... nurturing. I have my friend Amber – although I think I've messed things up with her. And my work is a disaster. I'm a disaster. And now I've made a mess of this too.'

Her head fell forward, partly from tiredness, partly from misery. But Pascal reached out and lifted her chin gently with his fingertips. '*Non*,' he said. 'You are tired. And perhaps have chosen a bad time to paint. But nothing is so bad. It is just paint.

It will dry. We will correct it. In ten years, maybe less, someone new will paint it again. It does not matter.'

She nodded miserably.

'Let me clear this up,' he instructed. 'You go to bed. Things will be better in the morning, you'll see.'

She nodded again and got to her feet, standing for a moment to test her balance before finding that she was OK to walk. 'Thank you,' she said.

'It is nothing. Just a paintbrush to wash.'

'No. For everything. For being kind to me. It's... well not many people in my life are kind. Or maybe they are, and I'm too busy to notice.' Her eyelid flickered again, and she felt suddenly just how tired she was of all of it.

'Of course,' he said. 'Do not think about it. And I am sorry you have so many horrible people in your life. Maud, when I got stressed about my work, she always used to say that it is OK to get things wrong. To fail. This is how we grow.'

'Well, looks like I'm going to be growing A LOT,' she said with a watery smile.

He laughed, lightly. 'Perhaps,' he said.

Before leaving the room, she turned and looked at him, earnestly clearing up her things, and felt a rush of gratefulness before turning and making her way to bed.

12

The next morning there was a tentative knock on her bedroom door. She groaned, rolling over, feeling her head throb. 'Yes?'

'No rush, but I have some breakfast for you in the kitchen when you are ready,' said Pascal from behind the thick wood.

'Oh! Thank you!' she said, sitting up slightly. 'I'll just be a moment.'

She climbed out of bed rather reluctantly, and pulled on a pair of jeans and a sweater. She'd have her usual weird bath after eating, she decided, and made her way down the stairs.

After Pascal's kindness the night before, she felt a little shy to see him, but he beamed at her as she came into the kitchen as if nothing untoward had happened. He gestured to a plate of pastries on the table, a carafe of coffee, a plate and – in an apparent gesture of solidarity – one of her enormous white mugs.

Through the open door, she could see the interior of the still closed café; her eyes rested on the wall she'd nearly collapsed against last night. And she gasped.

'But it's...' she said, looking at the smoothly painted wall. 'You...'

Pascal joined her in the doorway, folding his arms. 'Yes, perhaps I tidied it up a bit.' He smiled and raised an eyebrow.

'It looks... Thank you.'

'Ah, it is nothing. I did a lot of painting for my mother in the past. And I had some time.'

'In the night?'

He shrugged. 'What is that you said? That rest is overrated?'

She turned to him, grinning, and gave him a playful slap. 'Now you're being facetious!'

'Perhaps a little.'

She looked at the wall again. 'Thank you,' she said. 'Really. But... why?'

He touched her shoulder lightly, gently. 'Last night you felt alone,' he reflected.

'Yes.'

'When I came here, that's how I felt too. A little lost.' His arm rubbed her back lightly. 'I wanted to show you that even when we feel we are alone, it is often not the case. I may not feel that the renovations you wish to do are necessary. But I will help you, Becky.'

Relief flooded through her and she stood on tiptoes and kissed him firmly on the cheek, flinging her arms around him. 'Thank you,' she said, seeing his neck redden.

'It is nothing. Let's get the café open,' he said. He turned and walked back into the kitchen, his hand subconsciously rising up to touch his skin where her lips had been.

Becky pulled out a chair and sat at the table. 'Wow, thanks for this,' she said a few minutes later when Pascal wandered back through with an empty jug.

'I do not always start my day this way,' he replied, turning from the fridge with a bottle of milk and smiling. 'Or I would probably not fit through the door into the café. But sometimes you need to do breakfast properly. This is one of those times.'

'Well, it's appreciated,' she said, picking up a still warm croissant and pulling it gently apart on her plate. She popped a piece in her mouth and closed her eyes. It was delicious – buttery, fresh, just the right amount of sweet. 'Are these from the *boulangerie*?'

'*Non*, I made them myself,' he said.

'You didn't!' He truly was talented.

'*Non*,' he said mischievously, 'I didn't. They are from the *boulangerie* as you thought. I am an artist with words, but not so much with pastry.'

She laughed. 'You'll have to let me read your stuff.'

'In French?'

'Ah, perhaps not. Maybe if you get a translation some time?'

'You will be top of the list.'

She sipped coffee in silence for a moment, still feeling around the edges of what seemed to be the beginning of a friendship. 'So, tell me about Maud,' she said. 'How exactly did you meet?'

'Well, I came here from Paris, two years ago,' he told her, leaning against the counter, the milk forgotten. 'I was given the opportunity to be a writer in residence at the *Centre d'Arts* and everything seemed wonderful to me. But the placement ended after six months and I was no further forward with my work. I was embarrassed to go back to Paris empty-handed, so I rented a small room in Vaudrelle and was determined to finish my book and go back triumphant!' He gave a wry smile. 'Clearly this did not happen.'

'Oh. I'm sorry.'

'It is OK. I wasn't ready then. My work, it was too shallow, too young. Now it is better, I think.'

She nodded. 'So you met Maud in the café?'

'Yes. Sometimes I would come here in the daytime. It was winter and my room was often very cold – I was a cliché of a poor writer, slaving away for my art. Maud would serve me coffee, and we got to talk, and she was very sympathetic to me. She read some of my work and she said she liked it – perhaps she was just being kind? I am not sure. Then when my tenancy ran out, she offered for me to stay.'

'That was nice of her.'

'Yes. She was always a very kind person. And also, she told me that I could live above the café, instead of paying rent, which was kind. She became like a mother to me, perhaps. My own mother, in Paris, she wants me to work in a bank, or become a lawyer. And maybe I will one day. But I want to give this a chance first.'

'Your mother doesn't like your writing?'

He shook his head, smiling. 'I do not know, she has never read it! My mother doesn't think that being a writer is a proper job. She thinks I'm a silly boy.'

Becky gave a smile. 'Well, I guess mums don't always know best.'

'*Non*, this is true. Anyway, over time I became Maud's friend. And I saw that she was not just an old lady, but a kind person with a big heart. And perhaps a little lonely too.'

'Oh.'

He shrugged. 'Maud was very popular in the village. She spoke beautiful French, had many friends. But no lovers. And no family around. I think she sometimes felt that... absence. She would talk a little about you – your mother was her niece, yes? – and sometimes tell me that she was sad that you stopped coming to see her. Because she didn't really have a connection like that – of blood – with anyone else.'

Becky laid down the piece of croissant she'd been attempting to eat, feeling rather sick. 'I didn't know,' she said. 'I suppose, I never really thought about Maud. I was so young when we stopped coming. I sort of forgot about her. Forgot to think of her.'

Pascal nodded. 'It is easy to do this when we are young. We think that all adults have full lives and make the right choices, and that we have much to learn. Then we become adults ourselves and...' He gestured to himself as if indicating that he was definitely an unfinished product.

'Still. I should have written. Or come over when I was old enough. Just... well, not everyone in the family would have wanted me to.' She couldn't go into the issue of her mother right now. Pascal would never have time to serve coffee. 'But it's no excuse, really.'

'You could go to see her now, to say sorry perhaps? It might make things feel a little better?'

She nodded. 'I will. Soon.'

'That is good,' he said, softly. 'I can take you, when you are ready.'

'Thank you.' She hated the thought of visiting a graveyard alone, scouring the headstones for her great-aunt's. 'And where will you go after this?'

'I am about to open the café... then—'

'No! Sorry, I mean, after you leave here. Sorry, that sounds really crass. I'm not being... I don't know, pointed. I just wondered what your plans are.'

He smiled. 'It's OK. I think I will go back to Paris when I leave here. It has been a long time now. I have friends there, family. My mother.' He rolled his eyes to suggest that perhaps not everything was good between them. 'And now I have an agent and possibly a publisher, maybe I will be successful enough for my mother to acknowledge.'

She smiled. 'I do feel bad, you know. Kicking you out. Making you leave.'

'Don't. It is time for me to move on. I just want to do it properly. To fulfil my promise to Maud to make sure the café is in good hands. Perhaps it's stupid – I am sure another owner will take the café and it will be just as successful. But sometimes I think that Maud gave me a home, and because of her I have a chance to make a success of my writing. And I am superstitious about it – I need to fulfil her dream because it will make it more likely that my dream will come true also!' he laughed, self-deprecatingly. 'As you can see, I am completely mad.'

'Well, maybe not completely...' She grinned. Pascal looked up, their eyes locked and he returned her smile. It felt good to feel on the same side, not to be at war, as she'd assumed at first.

'Can I share one more thing?' he said, finally filling the jug with milk to take into the café.

'Of course!'

'Your aunt, she told me once she was worried about you. Because of your mother. Because she felt that your spark would be extinguished.'

'My spark?'

'Yes. Perhaps I am not explaining very well. But I think that Maud felt when you were younger, the two of you had so much in common. You used to paint together, yes? And you were creative?'

'Well, everyone paints as a kid, I suppose.'

'Well, she felt a bond. And she felt that your mother perhaps was not so keen on you being artistic. She was always seeking out money, success! I remember it clearly because I thought *Ah, perhaps I am not the only one with a mother like this!*'

Becky smiled. 'Perhaps not.' She was silent for a moment. 'But how did Maud know about my life? I... I mean, I was ten when we stopped coming.'

Pascal grinned. 'Well, even here in rural France we have the internet. Instagram. Facebook. All of those things. She saw you sometimes online. She used to show me your picture and tell me about you.'

'Oh.' Maud had always struck her as so old, the village she lived in so backward, that the idea of her looking Becky up on Instagram seemed bizarre. 'Well, luckily she was wrong. I never really missed the art.'

Pascal nodded, straightening up. 'That is good.' He smiled. 'Do you want to help in the café today? Perhaps learn to serve coffee?'

Something inside her dropped. She really, really did not want to help in the café. She wanted to find a decorator, to sort out the paint job. To check that the tables were still coming. But now that Pascal had been so nice to her, she ought perhaps to show a little enthusiasm. 'OK,' she said. 'I'll just get ready, then... for a little while?'

He nodded. 'Good. I can perhaps do some writing while you serve? I can edit some pages before I send them to the publisher. They are ready, but I feel the need to check them just one more time. This could be *ma chance en or*.'

'A golden opportunity?'

'*Oui.*' He smiled, modestly. 'It has been a long time coming, perhaps.'

She laughed. 'Well, it sounds great. I'll just freshen up first.' She pointed to the stairs before turning and making her way up.

As the bath filled, she rang Amber. Usually by this time of

the morning, both of their message threads would be filled with silly comments and GIFs, little jokes or anecdotes. She hadn't realised they had become such an important part of her everyday life until she'd missed them. The first thing she'd done on waking was send a GIF of a puppy with enormous eyes, pawing at the camera with the words 'I'm soweee' written across the picture. But she'd had no response, despite the fact a little icon told her that Amber had seen it.

As the line rang out, she felt a kind of sick feeling rising up in her. The answerphone cut in and she rang once more. This time she left a message.

'Hi, Amber. It's Becky. Well, you know that, obviously. I just... can you call me when you get a chance? I hope you're OK. Sorry again. Bye!'

Then, stepping into the warm water and taking her habitual cat-in-a-cardboard-box position, she began to wash off the debris of yesterday and tried to focus on moving forward.

13

'So, is it all sorted?' Her mother didn't even bother with a hello. Becky, who had had quite a relaxing start and was just enjoying a cup of coffee in the kitchen before a quick shift at the café, felt tension return to her body immediately.

'Not quite,' she said, thinking of the beautifully finished wall Pascal had somehow made good, and trying not to panic at how she might fare when she wielded a paintbrush again.

'Well, what are you doing? You've been there a week. Surely it's time to up sticks!'

'Mum, it's going to take a bit of time, I think.'

'Oh, tosh! Rebecca, think about it. What if that firm of yours comes to its senses and needs you to come back in urgently? They're hardly going to warm to the idea that you're lazing around in France, are they? And I don't see what you can achieve there that you can't achieve back here. It's one world these days with technology. I think you should get yourself back home.'

'I'm aiming to come soon...'

'Well, good. Darling, I don't mean to be pushy. It's just that I worry about you there, what with your health.'

This was news to Becky. Surely her mum hadn't bought into the idea of her being burnt out. 'I'm fine! You said so yourself. It was just the doctor being overzealous.'

'Still, I'd prefer you to be here for me to keep an eye on you.'

Becky's mum worked such long hours that they barely saw each other – the idea of her mother actually hovering over her, looking after her was almost laughable. Plus, she didn't need that. She was perfectly fine. 'Mum, you know I'm thirty now, so... honestly, I can look after myself.'

'Hmm.' Her mother didn't sound convinced. 'Yes, I daresay. But it's that place, Rebecca. It had an effect on you and your father. Both of you became complete slugabeds whenever we went there!'

'Slugabeds?' Despite her mother's stern tone, it was impossible sometimes to take her talking-tos seriously.

'You know, you laid about like a couple of dilly-dalliers. And then your father – God rest him – started to talk about moving there. I mean. Can you *imagine?* What on earth would we have done?'

'It might have been OK?'

The silence prickled on the line.

'Rebecca Thorne, are you telling me that you think I should have done things differently?!'

'No, no – I understand.' Becky rubbed her forehead with her fingers, wondering how they'd got here, conversationally. 'Look, I do mean what I say. I want to come back as soon as I can. I just... things are complicated.'

'Well, work a bit of that Rebecca magic on them all,' her mum said firmly. 'You'll soon show them what's what.'

'Great. I'll just do that then.'

But her mother didn't seem to pick up on the sarcasm. 'Atta

girl. You show that squatter who's boss. And get back here, to reality.'

'Will do.'

Once the call had ended she sent another message to Amber.

BECKY

Are we OK? You still complete me!

They'd argued before, from the get-go. Squabbling over balls and games in the school playground, fussing over this and that. Living together in their shared flat, they'd often had disagreements about teabags, or mess, or whose turn it was to take out the rubbish. But they'd never fallen out properly, not like this.

It was hard to remember what it had even been about. She'd rung up upset from her argument with Pascal and Amber had given her short shrift, she remembered that. Amber was stressed about work, Becky got that. But what had she said that had upset her friend so much? She'd been in such turmoil she couldn't really remember.

She felt a pang in her chest, probably indigestion from rushing her coffee, and rubbed it absent-mindedly, wondering what she could do to make things OK again between them. If she were home it would be easy – bringing a cake home after work, offering to get a takeaway. Here, she was at a disadvantage. Especially if Amber wouldn't even speak to her.

Then a beep from her phone.

AMBER

It's OK.

She seized it and began to type ferociously.

BECKY

> Oh! I'm so glad. Amber, you can't imagine how difficult it's been! I have so much to update you on here. Pascal's actually a great guy and I've been serving coffees, can you believe? I've got stuck in with the decorating too. Not that successfully. But I'll explain when we speak. Oh God, and Mum is on the warpath! I think she worries I might ditch my job altogether and come and live a life here like mad Maud.

The little icon appeared, confirming that her message had been seen. But Amber didn't respond. Becky waited for a moment, to see whether the three little dots that indicated someone was typing appeared, but nothing did. Then again – she checked her watch – it was 8 a.m. back in the UK now. Amber was likely on her way to work. That was probably it. Still, it was odd that she'd texted so much only to be ignored once again. She noticed that her knee had started its habitual tremble and stilled it with her hand.

Amber had become so much part of the furniture of her life that she hadn't realised how crucial her presence in it was; how vulnerable she felt without the woman she jokingly referred to as 'my other half'. Perhaps Jerry Maguire was right, perhaps some people really did complete each other.

Trying to take her mind off things, she got up, tucked her phone into her pocket – resolving not to look at it until at least lunchtime – and took her cup to the sink. Then she went and unlocked the front door of the café and prepared for the morning's trade.

Pascal had already shown her how to work the espresso machine – which had been pretty straightforward all in all – and she had enough French to take basic orders. To her surprise, she even quite enjoyed the process of getting out cups, filling them, taking them to tables, collecting empties.

The café's offering was basic – black coffee, herbal tea or water; sometimes a pastry or a biscuit. Once in a while a customer would request hot chocolate which would mean whisking spoonfuls of cocoa into warm milk. But most people just requested '*un café*' and seemed quite content with the inch and a half they were served. Prices were low, but the café usually had at least ten people – some of whom stayed and became a kind of backdrop to the day, conversing with new people as they came and went, some of whom were in and out in an instant.

Mum had nothing to worry about – working in the café wasn't Becky's dream – but for a few hours on a few days, it could be quite dreamlike in its own way. Methodical, and busy in a way that didn't tax her too much. It was kind of relaxing: not the 'overrated' kind, but the kind that enabled her to simultaneously make people's day a little brighter and give Pascal the time he needed to work on his manuscript.

He took over at midday, looking thoroughly refreshed, and thanked her profusely. 'Don't be silly,' she found herself saying. 'It was my pleasure.' And, she realised, it really had been.

Her mood shifted downward as she checked her phone and saw a brief message from Amber.

AMBER

Try not to stress

But nothing more. At least it was a response of sorts, Becky thought.

She'd just slipped her phone back into her pocket when it began to ring, and she was so certain it was Amber she barely glanced at the screen before answering. 'Hello, you!' she said, smiling, as she put the phone to her ear.

'Is this Rebecca Thorne?' an efficient-sounding voice asked.

'Oh,' she said. 'Yes. Sorry.'

'Oh good. It's Michelle, from the London office. I've been covering some of your work on the Tudors account and wonder whether you'd got the latest magazine copy signed off, or whether I need to finish it up for you.'

Her head started to spin. 'Oh. God. Yes.' She racked her brain. In reality it had only been a week or so ago that she'd been all over this thing and now it was as if she'd wiped it from her mind. 'Um... I can't remember... let me think.' She scrunched her face with effort. 'Yes. I think it was all sorted before I left... but perhaps run it past Geoff to make sure.'

'So it's not complete, then?' Michelle sounded impatient.

'I don't have the files in front of me so...'

'Fine. Thank you.'

The line went dead without a goodbye. Although what was she expecting? Everyone was so rushed off their feet in the firm, there was no real time for niceties, especially for employees who'd chucked laptops and been given sick leave and left everyone else in the shit. Luckily, they didn't know she was in France. Not that she wasn't entitled to be here – of course she was, she was meant to be relaxing after all – but there was something too flagrant about it. She should be sitting in a white room with only calming music, water and the odd grape, not living it up in the sunshine.

Unless they could tell. What if they'd realised they were calling internationally? How would it look?

Suddenly she felt odd. Her breathing seemed to become more erratic; her head started to spin. She sat down, head in hands, and tried to slow her gasps down, but it seemed her body had taken control of things and she was at its mercy.

Thoughts spun around her head – Maud, whom she'd let

down without knowing; Mum, whom she seemed to disappoint on a daily basis. Amber who was being cold and she wasn't sure why. She was here, alone, without anyone who had her back. What was she actually doing here? What would happen when she went back? Would there even be room for her?

Somewhere beyond her hot, hyperventilating state, someone appeared. The person crouched in front of her, encouraging her to match his breathing. In and out, in and out. And gradually the mists cleared, her heart rate dropped to its normal rhythm and she was able to open her eyes again.

14

'What happened?' Pascal said once her breathing had steadied and she was feeling a little better.

'Nothing, really. I was just here, and there was a phone call. And then...'

'From your mother? She upset you?'

This assumption at least, made her smile, although it was a genuine enquiry. 'Well yes, she was first,' she said, 'but I was fine after that. It was actually a call from work asking me a question. Which is weird because I've been hoping they'd call, really; it's nice to be in the loop, you know?'

He looked at her confusedly and straightened up, moving to the fridge to get a bottle of water and handing it to her.

'Your work called you? When you are on holidays?'

She found herself flushing. 'Well, not strictly a holiday. It's... more of an enforced absence,' she said. Then realised that this sounded even worse than the truth. 'Look, I'm actually signed off work sick,' she admitted.

'You are not well?'

'I'm fine. Honestly. It was all a bit of a mix-up.'

Pascal looks even more confused than before. 'I don't understand,' he said. 'Are you sick or not? Should you be at work?'

Sighing, she explained about the doctor, about her overzealous diagnosis. About the fact she was making the best of it, although she'd honestly rather be at work. And now this ridiculous panic when she'd just been asked quite a simple question. 'The crazy thing is that I would have been able to answer it easily a week ago,' she said. 'I practically know my files off by heart. But I was so surprised that my mind went blank.'

Pascal nodded.

'Now they probably think I'm incompetent as well as crazy,' she said, rolling her eyes.

It was meant to be a joke, but Pascal doesn't laugh. 'Why do you say these things about yourself?'

'Oh. It's... I'm joking, sort of. I just... I'm imagining it through their eyes I suppose.'

'Or perhaps your mother's eyes?' He cocked an eyebrow. 'Do not be offended. I am just thinking of myself, how I sometimes used to call my work useless or say I was wasting my time. One night, Maud asked me why I would say such things about myself. She told me that I had to try to believe in myself no matter what. Because nobody else would unless I started to. It really hit me here,' he tapped his chest. 'And I realised that I had been brought up with so much negativity around my work – not my academic work of course, but my passion – that I was looking at things the wrong way.'

'That was nice of her. Of Maud.'

'She told me that her mother was similar. And Maud, you know of course that she was a lawyer before she came here. Then her sister – your grandmother – got sick, and she died quite young, I think. Perhaps fifty? And Maud realised that she wanted a different sort of life.'

'That makes sense.'

'*Oui*. Of course some people, they dream of being a lawyer. And some people dream of having a career like you have or my mother. But it is not for everyone.'

'Oh, it's definitely for me,' Becky said. 'I was just going through something.' She didn't mention that the fact she'd found out he was living in the café was the catalyst for *Laptop-gate*. It didn't seem fair.

Pascal nodded. 'Well, if you ask me, your work are to blame. They should not be calling you when you have been diagnosed sick by a doctor.'

'Yes, but I think everyone knows... I mean, "burnout"?' Becky uses her fingers to create air quotes. 'Seriously, it's not really something that people in my industry buy into.'

'I'm sorry. Burnout?'

'Yes. You know. You work too hard, you get sick.'

'Ah! *Surmenage*.' Pascal nodded. 'But this is a genuine problem for many people.'

She nodded. 'Yes, I know. It's just... you have to be quite tough in my firm.'

'I do not know much about it, but I don't think that burnout is for weak people. Perhaps it is for strong people. Because they push themselves too hard. Everyone has their limit.'

'Maybe.' She shrugged. 'Anyway, I'm feeling better now, so...'

'No, you should rest.'

She shook her head. 'Honestly, resting is like my... kryptonite.'

He laughed. 'Ah, so you are Superman?'

'I just mean I can't do it.'

'You cannot rest?'

She shook her head, realising both that her words were true and that this wasn't normal. 'I sleep OK at night most of the time. But during the day... I just feel better when I'm working, when I'm *doing*.'

'Yet your body is perhaps telling you otherwise?'

Why did he have to be so bloody perceptive? 'No,' she said. 'It was a blip.'

'OK. Of course.' Pascal set his empty water glass down. 'But still, it would be a good idea perhaps just to take a little time off.'

'No.' She said this more firmly now.

'OK.' Pascal smiled a little sadly and walked towards the café door. Then, turning, he said: 'But answer one question for me. Why are you afraid to stop?'

'I'm not afraid to stop!'

'You are afraid to relax.'

'Relaxing is over—'

'*Non*. These are not your words. Why are you, Becky, so afraid to be with yourself, without a distraction?'

Was she afraid? She pictured lying on her bed – not to sleep, not to read or scroll her phone but simply to rest and shuddered. 'I guess I probably think too much,' she said at last.

'And you are afraid to think?'

It did seem a bit weird when he put it like that. 'Not exactly. Just... I suppose I'm not used to it. Being idle. It feels better when I'm doing something.'

'And were you always this way? Perhaps as a child?'

She shut her eyes, picturing her life at home: colouring books, piano lessons, ballet, homework, reading more and more challenging books. Then holidays – football clubs, Girl Guide camps. Those breaks in Rome and Greece her parents took her on. Never the pool. Always guidebooks and tours and ancient ruins. Except in France. She tried to picture those holidays all those years ago. Painting and running in grass. Sitting on Dad's knee and looking at the sunset. Restaurants and walks and playing silly games. Her eyes snapped open.

'Not always,' she said.

He nodded. 'Perhaps you need to find that part of yourself. The part that can stop for a moment and really feel. Perhaps that is what the burnout is trying to tell you.'

'What are you, a therapist?' She was half joking, half annoyed.

'*Non*, but I am a writer. I think a lot about things. And it makes me sad that you cannot do this, that you are afraid to stop and be with yourself.' He shrugged.

'But you know, I am happy. My life is... good.'

'Except that you have burnout.'

'But I don't! That was just some stupid doctor who...'

'Are you sure?'

'Yes! I just had a bad day at the office and...' Pascal's eyes remained on her and her words petered out.

She thought about the eye, which handily twitched her a reminder, the trembling leg. The panic. The fact that she'd been here for more than week and hadn't really stopped, explored the town properly or done anything other than try to push forward her plan to get Pascal out and the café sold. 'I don't know,' she said quietly.

Pascal nodded. 'OK. Well, perhaps be gentle to yourself just in case?'

She nodded, feeling suddenly teary.

'I will go to work. But you must call me if you feel unwell.'

'OK,' she said, looking up at him, feeling the warmth of his soft, concerned gaze. 'And thank you.'

'*De rien*. It is nothing.'

* * *

After a morning's work and a light lunch, she returned to her room and changed into some fresh clothes. If they were going to use the evening to update the decor, then maybe she really did have time to take a walk and look at the town properly, in daylight. She could label it research to give herself permission.

Checking her watch, she realised that Amber was likely on her lunch-break: 1.30 p.m. in France would be 12.30 p.m. back home. Tentatively she scrolled through her contacts and pressed *Call.*

'Hi,' Amber answered almost immediately. She sounded as if she were walking; Becky could hear traffic, the background hum of the city. She felt a wash of homesickness for the polluted, crowded, bustling melting pot of home. Or perhaps just for her best friend.

'Thanks for answering.'

Amber laughed. 'It's OK. Sorry for being a bit short with you. It's been a difficult time at work. And I've been—'

'Don't say any more, it's forgotten,' Becky interjected.

'I know, it's just I really wanted—'

'Nope. Not listening!' Becky joked.

'You,' said her friend, 'are bloody infuriating at times. You know that, right?'

'Guilty as charged.' Becky said. Then, 'Sorry though.'

'It's OK.' Amber's voice was exaggeratedly weary. 'Apparently you *never have to say you're sorry* when you love someone.'

'Ha! *Love Actually*?'

'*Love Story.*'

'The oldies are the best, right?' Becky smiled.

'So they tell me.'

'Anyway, I've made some progress here.'

'Yeah?'

'Yeah. I'm actually serving coffee, can you believe.'

'Really?' Amber sounded genuinely incredulous. 'What's that like? Driving you mad?'

'Actually no. I'm quite enjoying it.'

'Wonders will never cease!' There was a laugh, but suddenly Amber's voice seemed to change. 'Look, I have to go. I'm back at the office, but talk later, yeah?'

'No. Wait. Just a sec. Look, I've been thinking and... I wondered if you wanted to come out. Just for a few days. My shout.'

'Oh. No. I just couldn't.'

'Look, I know you don't have any leave. But I've checked and there's a flight this Friday, late afternoon. It's only a couple of hours. Then one back on Sunday. My treat.'

'Oh, I couldn't let you pay.'

'I insist. It's my way of making it up to you.'

There was a silence.

'It would be nice to talk to you properly,' Becky wheedled.

'That's true. Because you know—'

'There's wine...'

Silence.

'Say you'll come.'

'OK,' Amber said. 'Thanks. Why not.'

'Brilliant,' Becky grinned. 'I've really missed you, you know.'

'Me too.' And this time, although it was just an audio call, Becky was convinced that Amber was smiling.

15

It felt odd to be in the airport: bright lights and screens and stark white walls after spending so many days in an environment where the newest building must be at least eighty years old. Standing in her slightly paint-scuffed jeans and hoody, Becky felt slightly out of place. She'd meant to smarten up a bit more for Amber's arrival, but had run late painting a bit of skirting board and had had to rush.

Pascal had offered her a lift, but she'd turned him down – he'd have had to close the café and she knew he'd hate to do that. He'd then offered her his car, and she'd almost accepted until he'd pointed out the ancient Citroën parked up on the opposite side of the street. Its tyres were slightly deflated and the whole car was leaning slightly to the side. 'I haven't serviced it for a little while,' he'd said, grimacing.

Instead, she'd paid 150 euros for a round trip in a taxi, and prayed that Amber's flight would come in on time to avoid having to cough up anything more. As promised, she'd also paid for Amber's tickets and had vowed that she'd pay for everything this weekend too. After all, having her best friend there would mean the world.

People started to emerge through the double doors by passport control, their eyes scanning the faces outside for their family or friends, or the taxi that would meet them to take them to their next destination. Each time the doors slid back to reveal more people, Becky's heart leapt. Then, as they closed, she practically bounced with impatience.

As if prompted by the stress of everything, her eyelid started to twitch; she realised that it hadn't done so for a little while. Perhaps France was agreeing with her after all. She had to admit she'd quite enjoyed the last couple of days, since her panic attack and Pascal's insistence on helping her. They'd split shifts in the café, him returning to his writing between serving, her taking the time to walk or explore, or look up soft furnishings online; then come together for a couple of hours each evening to paint or rearrange furniture or plan things.

The yellow chairs looked a little out of place, but had been well received by customers; once they were assured that it was OK if a little mud got onto them, they'd relaxed. One old lady had even fallen asleep and had to be gently woken after an hour had passed.

Despite the fact she'd been busy – and definitely out of her usual comfort zone – Becky had found the time relaxing and had even managed to push thoughts of work to the edge of her consciousness, so she wasn't always accompanied by the perpetual feeling of unease she'd thought she'd never shift. It was nice coming to, sometimes, and realising she'd drifted away in a pleasant daydream rather than finding her mind chewing over the latest ad boards for Tudors.

When Amber finally stepped through the doors, Becky's heart leaped as much as it might have had she been a long-lost love. She found herself grinning and walking towards her friend, arms outstretched, and gathering her up in a hug. It was ridiculous in some ways; it had only been ten days but she hadn't been away from her friend for that long for years.

'Wow!' Amber said, breaking away. 'That's quite a welcome!'

'Well, I've missed you,' Becky grinned. She studied her friend's face for a moment. Amber looked different. Drawn, somehow. Slightly thinner. 'Are you OK? You look a bit... tired.'

'Yes, I'm fine. Just had an early one,' Amber said, stretching her lips into a reassuring smile. Perhaps that was it, thought Becky. Perhaps that, and the fact that everyone around here seemed to have more of a tan than their washed-out British counterparts. Amber's skin was pale from too long each day in the office, and it stood out more among the healthier-looking complexions on the continent.

'Good, glad to hear it,' Becky said. 'I've got a taxi waiting, so we'd better...' They walked quickly to the double doors that led out to the rank and beyond, to where the rather banged-up looking car that passed as a taxi in Vaudrelle was waiting.

An hour and a half later, they finally drew into Vaudrelle. Becky nudged Amber, who'd fallen asleep ten minutes into the journey, and whispered, 'We're here!'

Amber sat up straighter, bleary-eyed, and looked out of the window at the quaint streets, the mismatched buildings, the few inhabitants who were coming back from evenings out, or walking dogs or simply promenading. 'It's very sweet,' she observed, and Becky felt a rush of pride as if she'd invented Vaudrelle all by herself and was showing it to Amber for approval.

She'd hoped they might stay up for a drink when they arrived, but Amber looked fit to drop. It was only 9 o'clock, and just 8 o'clock back home, but Amber had had quite a week at work by all accounts. Becky hid her disappointment and instead showed Amber to her room where she'd made up her bed with fresh sheets and created a makeshift bed on the floor for herself. Initially she'd wondered about using Maud's room, but hadn't felt able to touch it, or even go in properly. But they'd shared before on many a sleepover – this would be just like old times.

'Sorry to be such a lightweight,' Amber said. 'I'm so perpetually exhausted at the moment.'

'Well, hopefully you can get a bit of a rest this weekend.'

'A rest? Never thought you'd be one for advocating that!'

* * *

The next morning, after breakfast and a quick meeting with Pascal before he went to open the doors to the Saturday morning rush (six people who'd already been to the market and needed a caffeine fix), Becky gave Amber the 'grand tour' of the building: the large kitchen tucked behind the café itself; the small, annexed living space with a couple of sofas – neither she nor Pascal tended to spend time in there and it felt a little chilly and unloved. En route downstairs this morning she'd shown her the door of Pascal's room but hadn't offered to show her inside, and then nodded towards Maud's; and Amber was already familiar with the bathroom they'd share with its special, tiny bath.

'It's cute,' Amber had said. 'And I love the pictures in the hallway and sitting room.'

'Yes.' Becky had realised she hadn't really acknowledged the photos properly. She enjoyed seeing the artistic prints on the walls but hadn't given them any more thought. Amber, however, had gone up to them. 'Who's the photographer?'

She'd squinted at the little strip of writing on the border. 'Oh. Is that your aunt, your great-aunt? Maud something?'

Becky looked. 'Oh! Yes, it is.'

'There's another! Wow, are they all hers?'

'I think they might be.' Becky had felt a little flush on her cheeks – fancy not noticing that! Although she'd had so much on, perhaps it was forgivable.

'She was good, wasn't she?'

'Yes. Really good.' Becky had examined one of the pictures – a favourite – and admired the composition, the way the landscape fell away, the fact that your eye was drawn to the little shape of a dog in a distant field. She'd felt a sudden, unexpected, wave of emotion.

'Are you OK?'

'Yes, just... it is sad, isn't it, that I hadn't seen her for so long when she died. I wish now that I'd tried a bit harder.'

'Come on, it wasn't as if you were close.'

'We were once though. And she was fond of me, fonder than I'd realised.' Becky had raised her finger and traced the outline of a tree over the glass. 'I didn't know she didn't really... have anyone. I mean, she had lots of friends. But no real family.'

Amber had put her arm around her friend. 'Well, sometimes friends can be just as important than blood ties,' she'd said.

Becky had nodded. She hoped what Pascal had said was true, and that Maud had had some friends who'd become like family. 'Still...'

'Come on, Maud wouldn't have wanted you to feel guilty, I'm sure,' Amber had said.

'I guess.'

'Perhaps it's the universe's way of telling you to spend more time with your mother?' Amber had suggested, looking at her friend askew.

'Yeah. No. I don't think that's it,' Becky had replied, laughing. 'At least we know where you get your artistic flair from.'

'My artistic flair?'

'Yeah. You know. Advertising. Thinking up new concepts. Thinking about what appeals,' Amber said, shrugging as they turned back towards the stairs. 'And your drawing.'

'My drawing? I never draw!'

'You're kidding, right? All those doodles on our shopping lists, the pictures you put on that little white board where we're meant to write reminders. I always thought they were really good.'

'Yeah?'

'Yeah. Maybe you should experiment a bit.'

Once they'd finished, Pascal made them coffee and they both joined him at the counter, leaning against the worn wood and chatting. 'It's a lovely place,' Amber said. 'I can see why you wanted to stay here.'

Pascal nodded. 'Yes. I have made a good home here. Although I'm leaving soon. I will miss this place.'

'Becky's been showing me Maud's photographs,' Amber continued. 'She was pretty good, wasn't she?'

'*Oui*, she is an artist, it is sure. It is a little messy down in her studio, but I left it just as she liked it. And have you seen the pictures in her bedroom?'

'Studio?' Becky said, confused.

'*Oui*, of course. I thought you said you had shown Amber Maud's works?'

'Well, yes, the ones on the walls.'

Pascal laughed. 'Then you have not seen anything! Let me get Stéphane to mind the café for a moment and I will show you!'

Moments later, Pascal opened a door she hadn't acknowledged before and saw, instead of a cupboard interior as she'd imagined, that there was a set of stairs leading down into darkness. Snapping a light on, he gestured that they should follow him.

'This is where we get murdered,' Amber whispered into Becky's ear, and she almost laughed out loud.

The dark stairwell opened out into a generous cellar space. The building was built onto a slope, meaning that one side of the basement was officially underground, the other had window spaces at the top where the room emerged from the soil. Light flooded the room and illuminated the white walls, lines stretched with photos pegged as if Maud had just stepped away. There were piles of paper, a door reading 'Dark room' and camera equipment piled on tables and shelves. 'Oh,' Becky said suddenly. 'I remember this!'

She did – following Maud into the darkness, feeling a little frightened until the light had snapped on. The memories were vague, like a whisper of fog on a winter's evening. She breathed in the air and inhaled the specific mix of ink and paper and purpose; all with just a touch of Maud's lavender perfume still lingering from the last time her aunt was there. Her mind raced – and then she was there, sitting by Maud's side in the garden, sketching a sunset. Trying her hand at mixing paints and coming up with brown almost every time. Another summer, somewhere in a field of sunflowers. Maud laughing and taking her picture. The feeling of being seen and cherished and just so utterly happy.

The tears were unexpected, welling painfully in her eyes and spilling over almost before she knew it was happening. With Pascal and Amber still looking at propped up paintings and studying the room, Becky was able to wipe the wetness with her sleeve and steady her breathing. Still, when Pascal turned, it was clear she was upset. 'What is wrong?' he asked.

'Just... remembering things. Silly, really,' she managed to say.

She paused at the back of the room to look at some photos and artwork scattered around the walls. It was less uniform than in the corridors – the frames were mismatched and although there were a couple of landscapes, there were pictures of pyramids and sun-drenched Moroccan markets; of small children playing on a dusty street, a man silhouetted under a street light, printed in black and white.

'She travelled?' Becky's voice registered surprise. Somehow, she always imagined Maud having a rather small life; lovely, of course. But small.

'*Oui*, yes, when she could,' Pascal nodded. 'She loved to travel, meet people, take photographs.'

'Look at this one,' Amber said, touching a small frame close to the work surface.

Becky looked. A picture of a child, barefoot, in a muddy dress, her hair tangled and tousled from play. Her face, despite her unkemptness, beautiful and open and smiling unselfconsciously.

'Recognise it?' Pascal said, as Becky picked up the frame for a closer look.

Becky's mother's photo collection contained shots of them at weddings, on holidays. Neat, orderly, obediently saying cheese. This photo was like nothing she'd ever seen. Yet she knew instantly who it was and where it had been taken.

'Of course,' she said. 'It's me.'

* * *

A few minutes later, they were up in the kitchen again, Pascal returning to the café.

'Well, that was a turn up for the books!' Amber said. 'Your aunt was amazing!'

'Yes, she really was.'

The sun was shining almost directly through the kitchen window now, and as it fell against Amber's face, Becky was struck again at just how pale her friend looked. 'Shall we go for a walk or something?' she suggested.

'Yes, why not. Not too far though, I haven't been to the gym for about two months and I'm so unfit!' Amber replied, linking arms with her friend. 'I got breathless climbing the stairs to the flat the other day – did I tell you? Such a couch potato.'

'I'll go easy on you,' Becky said, trying to smile. In truth, part of her wanted to sit and have a good cry – at the missed opportunities, at the innocence of her past self and for the woman she was only getting to know properly now it was too late.

But Amber was here, now. And she didn't want to waste a minute with her friend. 'Let's go.'

16

Amber hadn't been lying when she said she was tired. The next day, despite retiring at just 9 p.m. the night before, she slept until almost 10 a.m.

And although they took things slowly, meandering down to the restaurant for a light lunch before Amber's taxi arrived, the exercise seemed to absolutely exhaust her. 'Are you feeling OK?' Becky asked her, as she stopped for the second time to catch her breath.

'Yeah,' Amber said. 'Too many late ones at work, not enough good food. You know what it's like when you're cooking for one.'

'Sandwiches every night?'

Amber nodded. 'That's about the size of it. I've put on a ton of weight recently.'

'Really?' Becky glanced at her friend's still slender frame. 'Well perhaps you needed it.'

'I need muscle mass maybe, but not... mayonnaise mass.'

Becky laughed. 'Well, how about when I get back, we hit the gym together?' she suggested, putting her arm around Amber's back.

'So you are coming back then?'

'Of course I am!'

'Just... you seem really happy here.'

'Well... I am. Perhaps it's just because I didn't expect to be happy at all. It probably makes the happiness more noticeable. But you may have forgotten I have a job? A mother? A flatmate? I can't abandon any of them.'

'I don't know, I've heard some strange rumours about the flatmate,' Amber joked.

'Don't believe a word of them.'

After a simple meal of croque-monsieur, they took a walk a little farther down the village, meandered around the tiny, picture-book streets, before taking a seat on the cool stone of the fountain. 'I can't believe this is practically over already,' Amber said. 'I've really enjoyed getting away.'

Becky nodded. 'Well, come again. Come every weekend. It's been so nice having you.'

'Sure I'm not cramping your style?'

'What do you mean?'

'That Pascal's quite the hottie!'

Becky laughed. 'Pascal! I'll admit, he's gorgeous. But there's zero chance of anything happening. He's just tolerating me, I think. We didn't get off to the best start.'

'You seem pretty friendly now,' Amber said, raising an eyebrow.

'Well, he's a nice guy.' Becky thought again of Pascal's deep brown eyes, his earnest expression. The way they were able to talk to each other so easily. 'Maybe in another lifetime.'

'One where you live in France?'

'One where he lives in London.' Becky gave Amber's arm a little squeeze.

'I'm not sure I'd come back.' Amber tilted her head to let the sun play on her face. 'Aren't you tempted to just – I don't know – run away?'

'Become a barista?'

'Become whatever you want to become,' Amber said, her eyes sparkling and slightly wet. 'You have this amazing chance – an income, a home with very little upkeep required. It was just... looking at Maud's pictures. She was so free, wasn't she? She had the life she wanted, on her terms. She could do anything.'

'Seems so. Are you OK?'

'Yeah. Just not many of us get to do that,' Amber said, kicking a stone with her foot.

'No. I suppose not. But you know, we're young. We've got plenty of chances ahead. And I'm pretty happy with what I've achieved so far.'

'But what about the burnout?'

Becky shrugged. 'The price one pays for success.' She imitated her mother's voice.

But Amber didn't laugh. 'Are you sure it's one you're willing to pay? I've been thinking about that recently. How we're willing to sacrifice years for the promise of things getting better.'

'What about it?'

'Well, whether it's actually worth it? Selling our time for money when time is the most precious thing we have.'

''Course it's worth it. Come on, that's what people do, isn't it? In our early careers. Work hard, reap rewards. You of all people should know that. Financial year-end last year, I didn't see you for about three days.'

'Yes, I remember.'

'Well then.'

'You can't help wonder whether it's worth it sometimes though.'

Becky put her arm around her friend again. 'Come on,' she said, firmly. 'We're on the path to living the dream.'

Amber laughed. 'If you say so.'

The café had been closed for an hour, Pascal had gone out to a friend's, so it was a surprise to see a figure outside when they drew closer. He had his back to them, and seemed to be leaning against the wooden window frame, checking his watch.

'Visitor?' said Amber, her voice slightly breathless again.

'Not an expected one.'

'Nice arse.'

'Amber!' Although she had to admit, she thought, looking, that her friend wasn't wrong. The man wore well-cut beige trousers, a white shirt. Had some sort of blue jumper or cardigan tied around his shoulders so that the main torso part fell down his back. His hair was black and thick, the back of his neck slightly red from too much sun earlier in the day.

He turned, and her heart sank. She recognised the black beard, the solemn expression. 'Oh no. It's Georges, the *maire*,' she said. 'Remember, he was really rude to me the other day when I popped in.'

'Yes, but you didn't mention he was... gorgeous,' Amber said, fanning her face with her hand.

'Really?' Becky looked again. Perhaps, objectively, he was. But the way he'd treated her the other day – making her feel foolish – had completely overridden any physical attraction she might have felt. She wondered what he wanted now.

'*Bonjour*,' she said, smiling, as they approached. He might be a grumpy sod, but he was still the *maire*. She didn't know much about the administration in France, but it seemed sensible to try to keep on the right side of authority figures just in case.

'*Bonjour, madame...*'

'Thorne. And this is my friend, Amber.'

'*Enchanté*,' he said, nodding his head. He smiled, looking completely different from the way he'd seemed in the office the other day. More relaxed, somehow. His startling blue eyes rested on hers and for a moment things seemed to pause.

'Can I help you?' Becky asked.

'Oh, sorry. Yes, of course!' He grinned. 'Do not worry, I am not here in a professional capacity.'

It was a little relieving. 'Oh,' she said.

'Although I did want to tell you that I appreciate what you are doing with the café,' he added. 'It is looking *très respectable*. People are talking about it in the town.'

'Well, that's good.'

'*Oui*, it is nice to see people making improvements. And you will still sell in perhaps two weeks?'

'That's the plan.'

He nodded. '*Parfait*.'

Obviously, she'd wanted him to support her desire to sell the place, but it was a bit rich saying 'perfect' to someone's face when they told you they'd be disappearing in a fortnight. 'Well... OK,' she said at last, adding, 'What did you want, by the way?'

He seemed to shake himself. 'Sorry, I am going to see your great-aunt. And I wanted to know if you have any message for her. Or perhaps if you would like to come with me. It is not my business perhaps, but it seems strange that you haven't yet gone to see her.'

'Oh.' It seemed odd that he would visit Maud's grave again. Had they been close? She'd have to ask Pascal. And a message? Unless he was going to conduct a seance, she couldn't see how that would work out.

'Yes,' Georges nodded earnestly. 'I will tell her all about the café, of course. And how you have settled. And I realise you have not been here long. But if she asks me where you are, I am not sure what I will say.'

Becky gave a little surreptitious glance at Amber. This was actually getting a little bit weird.

'Look,' she said. '*Monsieur*, um...'

'Call me Georges.'

'OK. Look, Georges. I know that I should have been by now. It's important to... pay respects. And you're right, I've been busy. But I could probably have found a moment by now. I'll try to go tomorrow, or the next day.'

'So I can tell her this? Because,' he grimaced, 'she doesn't have so much to occupy her at the moment and if I say that you will be there on Monday or Tuesday and you do not come, I know she will be disappointed.'

Clearly, Georges needed some professional help. Becky smiled. 'Um, well, I'm not sure what you believe. And I respect your feelings. But in honesty, she's not going to know if I am there or not, is she?'

Georges's brow furrowed. 'But of course she will know!' he said. 'Maud's body has failed her a little, but her spirit is still strong.'

Becky took a step back. 'I don't mean to offend you,' she said. 'But I don't believe in spirits.'

'No?'

'No. Not spirits, ghosts, whatever you want to call them.'

'Ghosts?'

'Yes. That's what you're saying, right? That you visit her grave and talk to her? That you sense she still understands you? Look. I know lots of people feel that way.' She held her hands up as if to say she wasn't trying to interfere with what he believed. 'But I just can't...'

'Her grave?'

This was getting weird. Perhaps it was something to do with English being his second language. She wished she knew more French, but unless he was going to serve her a drink or tell her the way to the tourist information office, she was all out of vocabulary. 'Yeah,' she said uncertainly.

'*Madame*,' Georges's voice was soft. 'I am sorry. But I think there has been a misunderstanding.'

'You can say that again,' Amber said in a low voice.

'*Non*. There is no grave. There is no... spirit or ghost. Maud is not dead.'

'I'm sorry... what?' Becky became acutely aware of her heartbeat, its rhythmical thud inside her chest. Time paused, the air around her became thick and she put a hand out and gripped Amber's arm. 'She's... Maud's alive?'

'*Oui*. Maud is a good friend of mine. And I visit her every few days, along with another woman from the village who is at the same home. She is quite happy there. So I know that when she offered you the café and she did not hear from you, she was a little sad. When she heard that you came over, she thought you would visit. Did you truly think she had died? Because I am not sure how this misunderstanding happened. Or do you mean in a metaphorical sense? That she is dead to you? Is there some argument between you? Something I can help with?'

Becky felt her knees buckle slightly and leant against her friend. 'Maud's... she's not... dead?' she said.

'Your aunt is not in the best of health, it is true. But she is very much alive.'

17

'Are you sure you're going to be OK?' Amber said, standing by the taxi. 'You know I'd stay if I could...' They'd spent some time in the empty café, coming to terms with what they'd learned. Becky had laughed, cried, laughed again, could barely get her head around the news. But then Amber had checked her watch, grown paler, rushed upstairs to pack in time for her taxi.

'You can't stay a couple more days?' Becky had asked her earlier.

'I wish I could.'

'It's all good,' Becky said now, trying to keep her voice from wavering. 'I get it. Work comes first.'

'Well, not always. Just...'

'Seriously. It's OK.' She hoped her tone sounded convincing to Amber. In reality, she needed her best friend more than ever. But if Amber couldn't see that this was the time to call in sick for a couple of days herself, or request unpaid leave or something, she wasn't going to beg.

'I really am sorry.'

'It's fine. Honestly. I know your work is a bit... there's a lot of pressure.' Becky forced her lips into a smile. It wasn't fair of her to expect so much of Amber. It was just that every fibre in her being needed someone familiar at her side while she dealt with this unexpected twist in her life.

'There really is. A lot of pressure. And there's more. I was going to...' Amber put her hand to her chest. 'I wanted to talk to you about it all. There just wasn't a moment. And then the *maire* guy said... well, you know.'

Becky nodded. 'We can talk later if you want?'

'OK.' Amber checked the time on her phone. 'I really am sorry.'

'It's OK,' Becky said again. 'At least you were here when it happened. You might not have believed me otherwise.' She gave a weak smile.

'Very true. I think if you'd called me and told me Maud was alive, I'd assume you were having a breakdown,' she admitted.

'A burnout *and* a breakdown?'

'Why not? You always were an overachiever.' They smiled genuinely at each other now.

'I will take care of her, don't worry,' said Pascal who'd arrived home shortly after Georges had departed to find Becky yet again red-eyed from crying and sipping water.

'Thanks. But I don't really need it. I'm fine, honestly,' Becky said.

'Well, then I will be there to help you if you need.'

'Thanks.' They'd both said in unison. Then laughed. 'Jinx!' Becky said, harking back to a playground game they'd used to play.

'Yeah, that doesn't work in your thirties,' Amber had said.

'Damn!'

The taxi driver revved the engine, just enough to remind

them that he was on the clock and that Amber did need to start her journey to the airport.

'Have a good flight.' Becky stepped forward and gave Amber a hug. Her friend gripped her tightly, almost as if trying to communicate how strongly she felt through the strength of her hold. 'You really do complete me,' she whispered, and felt a reciprocal squeeze.

When she stepped back, Amber gave her a small smile and slipped into the taxi, turning her face forwards as it pulled away and took her towards the airport.

Then it was just Becky and Pascal in the early evening sun.

Becky sat down on the edge of the pavement and hugged her knees, watching orange rays turn the tops of the buildings a golden colour, flooding one half of the pavement with light, but sending the road into darkness.

If she was honest, she was struggling to hold it all together. Over the last twenty or so years, she'd barely given Maud a thought. But since she'd been here, certain her aunt was dead, she'd started to remember her. Mourn her in a way that she hadn't before. Now, suddenly, Maud was alive. And although it had always been the case, to her it felt surreal, as if something magical had happened, as if she'd been given a second chance.

Pascal moved forward and sat next to her, saying nothing. A physical reminder that he was there, even if he didn't know what to say.

And what could they say? She wasn't quite sure where the misunderstanding had come from. Receiving the solicitor's letter about the gift her aunt had bestowed on her, the language it had used. The fact that she'd been reading it as a foreigner and had been too stubborn to hire a translator had meant that she'd jumped to all the wrong conclusions. And Maud had seemed so old, even when she was a child, that she'd assumed the woman was at least in her nineties even back then.

Instead she was eighty-two, had moved to a retirement house – a kind of care home for those who needed minimal help – because she could no longer run the café, and had begun to struggle on the stairs. 'She had no one to care for her,' Pascal said. 'And I think she didn't want to be a burden. Besides, she is happy at this place – it is not for those who are waiting to die, not immediately. But in fact, it is full of people who are being cared for so that they can live.'

Becky's grandfather had been in a care home towards the end of his life. She had visited sporadically, hating the smell of the place, the fact that her grandfather had seemed to age rapidly once *in situ*, becoming more and more dependent and, eventually, confused.

Perhaps this was different.

'I did wonder why people kept saying they were visiting her,' she admitted. 'I thought it was nice that they paid their respects, but it did seem a little... excessive.' She gave a small smile.

'*J'imagine*,' he said. 'We must have seemed very strange to you.'

'I just can't... She must think I'm awful ignoring her for so long after she gave me the café. And then coming over but not visiting. Why didn't you tell me?'

Pascal shrugged. 'I believed you would come eventually. I thought perhaps you were nervous because you hadn't seen her. Of course I could not know what you really thought.'

'No.' Becky shook her head. 'What an idiot.'

'We are all idiots in our own way.'

'Thanks. That's... very reassuring.'

Pascal laughed. 'I love your British humour and – how do

you say? – sarcasm. How you find a reason to laugh even when the situation is bizarre or even sad.'

'I think we just do it because it stops us from crying.' Becky smiled, blinked rapidly and managed somehow to stop her tear ducts filling again.

Pascal nodded. 'But you have no problem with letting out your emotions?'

Becky laughed properly then. 'If I told anyone back home you'd said that, they'd be stunned!' she said. 'Honestly, I haven't cried in years until I came here.'

'It is that bad here?'

'No... it's...' she began, then looked at his face. 'Oh, you're joking.'

He grinned. 'See, I am learning the British humour.'

They were silent for a moment.

'Do you think you will visit her now?' he asked.

She nodded. 'I'm going to... try. Tomorrow, maybe? If you can show me the way? But I'm kind of terrified. That's why I was a bit down that Amber decided to go. You know, in spite of everything.'

'I think she felt bad too.'

'Yeah.' Becky nodded. 'Still, it would be so much easier going through this with her.'

'You are partners, perhaps?'

'Not in a romantic sense. Just been friends since... forever. We rent a flat together. We're stand-ins for each other's useless families who never seem to turn up to anything, or when they do turn up, seem to create difficulties...'

'You have known her since a child?'

'Yeah. We were five, I think. At school. She moved to the area and I was the one picked to look after her when she started class. We've seen each other through everything. Her parents' divorce, my dad... when he died. She was there for me. Kind of propped me up a bit. Until I could carry on.' Becky picked up a little stone and began rolling it between her fingers. 'Just wished she could have visited Maud with me. Selfish probably. I know she's got her own stuff on.'

'She has problems?'

'Nothing like that. Although I think work's a bit full-on right now. She's an accountant and I'm not sure she likes it that much. Only she doesn't have any holiday left in her entitlement, so she'd have had to ring in sick or take unpaid leave in order to stay. I do get it. But I'm still sad about it.'

'I expect she is too. She seemed sad for much of the time here, I thought.'

'Yeah?' Becky looked at him. 'I didn't notice that.'

'Perhaps you know her better than I do. She just seemed very... thoughtful. Quiet.'

Pascal straightened his legs, then turning slightly, clambered to his feet. 'Listen, I am no Amber, but I can take you tomorrow. Go with you when you see your aunt who has risen from the dead.'

'You will?' She got up too, touched his arm.

'*Oui*, of course. It might feel a little strange for you. Perhaps for both of you.'

'And do you think... would it be OK if you kind of explained to her what I thought. Maybe call her before we go? Because it's a lot to explain and might be kind of... awkward.'

He looked at her. 'Yes, if you want. Although I think Maud will probably find it very funny. She has a remarkable sense of humour. There is nothing wrong with her mind, it is sure.'

'Still...'

'Of course.'

Becky felt a flood of gratefulness rush through her. She

stepped forward and gave Pascal a squeeze, wrapping her arms around his back. 'Thank you so much,' she said. 'I'm sorry about when I said you were nothing, you'd done nothing.'

'And I am sorry that I said you were just a job.'

'Oh yes,' she remembered. 'I forgot you'd said that.'

'Ah, *merde*! Then I wish I hadn't reminded you!'

She looked up at him, hands still loosely around his waist. And in that moment, he bent down and let his lips gently touch hers.

Becky had felt adrift – lost without her job, away from home, away from Amber – and trying to come to terms with the wonderful, terrifying, strange news that her aunt was alive.

But as soon as their lips touched, she felt a jolt of connection. As if somehow all of the uncertainty, the feelings that fizzed and churned in her head, her stomach, stilled. And she felt suddenly rooted. That even though she was two hundred miles and a stretch of sea away from her London flat, from her mother, and even though her best friend was at this minute moving farther and farther from her, she was closer to home than she'd realised.

18

She awoke the next morning in a tangle of unfamiliar sheets. Bleary-eyed, she took in her surroundings: Pascal's room with its double bed, soft feather eiderdown and pillows, looked completely different from the room she remembered her parents staying in all those years ago. The pine cladding had been painted in light cream which, bathed in sunlight from the window, looked warm and inviting. There were pictures on the walls: paintings of sunflowers and lavender fields. And scattered around was evidence of the room's latest occupant: a jumper over a chair, a neat line of shoes next to the wardrobe. The space next to her was empty and, as she checked her watch, she realised that Pascal had no doubt already risen to open up the café.

Curling up luxuriously between the sheets, she relived a little of last night. The soft kisses, Pascal's gentle touch. The way he'd gathered her to him passionately once they'd reached his room. The way he'd softly, teasingly touched her until she'd felt almost desperate to have him inside her. The orgasm that had rippled through her body like a wave.

Then, later, sleepy in each other's arms, they'd made love a second time – more slowly – eyes fixed on each other's. It had been – without doubt – the most mind-blowing, body-fizzing sex of her life.

She stretched her arms out, feeling her body begin to come back to life, then forced herself to get up, pulling the sheets back over the bed tidily, before gathering her clothes and popping her head around the door to ensure that nobody was there to witness the naked dash back to her own space. Sure, Pascal had seen everything last night. But she was still keen he didn't clap eyes on her naked bottom in the cold light of day.

After a quick dip in the tiny bath, she stood in her bedroom, still sporting just her underwear. Everything she'd brought with her was laid out on the bed, but it was impossible to know what to wear. She'd already tried slipping on neat trousers and a short-sleeved blouse, then a long summer dress, followed by a pair of shorts with a casual T-shirt. Her bed was a jumble of discarded clothing, her floor scattered with sandals and shoes. She'd literally tried on every outfit she'd brought with her and nothing seemed right.

Earlier, she'd tried to ring Amber to get a debrief on her literal debriefing with Pascal, but there'd been no answer. Now, in the middle of a brand-new crisis, she tried again. But no reply.

She checked the time. Half past eleven. Soon they'd close the café exceptionally for the afternoon and head off in Pascal's rattling motor to the care home where Maud had moved just over a year ago. And although she knew it was unimportant in the grand scheme of things, it felt as if she needed to select the right outfit to ensure things went well. Every time she thought about seeing Maud again, she felt the flapping of a thousand butterflies in her stomach and chest; what would she look like?

How would she be? What would she say about the epic misunderstanding that had led to Becky thinking she was six feet under?

'At one point, I think we all thought we would lose her,' Pascal had said last night, leaning up on his elbow, his expression sad. 'She seemed quite young for her age, but when she fell on the steps and her hip was broken, I realised that she was frailer than I thought. She has such a personality that it made her seem strong, solid. But after the accident she seemed smaller.'

'Poor Maud.'

'*Oui*, but she has made a good life for herself now. And I began to run the café full time, but we both knew it couldn't be forever. Then she had the idea to make you a gift – in advance of her Will. I think her dream is to see you running the café before she dies. And if not, at least to see you.'

'And you don't think she meant to mislead me?'

'*Non*,' he'd shaken his head firmly. 'I suspect nobody ever told you directly she had died.'

Becky had tried to remember the wording in the letter. Had it mentioned a death? Perhaps she'd just assumed benefitting from such a gift must mean it had been left to her in a Will.

'She must have thought I was very rude not to reply to her.'

'Perhaps. But she did not say so. She still hoped, I think. Then the *notaire* told her you wanted to sell.'

Becky had made a face. 'She must hate me.'

'*Non*. Not at all! In fact, although I haven't called yet to prepare her for our visit, I imagine Georges has told her why you didn't contact her already. She is kind. And she is British.'

'Meaning?'

'She will probably laugh.'

Becky had smiled. 'But she wouldn't if she was French? Don't French people have a sense of humour too?'

Pascal had grinned and shrugged. 'Yes. We French have our own humour. But we are very good at embracing the darkness too,' Pascal had admitted. 'Perhaps too good. It means we have some wonderful literature. But it also means that we are too often sad.' He'd made a face to indicate he was joking, but Becky had felt there was truth at the heart of it.

'Is your book sad?' she'd asked.

He'd looked up. 'It is the first time you ask me about my book,' he'd said, seemingly delighted.

'Sorry.'

'*Non*. I am pleased you asked. *Oui*, there is melancholy there, but joy too. And there is a happy ending, so it is OK.'

Now, she finally settled on a pair of shorts with a neat T-shirt. Sandals, loose hair and a slick of lip gloss. Before she had time to judge it all wrong and rip off the outfit again, she forced herself to pick up her bag and walk out of the room, closing the door behind her. She then went to seek out Pascal and found him sweeping the floor of the café. He'd seen the last patrons out, and turned the sign to '*Fermé*', adding a little explanation underneath.

He looked up as she entered, and his features softened into a smile. 'Good morning,' he said, walking towards her and giving her a gentle kiss. 'I hope you didn't mind that I didn't wake you?'

'Not at all.'

'Georges called by just now,' he said. 'He wanted to know how you are. I think he feels very guilty to have given you such a shock yesterday.'

'Yes. It must have been odd for him too. Did he speak to Maud?'

'Yes. And it is like I thought. She found the situation quite funny once she understood.'

'Oh. That's good.'

'Yes, and he is very pleased to hear that you are seeing Maud today. He asked if you would talk to her about the café – whether it could now be put up for sale, but I said I don't think this visit is one for business.'

'No. Bit nosy of him to ask?'

'Nosy?'

'You know. Sticking his nose in.'

'Asking things that are not his business?'

'Exactly.'

Pascal laughed. 'Ah Georges, he takes his job very seriously. To him, in Vaudrelle at least, *everything* is his business.'

She smiled. 'I see.' There was a pause. 'Thanks for closing the café for this,' she added.

Pascal shrugged. 'It is your café.'

That was true. It didn't feel like hers though. And she had no idea whether it could weather the lost revenue an afternoon closing would cause. She'd learned how to pour a couple of coffees, but she had no idea of the profit and loss, the workings of the business. She should, really. Although he could show her the ledger books and she'd probably still be clueless.

'I'm so nervous!' she found herself saying as they climbed into Pascal's car. The vehicle smelt like polish and leather and dust and the kind of unspecific 'old' smell that you find in museums. The seats were cracked and sun-bleached and as she sat down, the whole thing wobbled on its dubious suspension.

'About my driving?'

She laughed, although he wasn't completely wrong. 'Mostly about meeting Maud.'

'It will be fine.' He reversed out of the space, the car emitting a puff of putrid exhaust fumes as he did, then began to drive along the slightly bumpy road through the village. Becky had never been in such an old car, certainly not one that was practically falling apart; but at least the fear of potential death or breakdown prevented her from worrying too much about her upcoming meeting. The route took them out of the village and left, along a road she hadn't yet travelled down. They passed a cemetery with ornate family plots, a farm where a dog watched them suspiciously as they drove by, but didn't bark. The worst moment was probably when they confronted a tractor head-on and Pascal was forced to reverse into a lay-by that had an enormous ditch just next to it.

Between these moments of trepidation though, she was able to take in the sun-drenched scenery, the sparkle of light on water as they crossed a river. And feel, with pleasure, Pascal's hand as he rested it briefly on hers from time to time for reassurance.

She wondered what he thought of the night before. He seemed completely at ease with her, but hadn't mentioned it directly. How did he view it? Had it been a one-night stand for him? Or the start of something more meaningful?

They stopped in a small convenience store, and she managed to pick up some chocolate and a magazine – feeling she ought to take something. 'Do you think this says, "Sorry I thought you were dead"?' she asked Pascal, waving the large bar of Milka and the copy of *Voici!*

He laughed. 'They are perfect.'

By the time they pulled into the car park of the residential home, her knuckles were white from gripping her seat, yet Pascal seemed completely relaxed and oblivious to the terror she felt winding around some of the sharper corners close to the residential home.

The building they'd parked next to was pretty – not what she'd been expecting at all. It had been created inside what had evidently once been a rather grand family home – not quite a chateau, but with aspirational turrets hinting that it was doing its best to be a luxury residence. Pascal closed his door without locking it, leaving the keys in the ignition. She nearly pointed it out, but decided against it.

The day was warm once again, and it was easy to forget that at home the weather was less than clement. The alerts that had pinged on her phone this morning had predicted twelve degrees and rainy in London – not the best June weather. Here, it was warm with an edge of heat that would only increase as the day grew into itself. She was getting used to it: no longer carrying a 'just in case' cardigan or coat, and ensuring she applied sun cream to her shoulders before stepping out.

As they walked together along the path that led to a giant wooden door, Pascal's fingers brushed hers, holding her hand briefly and giving it a squeeze, then dropping it, leaving her hand feeling somehow incomplete without his.

She let him lead the way into the building and to a reception desk made of polished mahogany. A woman behind the desk smiled her *bonjour* at him, dipping her head a little when they spoke, and barely acknowledging Becky at all.

'Does she always flirt with you like that?' she asked quietly as they walked away from the counter.

'Flirt? *Non*. She is just friendly,' he said, oblivious.

Pascal led her through to a bright, light conservatory scattered with comfortable chairs. In the corner was a grand piano, its keys bright in the sun, just waiting for the next set of fingers to tickle out a tune.

There were three chairs occupied. One by an old man, another by a woman who was holding a book and frowning at its contents. A third chair had a crutch leaning up against it, and was occupied by a woman whose face was turned away, looking outwards towards the sun-drenched garden. Seeing her, Becky gasped in recognition.

It had been twenty years. And Becky had worried she wouldn't recognise her great-aunt easily. Yet instantly she knew, even without seeing the woman's face. It was something in the way that she held herself, the arm that draped on her lap. The glimpse of an emerald earring in her ear.

And something in Becky's body changed, too, on seeing her. She'd been nervous, holding herself back, her limbs stiff and awkward. But it was as if her muscles, her subconscious, recognised Maud and she became the little girl who'd hugged her fiercely when they'd last left, with no idea it would be the last time for a long time.

Rather than lingering behind Pascal, allowing him to make introductions as she'd expected, she rushed to the woman's side. 'Auntie Maud!' she said, arms outstretched.

Maud looked up, her creased face breaking into a smile, her eyes dancing. 'My Becky!' She reached up and they enveloped each other without any self-consciousness at all. Anyone seeing them would have thought they'd been in each other's lives for years and years without a fracture. And that's how it felt, too, for Becky. She remembered Maud's arms, the way her head rested lightly on her shoulder. The sound of her breath. And the smell of lavender water. She might not have seen her in the flesh for years and years and years, and yet here they were, as if no time had passed at all.

'You're alive!' she found herself saying. 'You're really alive.'

'Yes,' said Maud, grinning as Becky straightened up. 'I rather think that I might be.'

19

Pascal quietly pulled a chair up for Becky and she gratefully sat in it. Maud held both of her hands and the pair grinned at each other. 'Thanks, Pascal,' Becky said, not looking around.

'It's OK. I think I might go for a walk now.'

'Oh, you don't have to!'

'*Non*, it will give you two a chance to talk.' He leaned down and kissed Maud lightly on the cheek, then turned to Becky, pausing as if deciding whether to do the same to her. He shook his head lightly and smiled before walking off.

Had he not wanted to kiss her in front of Maud?

Or did he already regret last night?

This was one of the reasons she'd stayed single for so long, she remembered. The exhausting second-guessing that came with meeting someone new.

'Such a nice boy,' said Maud when he'd gone. Was it Becky's imagination or did Maud give her a knowing look?

'He really does seem lovely.'

There was a moment's silence. When you have twenty years

of absence to unpick, it's hard to know where to start. In the end, Becky said, 'I'm so sorry.'

'What for?' Maud looked at her with interest.

'Well, all of it, I suppose. For losing contact. For not responding to your Christmas cards. For... well, for not realising you were alive. And I guess the kind of... monetary way I seized on the café.'

'That's a lot to apologise for,' Maud observed.

'Well, yep.'

'It's not your fault,' she said firmly. 'Goodness, you were only ten when I last saw you. You could hardly have defied your mother and flown to see me on your own. And memory is fickle at that age; your parents are your whole world. I never blamed you for any of it.'

Becky was determined not to let herself cry again, but she was having trouble keeping her resolve. 'Who do you blame?' she asked, more interested than anything. 'Mum? Cynthia, I mean?'

Maud shook her head vehemently. 'Poor Cynthia. Has she changed at all since I last saw her? Mellowed, perhaps?'

Becky snorted, unintentionally. 'Sorry. But no. She's, if anything, more forceful.'

'I'm not surprised. Losing Peter must have been quite awful.'

Any humour she had felt at Maud's observations on her mother faded. 'Yes. Poor Dad.'

'He was a good man.'

'Yes. Yes, he really was.'

'But Cynthia,' Maud shook her head. 'Not the easiest woman to love.'

'No.'

'God knows I tried to be there for her after her mother died.

And other times, too.' Maud's lips pursed slightly. 'Silly girl would never let anyone close.'

Becky felt a wave of sadness. 'But she's happy, I think.'

'Yes. I expect she is, on a level. But...' Maud shrugged. 'Perhaps this isn't the best subject to discuss right now.'

'Go on. It's OK.' In fact, Becky was intrigued. It was years since she'd been able to talk to anyone else who knew her mother, properly; someone who knew the heart of her.

'I was just going to say – it's a shame that her happiness comes at the cost of those around her.'

'Oh.'

'You disagree?'

'She's my mum,' Becky shrugged. 'I wouldn't say she's cost me happiness. There are times when she could have been more thoughtful, maybe? But she is who she is, I guess.'

Maud nodded. 'I don't expect you to take sides,' she said after a beat.

'Thank you.'

'I think Peter was the tonic she needed. She certainly softened a bit when they first met.'

'Really?'

'Yes. They balanced each other out somewhat. Although they'd argue horribly sometimes.'

'Oh. I don't remember.'

'You know, he'd wanted to come and live here for a bit? A sabbatical, he called it. He wanted to write a book, I think.'

'Dad? Write?'

'Yes. I think your mother was equally surprised. Engineers aren't known for their creativity, after all. But your father had something... the stories he used to tell you at night-time. Off the top of his head! They were... I still remember some of them now.'

'I do too...' Becky hadn't thought of those stories for years. The little trains and their funny little stations. The world he created with words. He never wrote anything down, yet could tell her stories for hours. 'And Mum didn't want to?'

'You mustn't blame Cynthia too much. We're all a product of our upbringing. My sister – your grandmother – was the same. We had strict parents by today's standards. But they wanted the best for us. Things were different then. We needed to earn and they wanted a good life for us. It meant working hard; high expectations. All things that are quite admirable. And my sister, God rest her, only had the one child to focus on. I think she created quite an impossible situation for your mother.'

'In what way?'

'Well, your grandmother had a lot of regrets educationally; and she was frustrated in her work. She pushed Cynthia hard to save her from living the same life. And it worked, of course. She's enormously successful. But it took its toll in other areas. And on you.'

'Oh. I didn't know that about Grandma.' Becky's grandmother had died before she was born. She'd never felt quite real to her.

'She didn't mean it. You have to remember that in those days, we didn't know so much about child development.'

Becky nodded.

'Anyway, at one point, when you were eight or nine, I think that your mother was warming to the idea of the move. Just a little.'

'Really! Mum?'

'Well, she loved your father. And she could see how much it meant to him.' Maud smiled, remembering. Her eyes looked distant. She still clutched one of Becky's hands in hers.

'Yes.'

'But when it came to it, I think she was too afraid.'

'Of moving to a new country?'

'That, yes. But mainly of letting go of what she had. It was – is perhaps still – her safety net, you see. Her evidence that she hasn't let her mother down. I doubt she realises that even now.'

'Oh.' Becky looked at this woman who hadn't seen Cynthia for two decades, yet could see a side of her that Becky had never known. It made sense, from this distance. She felt a well of sympathy in her chest. 'You're being very... forgiving about it.'

To her surprise, Maud threw her head back and laughed. 'Oh, I'm sorry,' she said, after a moment. 'I wouldn't say I've completely forgiven her. I have my moments, even now. What could have been. Your father... his health. You. Perhaps it's just old age creeping up on me! When you're young, older people seem quite one-dimensional,' Maud said. 'You can't imagine they have a past. But you see things differently when you get to my stage of life. Everyone seems young. Everyone seems... forgivable.'

'Still, I wish we'd stayed in touch.'

'Oh, me too. Of course. But apparently, I was leading you astray. Your father too, I think, in your mother's estimation. When it came to it, she couldn't take the risk of a freer, less predictable life. And my being a bad influence, or a troublemaker, was her way of justifying it to herself, I think.'

'A bad influence?' Becky looked at the neatly dressed old woman in front of her.

'I know! It's laughable, looking back. Anyway.' Maud seemed to right herself. 'That's ancient history. Besides, I could have made more effort too – especially after Peter died. None of us was perfect, or is now. But hindsight certainly adds clarity.'

'It's not too late,' Becky suggested.

'Perhaps. Anyway, I'm sure you didn't come to map out the

mistakes from the last twenty years. Tell me about you. I've seen some things online of course. Lovely offices. But tell me about your work, your life in London. It looks like you're having a marvellous time.'

'Does it?'

'Yes, although I think those platforms are designed to make everyone look glamorous,' Maud admitted.

'Well, I'm a director,' said Becky, trying to suppress a proud smile. 'Youngest they've ever had, apparently. And, you know, well, on track to get onto the board. That's it, I suppose. It's going well – or it was.'

'On track? Sounds like something Cynthia would say.'

'Ha. Well, I suppose it's her who showed me how to write five-year plans, strategise, that sort of thing.'

'Oh, goodness. I'd forgotten about Cynthia's five-year plans!' Maud chuckled affectionately. 'Anyway, you said things *were* going well – do you mean the burnout? Pascal mentioned it.'

'Did he? Oh, it's nothing. I just... I had a bad day and things got out of hand.'

Maud looked at her, intelligent eyes reading so much more than Becky said. But she didn't offer a counter opinion.

'And you're enjoying this... break? Enjoying the café?'

'It's wonderful!' she said without thinking.

'And do you still paint?'

'Oh? No. I don't really do that any more.'

'I see. No time, I expect.'

'Yeah. Sadly.'

'You used to be quite the prodigy in that area.'

'Ha. I wish.'

Maud shrugged and smiled.

'The café,' Becky said then. 'What made you decide to give it to me?'

Maud smiled. 'I'll admit there was a part of me that wanted to... prompt something from you, or Cynthia. Force a response – solicitors' letters tend to do that.'

'Oh. So...'

'But I do want you to have it. If you want it. I haven't got anyone else – and I can't work there any more. I wanted to offer you... a lifeline.'

'A lifeline?'

'Well, an alternative. To the high-flying lifestyle.' Maud laughed. 'You may not want that, of course. But I had to be sure.'

'Sure of what?'

'Sure that your life choices are making you happy, rather than fulfilling some need of your mother's.'

'Oh! No. They're all my choices. I love my job! And...'

'Well, that's good then,' Maud said. 'So if you want to, you must sell the café. It's no good to me from here. I don't need the money. And it would come to you anyway when I die.'

'You don't need the money?' Becky thought about the rather shabby furniture in some of the guest rooms. The fact that the café looked a little run-down, at least to her eyes.

'No. I have plenty of the stuff. From my work as a photographer. I used to sell quite a few photos. Anyway, no matter. That's the truth. I don't need it. It's yours.'

'Thank you.'

'I suppose it's a little unfair of me to have brought you out here like this. Although I can't be blamed for faking my own death, that's for sure.'

'No! That was all in my head.' They smiled at each other, but there was sadness there.

'I don't have to sell it,' Becky said, suddenly. 'I could... oversee it. From England if I have to. Find a manager?' The beautiful flat she was planning to buy flashed up in her mind, but she pushed it away. It just wasn't an option – selling the café now simply to raise the deposit would be heartless. 'You could visit it still, sometimes? I can come over?'

Maud touched her hand. 'Becky,' she said. 'You do you.'

'What do you mean?'

'Don't do what you feel I might like, or Cynthia. Or anyone else who's important to you. Do what *you* wish. There are enough expectations on people of your age without me piling on more.'

'Oh,' Becky said. 'Thank you.'

The conversation petered out and Maud began to look a little restless.

'Are you OK?'

'Yes, it's a complete nuisance but I need the loo and I need to get one of the nurses to help me get there,' she said.

'I could...'

'Don't be silly.' Maud said. 'It's just so frustrating. It's what you fear most, you know, as you get older. Falling. As a child you don't care. When you're an adult – a younger adult at least – you just find it embarrassing. But now? It's the start of the decline.' She said the last words with a touch of humour, but Becky could see the fear in them.

'But you're getting better?'

'There's a limit.' A nurse noticed Maud's waving hand and came to help her, talking to her in rapid French. Maud replied fluently, but there was no way that Becky could keep up.

'I expect you'll be off, then?' Maud said, her tone sounding slightly sharper than it had.

'If you... I don't want to stay too long.'

'Right then. Well, it was lovely to see you.' Maud heaved herself up, the nurse's hands hovering, prepared to break a potential fall. 'Do visit again before you go.'

Compared to her welcome, it was cold. But perhaps Maud was tired.

'Of course! It really was lovely to see you.'

'You too.' Maud's tone softened as she took a couple of steps forward, leaning on her crutch, nurse at her back. 'Look after yourself, Becky. Burnout is no joke.'

Becky gave a nod. As Maud made her painfully slow way across the wooden floor she tried to avert her eyes, look out of the window, as if something interesting had caught her eye. It was only when Maud reached the door that Becky looked at her fully again and gave a little wave.

Moments later, she walked out to the front drive again, leaned against Pascal's car and hoped that he hadn't gone too far. They'd yet to exchange mobile numbers so she couldn't call him. Instead, she texted Amber, who'd left her on read the last couple of times.

BECKY

Can we talk? I've just met Maud! Miss you.

But there was no answer.

20

Georges was waiting outside the café when they returned. As Pascal parked his car approximately in the space it had left, he turned, frowning.

'Uh oh,' Becky said.

'Sorry?'

'He's back!' she said, dramatically. 'Again.'

Pascal laughed. 'Oh, Georges? But he is not a monster!'

'Still, he looks a bit...' She nodded at Georges, who had turned fully and was watching them both, his mouth a straight line.

'He probably misses his caffeine,' Pascal said. 'Don't worry.'

He exited the car and made his way over, as Becky undid her seatbelt and climbed out. After a quick handshake, the two men started talking quite rapidly together. It wasn't clear whether the conversation was friendly or hostile.

'*Non*,' she heard Pascal say. '*Pas maintenant.*'

Not now, she translated, missing the words that followed.

Becky walked over slowly, trying to take her time to avoid being caught up in anything. She smiled as she approached. The two men stopped talking abruptly and turned to face her, looking a little like two toddlers caught stealing cookies from a jar. '*Bonjour*,' she said to Georges.

'*Bonjour.*' He stepped forward and quickly pecked both of her cheeks. It was the first time anyone had greeted her this way in France, although she'd witnessed countless *bisous* in the café. She tried to pretend that this was a completely normal way to greet someone – although could only imagine what would happen if she started to welcome her colleagues back home in this way. A lawsuit, probably.

'Everything OK?' she asked, glancing from one to the other.

'*Oui*. Georges was just coming to see how things went with Maud,' Pascal said, giving Georges a look.

'Oh. Yes. *Oui*, I was here to find that out,' Georges said, seeming flustered. 'Was it all OK?'

'Yes. Strange, obviously. Because I thought she was... you know. But yes. Lovely. She's just as I remember her.'

Georges nodded. 'I am glad.'

Tell that to your face, she wanted to say, but didn't.

Pascal got out his key and unlocked the café. 'You will stay for coffee?'

'No. I must go. But again, I am very happy for you.'

Pascal nodded and pushed the door open fully.

Georges walked away, glancing over his shoulder at them as they went into the building. 'I will see you tomorrow?' he called to Pascal.

Pascal gave him a wave but remained silent.

'Was he OK?' Becky asked. 'He was acting a little... strangely.'

Pascal laughed. 'That is just Georges!' he said. 'I have known him some time now. His mannerisms take a while to read.' She noticed his neck was slightly blotchy – red perhaps from the heat in the car.

'OK.' Walking into the café, she put her bag down on the counter and sank into one of the contentious yellow chairs. It was extremely comfortable and sitting there, she realised she could feel her muscles ache. 'I'm shattered,' she said.

'Hardly a surprise. It was a big deal today, I think.'

'Yeah. It was.' She pulled out her phone and looked at her message to Amber. It hadn't been read.

'Everything OK?' Pascal said, walking towards the door into the main building.

'Yeah. It's just Amber. She normally replies and she's virtually blanking me.'

'She is busy?'

'Yes, but that doesn't normally stop her. Especially... she knows what I'm up to today.'

He shrugged. 'Sometimes things are not so important to others. I am sure she will reply soon.'

'Yeah, you're probably right.'

'Perhaps she is missing France.'

Becky laughed. 'Probably. It's raining again in London.'

'Did you ask her?'

It was an odd question. 'What? If she was missing France?'

'If she was OK.' Pascal said. 'Because I think sometimes it seemed like maybe she wanted to talk more about herself.'

'What do you mean?' Her voice sounded a little sharp.

'Oh, it is nothing.'

'No. Please. What is it?'

Pascal sighed. 'Perhaps it's rude to say, but as a writer I listen to conversations, I observe things. And it... I don't know you very well, but I have noticed that sometimes you talk...'

'Well, yes. So does everyone!'

'No. I mean you talk but you don't listen as much. You don't ask questions of other people so much.' He walked up and gently touched her shoulder, the back of her neck.

'Yes I do! I'm always asking questions!' She felt herself stiffen.

'OK. I did not mean to offend. It is just an observation. But for example, I told you that I was writing, but it was more than a week before you asked me anything about it. And when you decided to decorate... you did this on your own without consultation.'

'Yes, but I didn't know you then. I didn't think you'd want to help.' She shrugged his arm away. Her shoulder felt cold after the warmth of his hand.

Pascal's eyes hardened. He nodded. 'I understand.'

'Anyway, Amber's fine. We talked a lot when she was here,' she almost snapped. 'And quite honestly, you don't know her at all, so I don't see how you could sense how she feels.' All the while, inside, a little voice was telling her to stop; to alter her tone. Why was she talking to Pascal like this? He clearly meant well.

'I just thought I might mention it. I am an empath. I feel people. She seemed very sad.' Pascal's voice was close to monotone.

'Amber? No, she's fine,' Becky said firmly.

'Good.' Pascal made towards the door again, then turned. 'Oh, and you will be pleased to know, I think, that I have started to make plans.'

'Plans?'

'Yes, to return to Paris. The publishers my agent sent the novel to are very happy with my work and have made me a generous offer. Good enough for me to tell my mother about my book deal, and for her to even be a little pleased for me, I think.'

'Oh! Right.' She felt a sinking sensation. Was this his way of telling her that last night had meant nothing? It felt off, as if he were annoyed at her.

'So you definitely need to go to Paris for this?'

'*Non*. But it is time. As you say, I cannot stay here.'

'You can, though!' she found herself saying. 'I mean, there's no rush from this end.'

He raised an eyebrow, acknowledging her U-turn. 'Thank you. Well, I will stay for the two weeks you are here. I will help you to finish the works? The tables are coming soon, *non*? And your very modern coffee machine. I would like to help you finish, and I think Maud would want this.' He smiled thinly.

She nodded, somehow unable to speak. For a moment he looked as if he were going to say something more, but seemed to check himself, smiled, and made his way through to the kitchen. The door shut and she was once again alone in the café.

It felt odd being here with no customers, without the hustle and bustle of locals consuming coffee, without their cheerful *bisous* and general conversation. The sun still shone resolutely outside and its light streamed into the café, illuminating the first row of tables. But here, near the counter, she was in shadow. She didn't move to turn on the lights, preferring to feel invisible to anyone who might pass. Her stomach clenched as she thought of Pascal. How easily he'd managed to brush her off. Not that she'd hoped for more. Obviously, nothing long term could happen between them. Still, it would have been nice to be wanted.

She felt something stir inside her and for a sudden moment wished she were back at work where there were clear rules and where she could lose herself in the busyness of her job and forget that there was life outside the bright, white walls of the office building.

Drawing out her phone she scanned through her messages to Amber from the last couple of weeks. There were a lot of them. She tried to find a moment when she'd asked Amber something about herself. How she was, or how work was going. But other than, 'Can you talk?' and 'Let me know when you're free!' her messages did actually seem to be almost solely about her own experience.

But then she was going through quite a tumultuous time. Amber had to understand that.

She typed in 'How are you? Hope you're OK?' just in case. Then got up and made her way through the kitchen and upstairs towards her room. Drawing out her mobile phone again – although it hadn't been any more than five minutes – she saw her message had been read. But Amber hadn't yet replied.

It was odd, this separation from Amber. She'd seen her daily for years – a little less when they'd attended different universities of course. But then when they'd both been offered jobs in offices a stone's throw from each other and realised they could rent a place together, they'd jumped at the chance. And it had worked – they'd lived together seamlessly ever since. She never ordinarily had to second-guess text messages from Amber, because she'd see her every morning and evening.

She watched the message window for a moment as if by doing so she could perhaps telepathically encourage her friend to write back.

But no.

There was nothing for it. She'd have to go ahead and call Mum without a bolster from her best friend first.

She should, of course, have broken the news about Maud to Mum immediately. But she'd put it off, telling herself it would be better to wait until she'd actually seen her; so she could deliver a full report about how she was. Maybe even pass a message!

But now, calling up her mum from her list of contacts, she realised that deep down she'd simply been avoiding it. Whether it was to spare Mum the shock, or some other subconscious reason she was barely aware of, she didn't know.

'Now or never,' she said to herself as she pressed *Call*.

'Rebecca! How are you!' Mum answered before she even heard a ring on the line, making her jump.

'Yes. Good. Thank you.'

'Oh, wonderful! So you're surely back in the UK now? Fit for work?'

For a moment, Becky was confused. Then she realised: Mum had thought she was signed off for a fortnight, not a month. And she'd never corrected her. 'I'm a lot better,' she began cautiously.

'Wonderful! So—'

'Hang on, Mum. I think I might have made a mistake when I told you about... when I said I was signed off for a couple of weeks.'

'How so?'

'Mum, it was a month. I just... I'm not sure why I didn't say.' Becky held the phone a little away from her ear and screwed up her face, ready for the onslaught.

'What the dickens! Rebecca! I mean, gadzooks!'

'I'm sorry, I must have—'

'Don't give me that, young lady. You didn't tell me because you were ashamed, am I right?'

Becky felt her face flush involuntarily as if she were fourteen again and lying about staying out late. 'Not exactly, but—'

'The very cheek of it.' It wasn't clear whether her mother was now talking about Becky's lie or her being signed off for so long. 'Well, that's settled then, you have to come home immediately! Get back in there and fight for your job, my girl.'

'I am coming home. It's just... It's the café – things are... well, I'm still decorating and—'

'Really, Rebecca? Do you honestly need to be there for that? Surely you can just get a man in. I can always send some—'

'No. It's OK, Mum. It's well on the way!' She forced some positivity into her voice.

'You do realise the seriousness of the situation, I suppose?'

'Mum.' Becky tried to keep the impatience from her voice. It went against her nature to let someone talk to her like this; but she'd learnt the hard way that locking horns with her mother was both exhausting and pointless. Humouring was a better option. 'I am going to get back to work as soon as possible. I just have to finish up here. We're nearly done,' she lied.

'Botheration.'

'Yes.'

'I do actually have some news though,' she said, closing her eyes. Might as well get it all over with at once.

'You do? Well, come on! Out with it!'

'You know that we got the letter from the *notaire*?'

'Well obviously.'

'We assumed that Maud had... passed,' Becky said. 'But if you think about it, the letter didn't say that explicitly.'

'I don't understand... Why would the letter—'

'Mum,' she said, gently. 'Maud isn't dead.'

'Heavens to Betsy!' her mother exclaimed loudly. 'Maud is alive. Is she *there*? At the café? Why didn't you say anything before? What on earth would make you keep this from me? Did you know before you went out there? Is that why you were so keen to fly over?'

Becky waited for her mother to draw breath, then, 'No. Mum. Wait. I didn't know. And she isn't here. She's in a care home. I only found out myself yesterday.'

'Good gracious.'

'Yes, I went to see her.'

'Oh.' Her mum's tone sounded guarded. 'How was she? I expect her memory's not what—'

'Actually, Mum, she's doing really well. Her mind is completely intact. It's just a broken hip and I think a loss of mobility after that. She couldn't run the café and needed care so... It's a nice place, too.'

'Well, yes. Of course. Of course that was the right thing to do. But heavens! What a shock!' There was a pause. 'Did she... mention me?'

'A little.'

There was a silence.

'Rebecca, I really think it would be a good idea to come home. You clearly haven't inherited a café, and I'm going to investigate how the solicitor's letter got it so very wrong. And it'll be time to get back to the office soon, I'm sure. Perhaps we could get a second opinion on the burnout and...'

'No, Mum. Maud *has* given me the café.'

'Oh.'

'Yes. A sort of advance gift from her Will.'

'Sounds a little more like subterfuge,' her mother said darkly. 'Tax avoidance probably. And, it seems, a way to get you to visit her against your will!'

'A little strong, Mother?'

'You don't know Maud like I do.'

'Well, I suppose she did say she'd wanted to see me, hoped the gift would encourage me to visit. But obviously she wouldn't give me a café just to get me to book a plane ticket.'

Another silence. 'So you're coming home soon? Look, I've been thinking about the flat. And I could sub you the money – easily, in fact. I don't know why I didn't think of it before!'

'Because you wanted me to stand on my own two feet?'

'Well, perhaps Maud's inspired me. The money will be yours eventually, of course. After I've gone.'

'Mum, you're sixty-three.'

'I am aware of that, Rebecca!'

'You're not going anywhere. It's me who has all the health problems!' Becky said, trying to lighten the mood.

'Land sakes, Rebecca. You are fine.' Her mother's voice seemed to crack slightly on the final words. 'Look, come home. Let's get that flat of yours sorted, shall we? And perhaps we can pop back again together to see Maud at some point, if you'd like?'

'Thank you, Mum. It sounds… it's a lovely offer.'

'So, I'll see you soon?'

'I've got some things to do… some thinking. But thank you. It's so nice of you. And you know… I'll call you.'

'And book your ticket soon, too, I hope?'

'Yes,' Becky found herself saying. 'Yes, of course.'

'Good. Good girl.' Her mother hung up without saying goodbye.

Well, that was – as her mother would no doubt term it – 'a turn-up for the books.'

If only she'd known that all she had to do to get a bit more financial support from her mum was to suffer burnout, inherit a café in France, travel to the continent and resurrect an aunt from the dead, then she'd have done it years ago.

Her mum's offer would have simplified things enormously a couple of weeks ago. But now, she wasn't sure why, the choice didn't seem so clear-cut. And the flat didn't seem very important at all.

She tried to ring Amber again.

The phone cut to an answering service, but she didn't leave a message.

21

Two days on, when her phone trilled, she guiltily pressed *Dismiss.* It was the second time Mum had rung that day. As she looked at the screen, frowning, and pressed *Decline,* she saw Pascal looking at her from behind the stepladder.

'Everything OK?' he asked.

'Just Mum.' She made a face.

'You are declining a call from your mother?' His face was somewhere between impressed and aghast. 'I would never dare.'

'Not sure I dare myself. I'll be for it when I finally do answer,' she admitted.

'Have you had a fight? Argued?'

'No, it's just...' She dipped her brush into the tin of white paint and began to stroke it onto the skirting board, turning it from dull mahogany to something fresher. The walls were now finished, and this was the final coat.

She hated decorating. But spending time with Pascal, barely talking, just getting on with the job in hand, had been surprisingly soothing. There was something lovely, too, about seeing the café gradually become a new version of itself.

In the days that had followed their night together, they'd settled into something that felt like a friendship. Neither mentioned anything more and while for her, the question sometimes fizzed between them, she didn't let herself say anything out loud. What was there to say? *I wish you wanted to stay and be with me, even though I'd turn you down if you asked*? 'It's complicated.'

Pascal laughed. 'Complicated, I understand completely.' He stepped back from where he'd finished papering the back wall and inspected his work, hands on hips. She watched him – his narrow frame in its customary chequered (and now paint-splattered) shirt, messy jeans; hair with a few flecks of blue paint in it. And felt a sudden rush of affection for him, but forced herself to face facts. They'd had a one-night stand and now he was helping her decorate, probably more out of loyalty to Maud than anything else.

'Have you spoken to *your* mum yet?' she asked. 'About your book deal, moving back to Paris?'

She'd meant it to be a genuine question, but he turned and laughed. 'Touché,' he said. 'I am also guilty of withholding information from my mother. Although I would ignore her calls at my peril. But then it is complicated for me too.'

'Sorry!' she said, grimacing. 'You know what, if we ever have kids, let's make a promise never to... well, you know. Pressure them to the extent that they have to lie to us.'

'Kids?' He looked at her, eyes sparkling with mischief.

She flushed. 'I meant, with other people of course.'

He gave her a little grin that showed he'd already known how she'd intended the sentence to sound. 'Yes, we will have to make sure we do not use our children to right our own wrongs. Fulfil our regrets.'

'Is that what you think our mums are doing?'

He shrugged. 'My mother thinks she should have started younger, made more of herself. So it is my job to live her life instead of my own. At least, that's my impression.'

She nodded. She understood. 'With my mum, I suppose it's more about protecting me. She went through some hardship, and having money makes her feel safe. She just wants the same for me, I guess.'

Pascal nodded. *'Je comprends.'*

Straightening up, Becky inspected the section of skirting board she'd now finished. There were just a couple of metres to go. Pascal's eyes followed hers.

'It looks good,' he said.

'Yours too.'

'I think perhaps another day or two and it will be complete.'

And then what? she wondered. Would she start trying to employ a new manager? Tell Maud it was all too much, and that someone local ought to take it over? Leave Vaudrelle and return to work? Part of her still wanted to drop the brush, flag down a cab (a literal impossibility in Vaudrelle) and get back on a plane as soon as possible: reclaim her life, her flat, her best friend.

And her work too, she supposed. Although for some reason, although she loved her job, she didn't feel in such a rush where that was concerned.

She sighed more loudly than she intended.

'What is wrong?' Pascal said, walking over to the skirting board as if to take another look. 'It looks fine!'

'It's not the painting. Just... feeling a bit...' she said, shrugging in the place of an adequate word.

The past days had been spent visiting Maud, working in the café, then taking a break before continuing to decorate in the evening. Busy days. But productive. And they'd given her the kind of buzz her job had used to do before it became all-consuming, and she hadn't had time to think about whether she enjoyed it or not. She'd been struck on one of her walks yesterday when she glimpsed herself in the window of a shop and seen that she was smiling. She'd looked different. Lighter.

But that was because, she'd reasoned later, she was effectively on holiday. This wasn't real life. If she stayed – and she wasn't really considering that, not in any real sense – these exceptional, unusual days would become ordinary days. Would she enjoy them so much then?

She wasn't sure what the future held, or what the right direction was. But she knew that she wanted to see more of Maud while she could; that she wanted to find out why Amber was angry at her – if indeed she was. Against her better judgement, she still had this underlying desire to get Mum's approval; to make her proud. And all of these things fought one another daily in her mind. Except when she was decorating, or sometimes when she was talking with Pascal, and she found herself briefly existing only in the moment – the feeling slipping away the second it was noticed.

'You are unhappy?' Pascal asked. 'Homesick, perhaps?' He picked up a second brush and dipped it into the gloss she was using for the skirting board. Then, kneeling down a little farther along the wall, he began to help her with her task.

'I just don't know,' she said. 'There are so many unanswered questions, if that makes sense?'

'With Amber?'

'With everything! I came here with all these plans. This... agenda. And now Maud's alive, and there's no way I can sell the café. And Mum's offered me money – I could buy my dream flat, go back to my job. Live the life I wanted so much.'

'But?'

'I just don't know any more,' she said simply. 'All my life I've had this planned trajectory – this route that I was expected to take. And the easiest thing was just to take it. It's worked out great... on paper.'

'But you are not happy?'

'I'm just not sure I know what I want! How am I supposed to decide what to do if I have no idea where I'm headed?' She longed suddenly for the clarity of one of Mum's five-year plans. A recipe to follow to lead her life in the right direction.

'Your eye,' Pascal said, seemingly noticing immediately. 'It is vibrating.'

Not again! She touched her hand to her eye, before realising she had paint on her fingers. Instantly, it began to sting. 'Oh, God.'

'*Attends*,' Pascal told her, standing up and striding quickly to the sink. He ran a clean tea towel under the water then rushed back, kneeling down next to her and gently dabbing at her eye. 'I think it is OK,' he said, giving her the towel to hold over her eye, which was still stinging slightly. 'I don't think anything got into the eye itself.' He gently put his hand under her elbow and encouraged her to stand and walk to one of the yellow chairs. She sat down gratefully, not enjoying the throb of her eye, but if she was honest, enjoying his touch; his evident care.

'I will get the doctor,' he said. 'Just to be sure.'

'No! Oh, you really needn't.'

'He is a friend, he will come,' he said confidently, getting out his phone.

She was grateful, moments later, when he told her the doctor was nipping out of the surgery at the end of the village to make a quick house call. 'He will be here in five minutes.'

'Really? That's impressive.' She tried to remain stoic despite the throbbing and stinging sensation.

The doctor arrived, sporting jeans and a short-sleeved

chequered shirt. He looked to be around fifty years old, his hair still glossy and full, the lines around his eyes and mouth giving his age away. He looked at her eye and tutted. '*Mon Dieu*, you were lucky, *madame.*'

While adding a solution to some cotton wool and expertly dabbing at her sore eye, the doctor explained how while a tiny bit of paint had entered it, it had confined itself mainly to her lower lid. Any more and it might have been a catastrophe.

She felt her heart turn over. It was that serious? The idea of it made her feel a little shaky. The doctor created a makeshift patch from some gauze and plaster tape, leaned down and carefully applied it to her sore eye. 'You will be OK. I will send a nurse tomorrow to remove the dressing,' he said, straightening up.

Pascal shook the doctor's hand and walked with him to just outside the door, where the two men stayed chatting in the sunshine before the older man turned and walked back in the direction of his surgery.

Pascal re-entered to find her holding her hand over the gauze, feeling rather shaken. 'It hurts?' he asked.

'No. It's OK.'

'We should probably wear goggles.'

'Yes. Or maybe not put painty fingers into our eyes.'

'That sounds like good advice.'

She felt herself smiling a little.

'Let me see again,' he said, kneeling before her and gently lifting her hand and inspecting the gauze, his face just centimetres from hers, as if he were a doctor with X-ray vision to boot. It was nice, feeling his face so close to hers. She looked up at him with her one good eye and marvelled at his thick eyelashes, the depth and concern in his expression. 'You will live, I think,' he concluded, not moving his head. She gave the slightest inclination with her own and moments later their lips brushed in a gentle kiss.

She hadn't realised just how much she'd been longing for him to touch her again until that moment when she felt herself melt. She put her arms up and around him, pulling him a little closer for another kiss. Then another. Until:

'*Non*,' he said, standing up abruptly. 'We should not.'

'Oh!' she said, feeling her cheeks get hot. 'I'm sorry I...'

'*Non*, do not be sorry. It is not that I do not want to,' he said, crouching down again so they were the same height. 'But if I kiss you again, I will ask you to stay. And I know that you must go. And I will want to stay here too, but I cannot.'

'What if I did stay?' she said unthinkingly.

'You want to stay?'

'I could if I wanted to.'

He laughed. 'This is true. You are a free agent.'

'You too,' she pointed out. 'Didn't you say once that you could write from anywhere? Why does it have to be Paris?' She blushed. 'I'm not asking you to stay. Obviously. I just mean, sometimes I wonder why I tell myself I *have* to do this or that... I suppose we just know what's best, long term.'

'Perhaps,' he said. 'Or maybe we are afraid.'

She nodded, looking up at him.

'Jean-Paul Sartre, he said that being afraid is good... I think it was: "Fear is the consciousness of an anxiety in the face of the possibility of a choice".'

She nodded again. 'Letting a problem in can be the start of a transformation?'

'That is very wise. Which philosopher said this?'

She blushed. 'I've paraphrased it a bit but... Jerry Maguire.'

He looked confused for a moment then laughed. 'Well, I think this Professor Maguire must be a very intelligent man.'

She laughed.

And then they were kissing and for a moment she could let go of her future and just be present. Moments later, she gave him her hand and let him lead her to the bedroom. Whatever the future held for them, it would be silly to waste such a wonderful moment.

22

The next morning, Becky reached for her phone but found that her last few messages to Amber still remained unread. Surely Amber wouldn't ignore her though? The only other explanation she could think of was that there was some sort of technical fault on the line. Perhaps it was something to do with Becky being in France. She'd called the number a few times, too, but who's to say it wasn't ringing in some cyberspace void rather than actually in Amber's pocket or bag?

Becky couldn't think of a rational reason why Amber wouldn't be answering her. They'd parted on good terms, hadn't they? And in any case, Amber was more the sort of person to try to talk something out rather than sit and brood on it.

She had several missed calls from last night from her mother. But those could wait. To try to put her off a little, she'd sent a breezy text:

BECKY

> Sorry! I'm so busy with decorating! Will call soon!

She just needed a bit of time; a little space to think. To work out how she felt about everything that was happening. After living in London for several years, working at the same firm, seeing the same people, to be plucked out of there like a toy in a candy grabber machine and plonked into this totally new situation was a lot. She wanted to mull everything over herself rather than have her mother's forceful opinions and guilt trips in the mix.

But it would be a lot easier to mull things over if her best friend would pick up the phone and call her. The irony of being ghosted, while simultaneously ghosting someone else, wasn't lost on her. But she doubted her mother really yearned to speak to her the way she did to Amber. She would just be calling to berate and bully her into booking her ticket home.

She sighed loudly and flung her phone onto the covers.

Pascal, next to her in bed with a notepad open and wearing just a pair of briefs, looked at her. 'Amber hasn't replied?'

'Yeah.'

'It is early. Try not to worry.' He smiled. It was odd how she felt so comfortable around him, despite the fact he was nearly naked and that his body was even more attractive than she'd imagined it might be before she'd been confronted with reality.

Remembering last night – his gentle caresses, the ability he seemed to have to set her whole body alive with tingles at the slightest touch – she shivered, resisting the urge to reach forward and drag him back under the covers. Was it true what they said about French men making good lovers? Or was it that she and Pascal were so right for each other? All she knew was that when they were together, everything in her felt on fire. As if she suddenly realised what sex was all about.

'What's the matter?'

'Oh, nothing,' she said. 'Just thinking.'

They'd come up with the idea of the launch about an hour ago after waking up together. Pascal had fetched coffee and they'd sat up in bed, chatting and sipping, watching the early morning sky come into itself through open blinds.

She'd got used to early starts now. When she'd first arrived, she'd found herself sleeping – perhaps making up for all the years she'd spent reacting to six o'clock alarms. But there was something refreshing about waking up early and slowly coming to as the light turned from silver to gold, then bright brilliant white as the sun rose and began to gently wake the earth.

'We should have a grand opening!' he'd said.

'But the café is already open!'

'But we can do some... finishing touches. Then have an event. It'll bring new people to the café, and maybe demonstrate that what we've been doing is for the community – the whole community.'

'Even the yellow chairs?'

'Can I tell you something,' he'd said, his eyes on her face. 'Something I have kept from you?'

She'd felt a frisson of anxiety. 'Of course.'

'I am not sure what has happened to me, but I am starting to like the chairs.'

'Ah, you're just saying that,' she'd teased.

'*Non*! It is serious. The café, the whole aesthetic you've created. It's something really special, Becky. You have an eye.'

She'd basked in his praise. 'Thank you.' Then put a hand to the gauze. 'Hopefully I have two.'

He laughed. 'It is sure,' he said, gently caressing the skin next to her dressing. 'But you have truly transformed this place. That is why I think this launch is so necessary. To get people from farther away to come and try. To really show people what you have achieved.'

The Village Café in the Loire

'We.'

'You are speaking French, *oui*?'

'No! I mean "we". What *we* have achieved.'

Smiling, he'd leaned down and kissed her gently on the lips, before sitting up and picking up the notebook and pen.

'Do you think we should bring Maud here first, too? So that she gets to see everything before the party?' she mused.

'Maybe.'

She crawled out from under the duvet and sat next to him, wrapping an arm around his shoulders. His skin was cool to the touch. 'Time to open up in a minute?'

'*Oui.*' He looked at her. 'It was good,' he said. 'Last night.'

She nodded. There was something in his eyes, an emotion she couldn't quite put a word to. But she felt it too. They barely knew each other; but it felt somehow that they'd known each other forever. She'd felt it yesterday when they'd kissed, and again this morning when she'd woken up next to him and it had seemed the most natural thing in the world.

Somehow, things that hadn't made sense to her before were starting to fall into place here. 'I want to stay,' she said impulsively. 'I want to stay here with you.'

'I would like that too,' he said, maintaining eye contact for a moment, his dark eyes serious, watching hers. 'I wish it could happen.'

Moments later he went to get showered and dressed, ready to start work for the day, and she was left simply with his words – *I wish it could happen.*

What did he mean? That he wanted it to happen, but it couldn't? That he wanted it to happen, and would make it so? Was it a grammar faux pas or a gentle brush-off? And how was she supposed to know?

This was what best friends were for. Picking over important

words and working out what they actually meant. She pulled out her phone and rang Amber's number yet again. But nothing. Her thumb even wavered over Mum's number. But Mum would be no good for this kind of conversation. Becky knew exactly what Mum would make of all this, and she wasn't sure if she was ready to hear it.

It struck her, then, that she didn't have anyone else she could call, not really. There were friends, sure; people she'd have a drink with after work or meet up with occasionally. But nobody she could call in the early hours to try to pick apart Pascal's words and help her to decide what she ought to do about it all.

Amber, she said to herself. *Where are you?*

She tried once more. This time leaving a short message after the tone. 'Amber, call me back? Hope everything's OK!'

Then, not knowing what else to do, she bathed and dressed, made her way downstairs for breakfast. As she approached the large, tiled kitchen that served both the café and the house, she heard the sound of talking. Recognising Pascal's voice, she paused, listening out for the other person's voice. But there was only his; he was either talking to himself or on the phone.

Not wanting to interrupt, she waited. And although she tried not to listen, at least... a little bit, she couldn't help but overhear some words in French.

'*Oui, Maman! Je rentrerai bientôt!*' She closed her eyes, trying to grasp the meaning – he would be home soon. He must be calling his mum to tell her about the book. About his upcoming move to Paris. '*Oui, oui,*' he was saying.

She was just about to disappear back up the stairs until he finished the call when she heard the words. '*Bien sûr, il n'y a rien ici!*' – there is nothing here. What did he mean? Nothing holding him back? That it was boring in Vaudrelle? Or was this evidence that what had happened last night hadn't meant much to him at all?

Did he mean that? Hearing his words filled her with sudden doubt. And her idea of staying and having Pascal at her side – perhaps not running the café, but working on his writing, staying local – started to crumble. Was she kidding herself?

She crept back a few stairs, then re-trod them, making sure she was as noisy as possible. Then she flung open the door. 'Sorry,' she said. 'Didn't mean to disturb.' He ended the call and looked at her.

'Did you fall?'

Clearly, she'd overdone the banging. 'No. Not quite. Just, um, stumbled. Were you calling your mother?'

His face darkened. '*Oui.* You would think when I told her that I have this amazing publishing deal she would finally be happy for me.'

'And she wasn't?'

He shook his head. 'Well, perhaps a little. Perhaps if you had heard her, you would think she was ecstatic. She makes the right noises. But I can feel the heart of it. She is still disappointed that I don't work in a bank.'

'But she must be pleased you'll be living closer soon?' she prompted.

'*Oui.* I think so.' So he really, really was going.

'Well. Good,' she said.

'Perhaps after the nurse has called you could serve for a little? I can make invitations for the party. Then this afternoon we will close – it is often quiet in early afternoon – and go to buy things. It is very exciting!'

'Sure.'

Before she could say anything else, her phone rang loudly, making her jump. Fishing it out of her pocket, she saw it was

Amber's number rather than her mother's. At last. Feeling a surge of happiness, she answered immediately. 'Amber?' she said. 'Oh my God, I'm so glad you called. I...'

But the voice on the other end wasn't Amber.

As Pascal watched her, he saw her face fall, then turn pale. And in the end, her arm simply fell to her side, the phone still clutched in her hand.

'What is it?' he said. 'What's wrong?'

'It's Amber,' she said, before collapsing into tears.

23

Pascal was at her side instantly.

'Amber's in hospital!' Becky said. 'Someone heard her phone and saw all my missed calls and...'

'*Merde!*' Pascal exclaimed loudly.

Becky turned away from him, scrolling through her contacts until she found an old landline number. Hopefully Amber's mother would still have the same one she'd had back in the day. Sure enough, it rang twice before it was picked up by a rather hesitant voice saying, 'Hello?'

'Mrs... I mean, Hannah, it's Becky.'

'Oh. Becky.' Hannah's voice was rather flat. 'I take it you've heard about Amber.'

'Yes. Oh my God. How is she?'

'Well, she's not in any danger. So you needn't worry.'

'What? Of course I'm worried. She had a heart attack?'

'No. Not a heart attack exactly. Look, Becky, I understand you're busy. Perhaps it would be better to leave this to Amber's close friends and family.' The remark was pointed.

Becky had gone to Amber's house regularly when growing

up, had always liked her mother. She'd make them sandwiches or cups of tea or ask about their homework. Even now, she probably saw her once or twice a year when she came to London to visit her daughter. But in all the times she'd seen her, in all circumstances, she'd never been anything but polite and friendly.

'Look, Hannah,' she said. It felt odd to use her first name, even now. 'I understand that this must be a very stressful time. But you know that I'm Amber's close friend. Her closest. Can you please just tell me what's happening? How did she... What happened? When?' Her voice cracked on the last word.

There was a silence, then, and when Hannah spoke, her voice trembled. 'Well, you know all about Rufus at work, I suppose?'

'Rufus? Hannah's manager?'

'Yes. Nasty business.'

'What business?'

There was a silence. 'Amber didn't mention to you...?'

'She mentioned his name. She never said... I don't know exactly what's happened between them, no.' Had Amber dated Rufus? Had a crush on him? All Amber could remember was that her friend had described him as a bit of an idiot.

Hannah was silent again. 'Well,' she said at last, 'I'm surprised you didn't know about the bullying.'

'Bullying?'

'Yes. Rufus has been targeting Amber for the last few weeks. Making her life a misery. And on top of all the stress she was already under, it was the straw that broke the camel's back.'

Becky felt cold. If it had come to this, why had Amber never said anything? Surely she would be the first person Amber would reach out to ordinarily?

'Oh God. What a bastard. But I don't understand. You said

she was stressed? I mean, I saw her recently and she seemed... fine.'

Hannah snorted. 'Well, safe to say she wasn't. Amber's been under enormous pressure for months. She always struggled a bit with the rent for that fancy flat of yours, I suppose you know that? And with all the threats from Rufus, she was terrified of losing her job too. She started doing overtime, applying for extra work. And I suppose it all became a bit... much.'

'Oh God, Poor Amber. Why didn't she tell me?'

Hannah sighed. 'Well, she tried. But you were so stressed yourself. And it's harder than you'd imagine, admitting that you have financial problems. There's pride.'

Becky's face felt hot. 'And she's... it was a stress thing? A panic attack?'

'No. Worse than that I'm afraid. Pain. Some unusual cardiac activity.' Hannah reeled off these facts as if reading them from notes. 'They want to run tests. Think it's related to the build-up of cortisol. From stress.'

The last word sounded pointed. Becky opened her mouth to defend herself. She was hardly responsible for her friend's stress levels after all. But then Hannah was worried. A worried parent. She was entitled to snap a little.

'I just wish she'd told me,' Becky said. 'About Rufus, about the money.'

'I think...' Hannah said carefully, 'Rebecca, I think she was probably embarrassed.'

'Embarrassed?'

A silence. 'Well, things aren't perhaps as easy for her as they are for you. Financially. Her job... it's good, but she has a lot of debt from uni. And the flat... well, she was worried about covering the rent from the start... But you were so enthusiastic.'

'Why didn't she say?'

Another silence. 'It might be hard for you to understand. You have your mother. And now this inheritance in France. It's very different for you.'

'But...'

'I'm not saying you did anything intentional. Lord knows when I was your age, I was 100 per cent occupied with my own life. I didn't have time for anyone around me,' Hannah said in a gentler tone.

'I'll come home. I'll fly back today.'

'You'd do that?'

'Of course! She's my best friend. I...' Becky found tears in her eyes. She reached up and gently pulled the dressing from her eye. It would be fine. 'How long are they keeping her in for?'

'They said a few more days. They're not happy with some of her readings. But as I say, she's not in any immediate danger.'

This wasn't as reassuring as Hannah might have supposed it would be.

'What about her work?'

'Rebecca! Her work isn't important right now.'

'I know. I mean – is someone investigating this Rufus bastard? Are they being OK? Paying her?'

'She's quit. The day before the incident. Something happened. I'm not sure what. And it was the tip of the iceberg. But I think... I think threats were made. About references. And the poor girl got into a state, wondering how she'd pay the rent, how she'd... survive.'

'Oh, poor Amber.'

Hannah was silent.

'Well, I can cover her rent for the foreseeable.'

'It won't be necessary. She's coming home with me for a while. I'll look after her.' The clipped, defensive tone was back.

'Oh.' The Amber Becky knew wouldn't be too happy with

this scenario. But perhaps things had changed? It seemed as if she'd completely lost touch with how her friend was feeling. 'OK. Well, text me the details of the hospital, the ward? And I'll find a flight now.'

She ended the call and jumped slightly, seeing Pascal still at her side.

'So Amber is very sick?'

She told him, her words stuttering and failing at times. 'It's my fault!' she told him then. 'It's all my fault.'

He held her shoulders. 'Becky, it is not your fault. Of course it isn't. *Oui*, perhaps you could have listened more. But you would never hurt your friend.'

'I have to go.'

'*Bien sûr*! Of course you must. I can handle things here.'

She nodded and disappeared to her room, rapidly booking a ticket for the afternoon – thankfully there were plenty of flights – and shoving a few things into a bag. She texted her mother: 'Amber's sick, flying to UK. Will update.' But ignored her mother when she tried to call. She simply wasn't up to talking, speculating. She needed to see Amber first.

When she reappeared in the café, Pascal was chatting to some men in the corner. He saw her and came over.

'You have a taxi coming? I can give you a ride if not?'

'No, I've booked a taxi. You're busy.'

'Will you be OK?' he asked, brushing back her hair slightly and looking into her eyes. She blinked, hoping the tears would stay away. The last thing Amber needed was for her to fall apart. She needed to get to her. Then they'd figure everything else out.

'I'll be fine,' she said. 'Or OK at least. You mustn't worry.'

'Call me?' he said, ignoring a customer who'd come to the counter and was tapping his hand slightly on the wood. 'When you get there, when you are safe, when you have seen Amber?'

She nodded. 'I'll try.'

'When will you be back?'

She had hoped he wouldn't ask that question. She wasn't sure how to put the answer into words. Couldn't explain how the news of Amber had pierced through the bubble she'd been living in, exposing her trip to France for what it was. A distraction from real life. She'd had a sudden yearning, when packing her bags, for normality. Her normality. Life with Amber in the flat, her job. Feeling on top of things. Being present. She'd even started to miss Mum.

Yes, the idea of Maud – and her miraculous return to life – had been intoxicating. And she'd fallen for Pascal, she knew that she'd miss him. But there was no way to knit these two lives together, it was all or nothing on both counts. And Amber. Amber, who'd been there for her through thick and thin, needed her.

'I'm not sure,' she said at last, not ready to have that conversation. 'I'll know more when I've spoken to Amber.'

'But for the launch, I hope?'

She nodded. 'I'd like to be,' she said, figuring that this wasn't really a lie. She would like to be. Whether she was or not was another matter.

As she exited the building to wait on the pavement for her taxi, she stepped a little into the road so she could look up at it in its entirety. The polished glass of the window, the warm welcoming light inside. The light stone, the slightly sun-bleached shutters. The open window at the top that she knew was Pascal's room. The other one, hers. Closed. It was beautiful. It had been a beautiful adventure.

'Be careful, *madame*.' The voice in her ear made her jump. She turned to see a smiling Georges, then watched as his expression changed. Clearly her face was still streaked with tears. She tried to smile, not really wanting to talk about it to yet another person, not wanting to set herself off again. 'You are sick?' he asked.

'No. No, I'm OK,' she assured him. 'Just... I need to get back to England. To home. My friend is ill.'

'Oh no,' Georges said, shaking his head in sympathy. 'Your friend who was here? I am sorry to hear this.'

'It's OK.'

'Perhaps we can talk, when you have seen your friend. About the café. I have a solution for you. I think one that will be the best for all of us.'

Was he really talking about this now?

'Whatever you want. It doesn't matter,' she snapped.

Her taxi arrived then, its engine audible a good thirty seconds before it rounded the corner. She hoped it would get her to the airport in one piece. She had no idea what Georges wanted, but the last thing she cared about right now was the café.

Georges nodded. 'Well, I hope to see you soon,' he said, opening the door for her to slide in. He spoke to the taxi driver in rapid French, then tapped on the roof with his hand as if imbuing the taxi with the oomph it needed to get her to the airport in a timely fashion.

'Sure.' She tried to smile as he pushed the door to. Then allowed her face, finally, to fall.

24

Why were hospitals such mazes? Becky had been directed to the cardiac ward when she arrived at reception, but couldn't find it on the blue signs which seemed to point her in all directions but the right one. Visiting hours ended at 8 p.m., and she only had forty-five minutes to find her friend. She'd rushed from the airport and felt sweaty and frantic and exhausted. If she missed the chance to see Amber, she'd be devastated.

'Excuse me,' she asked a nurse. 'But can you tell me where the cardiology department is?'

'Next floor,' the nurse said, rushing by with a box in her hands.

Confused, Becky returned to the lift, waited an age for it to arrive, then got in. The interior was mirrored and she saw herself, bedraggled and red-eyed and not like herself at all. Her blonde hair, which had lightened in the French sun, looked wild and was tousled from the flight. She pulled it back as best she could and tried to smile. It was no use, she looked absolutely dreadful.

But it didn't matter, she told herself as she rushed out of the lift again. She found the right ward almost instantly and entered, slowing her pace, sensing a different tempo in the air. It was quiet. Machines beeped. There were six beds, curtains around two of them. A desk with a couple of nurses dressed in blue scrubs. Someone with a clipboard was talking to a man in a white coat in hushed tones. The air smelt like antiseptic and sweat, like the changing rooms at school.

It was, of course, raining outside and the large windows only revealed a grey sky dotted with the tops of buildings, through scattered water droplets. She wished she could whisk her friend back to France, sit her in the sun. Tell her never to go back to the job. Encourage her to talk about her worries. Prevent her from ever having to spend time in this place again.

At first, she thought that Amber must be in one of the curtained-off cubicles – but then the woman in the bed at the far end of the ward caught her eye. Her curls were flattened against the pillow, and there was a drip partly obscuring her face, but something about her called to Becky. It was definitely Amber.

Relieved, she walked over to her at pace. Amber was sitting, propped against a pillow, her eyes on a tattered book she was reading. 'Hi,' Becky said softly, not wanting to alarm her.

Amber looked up from the book, her eyes weary, and gave a double take. 'Bloody hell,' she said, giving out a heavy sigh. 'I take it my mother's been on the phone to you.'

'Well, yes. But... come on, Amber. Why didn't you tell me?' This was not the way Becky had wanted to start things.

Amber looked at her, her expression unreadable. 'Seriously?' she said. 'You're making things all about you?'

'No! No, of course not!'

Amber nodded. 'I know, really,' she said, looking down at herself in the generic hospital gown she'd been assigned by the hospital. 'I'm just feeling a bit shit.'

'Well, with cause.' Becky pulled up a chair and sat as close to Amber as she could. 'It must have been terrifying.'

'It was, a bit,' Amber admitted. 'I mean, I've had chest pains now and then for a while, but...'

'And you didn't get it checked out?'

'Becky, we're in our thirties. It just doesn't happen. I kept thinking it was indigestion or stress. And it kind of was... stress-induced. I just didn't realise it could have been... heart-related. Serious.'

Becky put her hand on Amber's. 'Pascal said you didn't look well, when he saw you,' she admitted. 'But I reassured him. Said he didn't understand what he was talking about. What an idiot.'

'You're not a doctor.'

'No. But I'm not a great friend either.'

'You realise we're still talking about you, right?'

'I'm so sorry!' Becky blurted, immediately feeling tears pool in her eyes. 'I just feel like this is all my fault.'

Amber looked at her dryly. 'I mean, you're capable of a lot of things, Becky, but I honestly don't think you can be responsible for my cardiac health.'

Becky laughed, slightly. 'Still.'

Amber smiled a little now. 'Look, shall we just agree you're a bit shit sometimes and then move on?'

'I will if you will?'

Amber wrapped her fingers around Becky's hand and gave it a squeeze. 'Done. Officially shit.'

'That's me!' Becky tried to smile.

'But you know I still love you, right? You're the only one who can make me laugh, forget about my problems. I know it hasn't been long, but I've really missed you,' Amber added.

'Aren't you going to say that I complete you?'

'We complete each other.'

Becky looked into her friend's eyes and felt the deep connection of their shared history. 'We really do,' she said.

Whatever had been broken between them seemed to be fixed for now.

'So, what's the...' The word *prognosis* came into her head. But it didn't seem the right thing to ask. 'What exactly is wrong?'

'They're not entirely sure. Not a heart attack, apparently. Thank God. But my heart was beating a little more quickly than it should. It might be all the stress hormones. They're worried about a bit of inflammation. They're just keeping an eye on me, honestly.'

'Shit though, Amber.'

'Yep!'

'And you've quit your job?'

It was brief, but she saw Amber blanch. 'Looks like it,' she said.

'Sorry, it doesn't matter, does it? Not under the circumstances.'

'Maybe not to someone like you.'

'What does that mean?'

'Oh, come on, Becky. We have very different lives. Very different circumstances.'

'Meaning?'

'Meaning, if you quit your job or needed some time... or had your career prospects thrown back in your face, you'd have a safety net.'

'What, Mum?' Becky made a face.

'Sure. Yeah. She's a pain. But she's wealthy and she has your back. You might not appreciate that. And, God knows, I realise the woman's driven you mad at times. But those are the facts. You are not going to starve.'

'Come on, Amber,' Becky said, trying to keep her tone gentle. 'Neither are you.'

'No. But my mum can't support me. Not for long. And it's fine. It's OK. It's normal, for a lot of people. That's why I've always worked so hard. But now this thing with Rufus...'

'He won't get away with it, you know! We can take him to a tribunal. Get some compensation.'

Amber nodded. 'Maybe. Eventually. But then what?'

'I don't know. But we must be able to do something.'

'The thing is, I didn't even like my job, not really. It was OK. But it was basically just fancy number-crunching. Stuck in a cubicle office in a faceless building.'

'I thought you loved it?'

'I thought I did at first. But it's amazing what having a suspected heart attack does. Sitting in bed, you think about things. And I realised I haven't been happy. Not for a long time. Not really.'

'Oh.'

'And *no*, it's not your fault.'

'Am I that bad?'

But Amber was smiling. 'No. Just busy. Preoccupied. In the middle of your own health crisis.'

'Health crisis?'

'The burnout. Like it or not, chick, you were displaying the signs. I've been worried about you.'

'Oh.' Becky looked down at her hands. 'I haven't got much going for me, have I? Shit, burnt out and self-obsessed.' She was only half joking.

'Ah, but you do have your good points. I mean, who else is going to let me indulge my obsession with 1990s Hugh Grant movies?' Amber smiled. Touched her hand.

'This is true.'

'Besides, you can't mess up a lifetime of friendship that easily.'

'I wish I'd listened more though, about Rufus.'

'Oh, he'll get his comeuppance eventually.'

'Tribunal?'

'Karma.'

'Do you want to talk about it?'

Amber shrugged. 'Not really. He was just a sleaze, basically. He asked me out about ten times in his first month at the firm, then when I said no, he started getting... well, mean. Finding fault, sending me emails. Making me feel... he made me feel as if my job were in trouble every single day.'

'What a bastard.'

'Yeah. And I've got a lot more to say about it, believe me. But right now, can we talk about something else?'

'Sure. Sorry.'

'It's OK. Just don't want to waste any oxygen on him.'

'So what will you do now? When you get out, I mean?'

Amber raised an eyebrow. 'Go back to Mum's for a bit. Get pampered and worried over. What else can I do? Try to figure out my next steps. Get some sort of online job if I can. If I can even do that.' Her face crumpled slightly on the last sentence, but she regained control of herself. 'I'll be OK. You can get back to your café, your Pascal.'

'He's not *my* Pascal.' Becky thought of his eyes; that moment of feeling they'd known each other forever, then the conversation she'd heard on the phone; his easy dismissal of life in Vaudrelle. 'And it's just a café.'

'Is it though? You actually seemed really happy.'

'Yeah. I thought I was. But all this... It made me realise it's not real life is it, Amber? This is. Being here for my friends, doing my job. Getting on in life. That... the French thing was a bubble. And it was lovely. And yes, perhaps I did have a *fantasy* that I might stay for a bit.' Becky laughed, softly. 'But it was a fantasy. Being back here, having distance, I can see it now. It was a bit like being drunk.'

'What, and this is the hangover?' Amber raised an eyebrow.

'OK, maybe more like having a daydream. But then coming to. Realising how things are.'

'You're seriously not going back to France?'

Becky shook her head. 'We've planned a launch for the new decor, so I might pop back to do that. Say goodbye.' She swallowed. 'But this is my reality, Amber. You and Mum and my job. My future here is... well, secure. Planned.'

'What about the flat?'

'I think Mum will lend me the money for the deposit if I want, but I'm not even sure I want it now. And our flat won't be the same without you. But that's life, isn't it! I'll find somewhere new to rent or whatever. It honestly, honestly doesn't matter.'

'Oh, Becky.'

'I wish you'd said,' Becky told her. 'I wish you'd told me sooner that the rent was too steep.'

'It was OK. I managed to pay my share all those years. Just some months, it was a bit of a stretch. But you loved it so much, it was infectious. I'll never regret living there with you.'

'It's only a flat. A gorgeous flat, admittedly. But I only enjoyed living there because of you. Not because of the en suites.'

Amber gave her a look.

'OK,' Becky smiled. 'Maybe a little bit because of the en suites too.'

It was nice to see Amber laugh.

Behind them, a nurse coughed pointedly.

Becky looked at the clock. 'I think I'm going to get chucked out soon.'

'It's alright. I'm pretty tired, to be honest.'

'You're feeling better though, right? I mean, you're going to be OK? There isn't anything else wrong?'

'I'm fine. Well, fine-ish.'

'Because if... I can't lose you, Amber. Without you I'm... well. Incomplete.'

'I know.' Amber said, smiling tiredly. 'Me too.'

As she exited the sterile light of the hospital into the fresh summer evening, Becky drew her phone from her pocket and booked an Uber. Then, after texting a quick, 'All OK. Speak tomorrow' to Pascal, she rang a number that she'd ignored for too long.

'Barringtons?'

'Hi, Julie. It's Becky. Can I speak to HR?'

It was time to get things back on track.

25

It was odd being back in the flat. Having been vacant ever since Amber's trip to hospital a few days prior, it had settled back into itself; walking in, everything seemed different, as if it were somewhere that belonged to a stranger. Becky started by switching on all the lights, then opening all the windows just a little, ignoring the fumes and the traffic noise, hoping to let some of the staleness out and welcome life into the place which felt barren and unloved. But it was no use: one way or another, she'd be leaving this place soon and already it had stopped feeling like home.

Three weeks ago, when she'd stepped out of the front door, she'd been a different person. Twitchy and stressed and desperate to prove herself at any cost. It was only now that she'd rested and gained a little perspective that she could admit that she probably *had* been suffering from burnout, or something close to it. An image of herself hurling a laptop across the office space, face contorted, phone clutched in a fist, flitted into and out of her mind. Had that been her?

Tomorrow she would be going into the office, meeting with HR. Starting to smooth the path to her return. Convince them

The Village Café in the Loire

that all traces of burnout had left the building. And they really had, she realised, looking at herself in her wardrobe mirror. She looked different. Healthier. It was more than just the fake, healthy glow delivered by additional time in the sun, and the fact that she'd started to wear her shoulder-length blonde hair loose more often than not; it was something about her eyes, the set of her mouth. The way that she could look at her reflection and smile.

She opened her wardrobe and ran her fingers over the rack of expensive corporate wear that she'd accumulated over the past few years. Neat, tailored trousers and skirts. Fitted jackets. Heels that were just high enough without being overly showy. Nothing particularly distinctive, but everything smart and orderly and on point. In these clothes she became someone else entirely – part of a collective whole. There was a comfort in that, somehow. In everything being the same day in, day out. Predictable and manageable – and not like life in France at all.

There was noise suddenly in the downstairs flat. Just a slight scraping as someone moved some furniture or dragged a chair nearer to the TV. But it reminded her that below her feet was another person, living the same sort of life, in the same sort of flat. And below them, another. And, to that end, another person above in the top flat. And she thought how odd it felt to be part of a building where people lived on top of one another, stacked a convenient distance from their various offices, with wardrobes probably similar to hers. And how tomorrow most of them would probably be donning their outfits, slipping onto the Tube and becoming part of the blood in the veins of London.

Part of the machinery.

She shook her head. Of course it was going to feel a little odd after spending time in France with the space, the freedom to work when she chose, to explore, to get a little sun and perspective. But nobody could serve coffee forever. It had been a holiday. And holidays were always better than real life.

Here, she had family. Her mother, but also Amber. The girl who'd held her hand at playtime. Who'd got in trouble for giggling in assembly with her. The girl she'd grown up with, laughed with, argued with, who was so essential because she knew Becky almost as well as she knew herself. The heart of her. And if her being in France had in some way contributed to Amber's situation, all the sunshine, freedom, happiness, fledgling romance and body-quivering orgasms were not worth paying that price.

She took a deep breath, sat on the bed and rang her mother, putting the phone on speaker and leaning back against her feather pillows, her body aching from the stress of rushing and flying and running down hospital corridors in a state.

'Rebecca!' her mother said immediately, answering within two rings.

'Hi, Mum.'

'So, how's your friend? How's Amber?'

'Oh. She's OK, I think. They're running a few tests. They think that it was stress-induced.'

Her mother let out a breath. 'Well, thank heavens. Such a lovely girl.'

'Yes. Yes, she is.'

'And you?'

'Sorry?'

'Do you have... plans?'

Her mother was nothing if not transparent, but for once she had an answer that she knew would please her. 'Yes. I'm going into the office tomorrow. Meeting HR. Start the wheels turning.'

'For...?'

'For going back to work, of course.'

Her mother's sigh exploded breathily over the speaker. 'Well, butter my biscuits! Darling, I am so very proud of you.'

The 'p' word was more surprising than the odd expression of relief that had preceded it. 'You are?'

There was a pause.

'As long as you're definitely well enough.'

This was fresh ground. 'What makes you say that?' Becky asked.

'Well, this whole thing with Amber. I know her circumstances are different, but I suppose it did make me realise how dangerous stress can be.' Her mother paused, took a deep breath. 'I want what's best for you. But not at any price. You know that, don't you?'

'Of course.'

'Daddy always said I pushed you too hard. But it's my way. I push myself.' There was a slight wobble of vulnerability in Mum's voice.

'I know, Mum. And it's fine. Honestly. I'm well. I'm ready to go back.'

There was a deep sigh, then her mother seemed to step right back into her usual role. 'Well, that's wonderful news. I must admit I was a little worried that Maud's ridiculous philosophy might have started to rub off on you.'

'Mum! Maud's lovely, she…'

'Fiddlesticks! That woman gave up a career at Archway. Top law firm in the city at that time. Amazing for her generation. Almost unheard of. And then she went on holiday and never came back! It was outrageous! Threw it all away.'

Becky pictured the café, the quiet but friendly town. Maud's photography career that had taken her around the world. 'I don't think she sees it that way.'

'Well, of course not. She's going to double down now.'

'It's OK, you know, Mum. It's OK that Maud chose a different life to you, to us. She hasn't hurt anyone.'

A silence. 'Well, you're wrong on that count.'

'What do you mean?'

'Oh nothing. It's just... when I was growing up, she was more than an aunt to me. My mother wasn't well. Even when I was tiny. She was in a lot of pain, didn't have time to really do very much with me. But Maud did. Maud really took me under her wing. And when Mummy died...' She took a deep breath. 'Well, I always thought of her as a mother figure to me. And then she... well, she left me and didn't come back.' Her mother's voice cracked a little.

'Oh Mum.'

'It's ridiculous, of course. I was a grown woman by then. Had met your father. And there was an open invitation for us to go over whenever we wanted. I tried to let go of that childish feeling of... I don't know. Abandonment. And I did! You remember, we went every year. And back then, it wasn't as easy or as cheap to do that as it is now.'

'But then you stopped.'

'Then we stopped.'

'Why? Why did you? Because of the things she said about education?'

'Partly, but it was much more than that. It won't make sense to you probably. You clearly love Maud. You'll take her side, no doubt.'

'Mum! I love you too, you know.' And she did, Becky realised. Despite the fact that sometimes talking to her mother was an effort, despite the thinly veiled criticism and completely out-in-the-open pressure her mum always brought to the conversation, she did love her.

'Well, all right. She started trying to take your father and you from me as well.'

'What?'

'We'd been going for more than a decade by that time. And it was always rather wonderful. A break from the routine. Then your father started talking about buying a property. Moving out there. You'd have loved the idea, I knew. You always became a little tearaway during our holidays – painting, getting dirty, rushing about with Maud. You'd had a tough time at school that year – a shouty teacher, a couple of bullies in the class – and when you'd got a bit teary about it, she'd told you that education wasn't everything. And suddenly I could see it.'

'See what?'

'Everything I'd worked for, everything I'd built for myself. My family, you. Yes – my work. I do love what I do, you know, Rebecca. I'm proud of what I've achieved even if nobody else appreciates it.'

'Mum! I appreciate it! I do.'

'Well, good,' her mother sniffed loudly. 'Anyway, at the time, I felt as if Maud had abandoned me all over again. And now she was stealing you and Daddy too.'

'Oh Mum, she's not like that.'

'Not intentionally perhaps,' her mother admitted. 'But what she suggested threatened to break up everything I held dear. My career. And my family too.'

'Did you ever tell her how you felt?'

'Not exactly. We just sort of... stopped going. Booked different holidays. Let things slide. Then Daddy died and...' Her mother's voice shook. 'I just couldn't face her after that.'

'Why not? Surely she would have been supportive? Looked after you?'

'That's as may be. But I couldn't bear the idea that she might think it was my fault.'

'Your fault?'

'Yes. That if Daddy had moved to France, relaxed more, he'd still be with us.'

'Oh Mum. Maud would never say that. And it's not true, you know that.'

'Do I? Does anyone?'

Becky felt a lump in her throat. 'So you blamed Maud?'

'No. I just couldn't bear her... judgement.'

'You were afraid?'

There was a sharp intake of breath as her mother crushed down the emotions from her past.

'Heavens, Rebecca! Not afraid! What rot! Anyway, it's all in the past now. No good dredging that up. You're back, you haven't decided to throw your life away. You're healthy. We can carry on as before.'

'Yes. I'm back. But you know, Mum, if I had decided to stay,' Becky ventured, 'it could have been a good thing. It was nice having... space. To think. To find myself. Maud wasn't trying to ruin my life or anything.'

'Poppycock! Finding yourself! Nonsense. I can tell you who you are right now, Rebecca. You are a young woman with a promising future, is what you are.'

'Maybe.'

'There's no maybe about it.'

'And a happy future?'

'One and the same,' her mother said firmly, all traces of vulnerability gone.

After the call ended, Becky felt drained. Leaning up against the headboard, she replayed everything in her mind. Her mum was hurt, that much was clear, but so stubborn, there was no obvious way of breaking down the barriers she'd put up between herself and Maud.

Sighing, she chose a safe outfit of black trousers and jacket, hung them over the back of her chair ready for the morning and, suddenly fatigued and aware how late it was, climbed between the cold sheets of her bed and tried to settle herself to sleep.

Her dreams were tumultuous and confusing; Maud at the café, Amber in her hospital bed. Her mother, chasing her down the aisles of a supermarket for no understandable reason. She rushed into consciousness to find it was just 4 a.m., but knew that she wouldn't sleep any more.

The night was just giving way to the first signs of daylight – a lighter grey hovered in the air. The city continued to move below her, almost at the rate it had in the daytime. Joggers pounded the pavements, people drove to work early. Nothing ever seemed to stop. She loved this about London and hated it in equal measure.

But she had to put all thoughts of France behind her for the moment. In a few hours she'd step into it, be pulled back into her old life. And perhaps that was for the best. This was where she belonged.

26

Stepping into the flow of people the next day, she realised she didn't feel part of the river of the city any more, but something caught in its current, observing everything around her with new eyes. The flood of human life heading down the escalators, their faces focused, expressions grim; people with headphones lost in their own world; bodies packed together, touching but not acknowledging one another. Nobody said hello – the trick was to focus your eyes on something else: a phone screen, a text, an advert on the wall, to make it clear to everyone around that you were not under any circumstances to be approached.

She compared it with her daily walks in Vaudrelle, where she'd been greeted by every person she passed. Of course, this wasn't necessarily a French versus English thing. More the city versus the countryside perhaps. People were so crammed in here, it was impossible to acknowledge one another without also acknowledging the strange, herded cattle sensation of being shoved so close to strangers, and the bizarre fact that you were paying for the privilege.

Two more Tube stops and then it was hers; she exited and

walked up into Holborn, feeling relieved as she found herself breathing the comparatively fresh air of the street, with its tinge of dirt and smoke and sweet-smelling vapes. She could see her office building, its glass front four times as wide as the café back in Vaudrelle, its reception open, the line of lifts that would take her up to her desk, to slot into this part of her life again: she was a USB stick, ready to be plugged into the socket of an enormous computer. The thought made her step back.

She'd loved it. Just a month ago, she'd been thriving. So what had changed? Having a holiday? Maybe the shock of Amber's situation? She wasn't sure. She only knew that she no longer felt like one of the people streaming in and out of buildings on autopilot. She'd been woken up.

She checked her phone, it was only 8.30 a.m. Her meeting was at 9 a.m. She had time to calm herself down before going in.

She walked past the entrance to her office building, aiming to keep her gaze fixed forward in case she made eye contact with anyone she knew, and imagined she was a tourist, visiting the city for the first time. Tried to see the beauty of the city as well as the busyness and chaos. A building caught her eye – a Tudor design stretching the length of three houses, buried between concrete block and glass. How had she never seen it before? She imagined what it might have been like once, before modernity rose up around it. Taking out her phone again, she opened the camera app and took a picture, then another. And had the sudden desire to see whether she could draw it. Where had that come from? She hadn't drawn for years. Hadn't had the time.

Taking a breath, she turned and headed back towards Holborn, back to the building where she'd spent years of her life. She stilled herself outside, straightening her jacket, trying to push her shoulders back and act confident. And then she went inside.

'So how are you feeling?' Julie, the HR lead, asked once Becky was settled into her office. Julie crossed her legs and smiled sympathetically. She had recently discovered contouring, but had not realised that the light she applied it in before she left for work was clearly a little duller than the light she sat under in the office. Dark brown stripes streaked her cheekbones, giving her the look of a soldier in camouflage paint.

'You know. OK,' Becky said, smiling. 'Ready to return, if that's possible.'

'Yes. Wonderful. Wonderful. And you're sure that all of the stress is... um, out of your system?'

'Yes. I've taken some time and really worked on myself.' Becky knew the right words to say to get herself off the hook and rolled them off her tongue with ease. It was a circus performance of form-filling and box-ticking and jumping through hoops.

'That's amazing. Well, well done you!' Julie said, giving a little patronising clap. 'So you were signed off for a month, that's up middle of next week. But it looks as if you're more than ready to slot back in!' She smiled broadly. 'How would you feel about starting tomorrow?'

This was unexpected.

'Tomorrow?' Becky had hoped to be deemed fit to work, but had assumed it would take more than twenty minutes with Julie to clear her for take-off; had assumed she'd have the time to fly over for the launch, say goodbye to Maud and Pascal properly.

'But the doctor said a month...?' Surely, legally, she'd need a doctor to sign her back into work.

'I know. It's tiresome,' Julie said, nodding sympathetically. 'But you know, it seems silly for you to wait until the exact date when you're clearly fine and ready to go. You'll have to see the doctor of course, to get her to sign you back in, but I can't see that being a problem.'

'Right, but—'

'Now, while you're here, I expect you want to go and see everyone, touch base?' Julie nodded towards the door then swivelled her chair back to her desk, leaving Becky with no choice but to do as she suggested.

Feeling slightly dazed, she walked across the main office space, smiling widely, saying hello to people as she passed, as if there were nothing wrong, and never had been. She stopped by Stuart's desk. The intern cowered slightly.

'Stuart,' she said. 'I really am sorry about what happened.'

He looked at her.

'You know, it was never meant to go near you. Go anywhere, really. The laptop, I mean.'

'It's OK,' he said, his face flushing.

'Well, still. It must have been horrible for you.'

She still remembered the incident, but it was as if it had happened to someone else. She couldn't imagine throwing anything in fury, let alone something heavy and valuable, and in the vicinity of other people.

She moved on, before he started getting into the brace position or crawling under his desk. And there it was, her little corner of the office. Neat filing tray, new laptop closed, mouse mat. Her little pot of pens. That ridiculous cactus Amber had given her with the googly eyes. Walking towards her old home-from-home, she felt herself step into her role. Becky, advertising whizz, queen of the corporate world. On the up. She pulled her chair and slid into it, feeling the familiar curves of the fabric against her back.

'You back?' said a voice, and Wendy lifted her head from behind her screen opposite. 'Nice holiday?'

'Great, thanks.' It was better not to remind her exactly why she'd been off.

'Glad to see you back,' said Maurice, moments later, passing from his glass-fronted office and perching a bum cheek on the edge of her desk proprietorially. 'Actually, I hate to nab you when you're first in, but Julie mentioned you'd returned early, and we've got rather a large presentation tomorrow at six. I'd love you to be present. Get you back up to speed, so to speak.'

'At six?'

'Yes. Only time we could fix. But it's such an opportunity.'

'But I can't. I need to... My friend's in hospital and visiting hours are...'

Maurice frowned.

'I mean,' she corrected, 'of course. I'll be there.'

'That's settled then! Great to have you on board!' he said jovially.

'Aw, your friend's sick?' Wendy said distractedly. 'Hope she's all right.'

'She's...' But it was no use. The office had swallowed her back.

Perhaps it was for the best. Perhaps she did need to get back up to speed. And Amber was going to be out of hospital soon. She opened her laptop and started the process of logging in.

Julie appeared at her side like a ghoul. 'Can I have a quick word?' she said, all smiles and warpaint.

'Sure. Of course.'

'Great.'

They walked towards Julie's office and the HR lead slipped a Post-it into her hand. 'Here you go,' she said. 'Doc confirmed for five o'clock. So that's good news!' she grinned. 'Just a formality, I'm sure, but with insurance being what it is...' She opened her office door. 'See you tomorrow!' A gentle but firm 'fuck off.'

It was something of a relief.

Back on the underground, workers had been replaced on the Tube by tourists and day trippers, their mood clearly contrasting with her own: the freedom and enjoyment tangible on their faces; excited chatter over maps; pointing out sights in guidebooks.

She'd go and see Amber, she thought. Amber would know what to say. But when she arrived at the hospital and found her way (easily, this time) to her bedside, she couldn't find the words. 'How are you?' she said instead.

'I'm OK. Hopefully out of here tomorrow,' Amber told her. She looked a little more upbeat.

'Are you sure you won't come back to the flat? I can pay your half of the rent for a bit?'

Amber shook her head. 'I couldn't let you do that,' she said. 'I need to start being real with myself. Not biting off more than I can chew.'

'I'll miss you though.'

'You'll have your brand new flat soon enough,' Amber said, squeezing her hand as if Becky were the patient and Amber was simply there to give comfort.

'Still, I'll miss you.'

'Even the ridiculous movie nights?'

'Especially those.'

Amber opened her laptop. 'Got the time?'

'Definitely.'

It was four by the time she left, after a healthy dose of *When Harry Met Sally*. The light was still bright, the city still bustling. She called her mum as she made her way to the doctor's office.

'Fabulous news!' her mother told her. 'Getting back in there will be the best thing for you.'

'Do you think?'

'Of course I do.'

'It's just... Mum, I've been wondering whether... whether it's right for me!'

'Twaddle! Of course it is. You didn't get where you are today without being a good fit.'

'I just feel like the job takes everything else away. I'm not a good friend, not a good daughter. Not even a good colleague. If I'm good at this job, it's at the expense of everything else.'

'Oh Rebecca. That's just being young. Trust me. You do the hard slog, and the rewards will come. Things will ease up. You'll have assistants, more money. The second decade is always the hardest.'

'I thought... Didn't you tell me once that the first decade was—'

'Oh, it'll pass in a flash!'

'But...'

'Rebecca,' her mum said seriously. 'Listen. You've been through a... tumultuous time. Your friend is ill. You've had all this Maud stuff to deal with. I'm guessing you don't know whether you're coming or going.'

'Well, yes. That's it. That's just how I feel.' *Did Mum actually understand?*

'Then don't listen to your thoughts right now. Put your trust in me. Get yourself back to work. Get back in the rhythm of life. And I promise you'll start feeling more like yourself. It's the best tonic. Push those pesky feelings out of the way.'

'You think?'

'Darling. I know.'

27

Doctor Fuller looked over her glasses in a way that she surely must have practised in front of the mirror some time. 'It's good to see you, Rebecca,' she said, smiling.

'Thanks.' Becky sat on the chair opposite her desk, trying to smile in return. In truth, her heart was hammering: nerves, probably. But whether she was nervous that her request to return early would be refused or accepted, she wasn't sure.

'It says here you feel more than ready to return to the office a little earlier than planned,' the doctor said, looking at an email on her screen. 'Your HR team certainly feel that you've made a full recovery. But obviously I can't sign off on it without a consultation.'

'I know.' Becky nodded.

'So, how are you?' The doctor clasped her hands together and looked at her earnestly. 'Any anger issues? Residual stress in the body? How's the eye?'

The eye hadn't actually twitched for over a week, Becky realised. It was funny that something that had plagued her so much had quietly retreated without her really noticing.

This was her chance, if she wanted it. To exaggerate her stress and get a few extra days under her belt. But Becky was hard-wired to ace any test she was set. 'Oh. It's fine,' she said.

'That's good.' Her doctor made a note. 'And how did you spend your medical leave?'

'I actually went to France,' Becky said, smiling genuinely for the first time as she pictured Vaudrelle. 'I have an aunt who lives in the country.' She elected not to tell the doctor that her aunt had been presumed dead a few weeks ago, but was actually very much alive. It probably wouldn't look too good on the notes.

'Great! And you certainly look rested. Must have been lovely to see your aunt too, I expect.'

'Yes. It was.'

'You know,' the doctor said, 'I thought about moving to France myself once. Doing something different.'

'You did?'

'Yes. Years ago, now.'

'And what stopped you?' Becky asked curiously.

The doctor threw her hands up. 'Ah, the usual. Work. Life,' she said. 'Nice fantasy though.'

'Yeah, definitely.' Although was it a fantasy? For Maud it had just been her life. And France wasn't a problem-free utopia. Being there, living there, had its own challenges. It was just a different choice, surely?

The questions continued – her physical symptoms, how she'd been spending her time. How she was getting on with her mother. When Becky mentioned Amber, she scribbled furiously in her pad for a minute before asking whether Amber's situation had caused additional stress.

At last, it was over.

'Is there anything else?' the doctor asked finally. 'Anything you want to share?'

It was now or never. 'Actually...' she said, sitting forward. 'Although of course I'm keen to get back, I wondered whether you thought it would be a good idea to have a few more days to get things together.'

'I'm sorry, I don't follow?'

'I've got some loose ends to tie up and...'

The doctor sighed. 'I'm sorry,' she said. 'As far as this interview goes, you're cleared for work. Anything else you'll have to agree in house, I'm afraid.'

'OK.'

'I expect you're itching to get back to your normal life.'

'Yes. Definitely.' Although would it be her normal life? The world had moved on while she'd been in France; the life she was returning to wasn't the same as the one she'd left.

'All OK?' the doctor asked.

'Yes. Just thinking about it all.'

'Right.' The doctor began tapping on her computer. 'Well, I'll just pop this information in...'

The café swam into her mind. Pascal serving coffee. Maud in her care home. It seemed odd, sitting here, that that world existed still; would exist even if she weren't part of it.

'So... anything else?' The doctor gave her watch a surreptitious glance.

Becky stood abruptly; embarrassed. 'No, that's great. Brilliant!' she blurted. Her mouth ached as she forced it into a smile. 'Thank you.'

* * *

She hadn't spoken properly to Pascal since arriving home. They'd exchanged text messages, but she'd deliberately missed his calls, writing instead to explain why: 'Sorry, was at the hospital, everything OK?' or 'On the train – did you call?' But now there was nothing for it but to confront things.

She took the bus home; preferring suddenly the natural light it afforded her over the gloom of the Tube and, sitting on a relatively uncrowded top deck, she pulled out her phone and finally rang his number.

'Becky!' The happiness was evident in his tone. 'You called!'

'I did!' She found she was smiling at his voice.

'Amber – is she still OK? You said in your message, but...'

'Yes. She's OK. She's being discharged soon, going to her mum's.'

'But this is wonderful news!'

'Yes. It really is.'

'And you will be back soon? Because I have been working hard for the launch,' he said, in the tone of someone confident that the person he was speaking to was on the same page. 'I think people are quite excited. I will close the café tomorrow to assemble the new tables and practise the machine. And then, *voilà*! You will be back and on Saturday, Vaudrelle will have a brand-new place to drink coffee!'

Something rose inside her and she pushed it down. 'Pascal, I...' She wanted to tell him that she couldn't come. That he'd have to do the last bit on his own. But she couldn't find the words.

'*Oui*? There is something you need?'

'Oh no. Just... I'm looking forward to it,' she lied, feeling sweat bead on her brow.

Her bus stop loomed and she ended the call with relief, not wanting to dig herself an even bigger hole. Stepping onto the pavement, she began walking towards the flat, her body fizzing with adrenaline. *You've really done it now, Becky,* she said quietly as she let herself in and dropped her bag and coat on the floor.

Tomorrow she would be back in the office; firmly back in her old life. She'd have to find a way to let Pascal down. It would feel absolutely awful. But perhaps once she stepped back into the fray, she would buy into that world again, forget about him. About France. These thoughts that were plaguing her would fade as her mind became occupied in strategy, and her days became filled with important phone calls, presentations, campaigns.

She'd lose herself again.

And maybe that was what she needed. It certainly seemed to work for her mum.

* * *

The evening stretched before her and she found herself pacing up and down. One minute resolving to get back to work and laying out clothes for the next day; the next, hanging them back up and pulling her suitcase from under her bed. She tried watching TV, reading, listening to the radio. Even resorted to a bit of cleaning, but nothing seemed to calm her.

In the end, she sat at the table and pulled an old letter from the bank towards her. Turning it, seeing its bright blankness, she pulled out her phone and brought up the picture of the Tudor-style building she'd photographed near her office that morning. She picked up a pen, propped her phone against the salt pot and began to draw.

And everything else stopped.

She took in the details of the wood, the contrast between the building's age and beauty with the modern chaos around and in front of it. She felt the hustle and bustle of the street and the calmness of the hundreds-year-old structure against it, withstanding the storm year after year.

When she next looked at the time, it was almost midnight and she'd produced a reasonable sketch, under the circumstances. Her heart rate had slowed and she'd created a gap in her mind, given it a chance to stop chewing over and over the same things time and time again.

Maybe that was all she'd needed. A hobby to give her a little headspace and calm her down. Not an escape to another country, another life.

She texted her mum:

> BECKY
> Got the go-ahead for tomorrow!

And soon received a response:

> MUM
> That's brilliant. So proud of you!

Then she texted Amber:

> BECKY
> Back to work tomorrow. Hope to see you after hours.

It wasn't a lie, was it? It was what she hoped. Even if it looked like she might have to let her friend down.

> AMBER
> Good luck! I'll be at home, at Mum's by 2.

That was a relief. If Amber was home, the pressure to visit would be off.

Finally. Pascal. 'Not sure I'll be able to make it back for the launch,' she drafted, looking at the words on the little screen – words that would sever that part of her life. And deleted them.

She'd talk to Pascal properly, however difficult it was, she thought. Tomorrow.

28

'Morning!' she said, beaming at the receptionist, Clare, who smiled back uncertainly. She showed her pass and walked confidently to the lift, pressing the button and waiting for it to reach her. Then, stepping in, making brief eye contact with the other passengers, she pressed button four and was whisked upwards.

She'd reminded herself on the way there that for the past eight years or more, this was what she'd wanted. She'd just lost her sense of direction. The key was to embrace it, fully. She'd printed out her latest five-year plan and with any luck, she'd still be on track despite the blip. And the flat wasn't important, not really.

Tonight, she'd tell Pascal her plans. Maybe they'd see each other again, who knew? She suppressed the slightly nauseous feeling that rose up in her when she thought about it, but quickly focused her thoughts on today's work. Once she got her feet back under the desk, her eyes on the files she had to work on, those thoughts would recede and she'd be back in her old groove. It was fine. It would be fine.

'Hi,' she said, walking past various desks. 'Hi, how are you?

Great. Good to hear.' She would hold her head high, ignore any curious looks or comments, and soon her outburst too would be written over like obsolete code and forgotten.

She drew out her chair and sank into it, feeling rather edgy, and fired up her computer. There were twenty new emails from this morning alone. Good. She'd have something to get her teeth into.

It took her a good hour to familiarise herself with where everything was up to, but she was soon on the phone, reintroducing herself to clients, informing them that she was back from her travels. At least she had been somewhere, she reflected, so she didn't have to lie about what it had been like. Most people sounded downright jealous, then the conversation would turn to facts and figures and arrangements and customer surveys, and they'd get bogged down in the numbing numbers they threw around all day.

She ignored a call from the *notaire* who'd sent her the original letter, and another from her mother, concentrating solely on work. And when Maurice dropped by in the afternoon to check that she'd read up on the client they were meeting, she was able to fire off some relevant data that had him nodding in admiration. 'Good show!' he told her. 'Sure we'll snag ourselves a new client.'

Perhaps, at some point down the road, she'd find a way to stop him perching on the end of her desk, she thought after he'd left. He couldn't surely get much rest from draping one of his buttocks onto the laminated surface, and there was something proprietorial about it that she didn't like. Yes, he was her line manager. No, that didn't mean he could put his bottom wherever he pleased. She resolved to think of a tactful way to prevent it happening again. Perhaps it was time to move the cactus?

By the end of the day, she was feeling more like her old self than she had in weeks – even before the incident, she'd been tired and run-down and not firing on all cylinders. Now, batteries recharged, she felt truly on top of her game. Good.

She thought about the café, briefly. It seemed distant, almost like a dream, from this perspective. She let the thought flit away and returned her concentration to the report she was reading.

Five-thirty came and the office thinned out. Half an hour until the meeting where she'd prove herself more than worthy; make them realise how good it was that she was back.

It was when she was exiting the bathroom, after restyling her hair and topping up her make-up in readiness for the meeting, that it happened. Her phone buzzed in her bag and she drew it out to check the screen.

AMBER

Home! Call me?

Becky stepped back into the cubicle – personal calls weren't forbidden at work, and this was after her allotted hours, but still it seemed unprofessional to be making them on the first day back. 'Hi, you!' she said as her friend answered. 'I'm so glad you've been discharged.'

'Me too.'

'So what are you doing? Lying on the sofa waiting for your mum to feed you grapes?'

Amber let out a rather hollow laugh. 'In bed,' she said. 'It's weird, I couldn't wait to leave, but now I'm home without people monitoring me, I feel a bit... strange, I guess.'

'That's understandable. But they must be pretty confident you're OK to have let you out?'

'I guess.' There was a silence. 'It's crazy, you know, being back in my bedroom. I swear Mum's going to tell me to go to bed at nine and stop me having my phone overnight, like I'm fifteen again.'

Becky laughed. 'She's just being protective.'

Amber's voice wobbled. 'Becky,' she said, 'I realise this probably sounds pathetic and you were back at work today so probably don't fancy a train ride, but could you come see me? I feel... it just feels so odd. I...'

'Oh, Amber.'

'Yeah, I know. I hate feeling like this. But can you? The train's quite quick out to Hatfield, if you go from King's Cross? I really need to see you.'

'I've got—' Becky began. But then, 'Of course,' she said. 'Of course I can. Hang in there.'

She slipped the phone back in her pocket and went to find Maurice.

In one of the glass-fronted meeting rooms, an IT guy was fiddling with some wires. Maurice was standing and watching him as if about to offer some sage advice, when in reality he barely knew how to send emails by himself. There were a few other junior team members there, sitting upright at the oval table, thrilled, no doubt, to be included. And Stevie, tapping away on a laptop.

See, there were more than enough of them to man the fort. Maurice asking her was just a courtesy, and a lovely one. But he'd understand, she told herself. She let herself in and his face broke into a smile on seeing her. 'Rebecca!' he said. 'I wonder if you could brief the team on the latest figures, I know you've been looking over them this afternoon.'

'Of course,' she said. 'I've put them all in an email so everyone can...'

'Still, nice to have it come from the horse's mouth, so to speak?'

'OK. Look, may I have a quick word first?' she said, jerking her head so that he understood he had to come a little closer, retreat to a private corner so they wouldn't be overheard.

'What's happened?' he asked once he'd made it to her side. 'Client problems?'

'Oh no. Not at all. More... well, *my* problem. It's a friend of mine, my best friend, Amber. Did I mention she was in hospital? Anyway, she's been discharged and she's feeling a bit vulnerable. I thought – given the short notice and that you clearly don't need me to join – it would be a good idea to go and see her.'

Her smile slowly faded as she looked at Maurice's confused expression. 'Sorry,' he said. 'Are you the primary carer for this friend?'

'Well, no.'

'And I take it she's being looked after.'

'She's at her mum's, but...'

'Well, then!' he said, breaking into a smile. 'She's fine. I'm sure. Perhaps if it were family... but it seems she's being well cared for. Shall we?'

'No!' Becky said, a little too loudly. The juniors' heads swivelled in their direction then quickly returned to their respective screens. 'No, Maurice. I'm sorry. I do have to go. She *is* my family.'

'You said she was a friend?' Maurice's brows knit together in a fluffy frown.

'She's more than that! She's my person. A sister.'

Maurice's forehead creased further. 'I'm sorry, Rebecca. I understand that you've been having some... emotional difficulties. And we're all thrilled you're back. But you must realise that this isn't the kind of job that ends neatly at 5 p.m. We all have to make sacrifices for the greater good. Besides, the client will be here in a moment so...'

The Village Café in the Loire

'No, Maurice. I'm not staying.'

'I'm afraid I insist.'

'No!' she said, no longer caring if it was loud. 'Maurice, you buy my time from me. My expertise. But you don't *own* me! I'm a free agent. And I'm going to see my friend. Because she needs me, and I've let her down too many times. She never, ever asks.'

'I really must—'

'And it means something, you know. That she's actually asking? If I don't go now, it'll just be another let-down. Another time I've not been there for her. I can't do it to her.'

Maurice's face was turning a deeper shade of red with every syllable.

'You realise this could be construed as gross misconduct,' he said, his mouth forming a sneer. The true snake coming out from under its fleshy, more personable, stone.

'Well then, consider me grossly misconducting myself,' she said. 'Look, if the last weeks have taught me anything, it's that outside this little microcosm of a firm, there is actually life. The world doesn't revolve around Barringtons!'

Maurice just about managed a contemptuous snort.

'This place isn't everything,' she said, feeling tears come. 'And if working here means I have to be someone I don't want to be... Someone who throws laptops, or has twitchy eyelids, or doesn't have time to visit an elderly aunt, or ends up being a crap friend, then maybe it's just not worth it.'

She got to the door, then turned and looked at the enormous fish tank installed to apparently 'calm the atmosphere'. Inside it, the poor tropical fish swam confusedly around an artificial environment, emitting calming vibes to the workers who were also moving around a confined artificial environment. She was tempted for a moment to make a grand, Jerry Maguire-like gesture. But in the end, she decided against it. She'd never liked fish much anyway.

Instead, she turned, eyes burning, and strode towards the lift. Pressing the button, she waited an inordinately long time for the lift to come, continually glancing over her shoulder, wondering whether someone might come racing after her to persuade her to stay.

But nobody did.

29

Clearly, Amber's mother was yet to forgive her for her neglect of her daughter, Becky realised when she was greeted by the rather stony-faced Hannah at the door of Amber's childhood home.

She'd managed to get the six-thirty train and although she hadn't been able to get a taxi at the busy station, had walked as quickly as she could to get here. Now it was almost half past seven and she was sweaty and uncomfortable. But she was here.

She tried to rise above Hannah's cold expression – after all, the woman was worried about her daughter and, rightly or wrongly, felt that Becky was partly responsible for what had happened. Hopefully she'd thaw once she heard that Becky had walked away from a six-figure salary to visit her friend.

Oh my God, she thought as she climbed the stairs to Amber's childhood bedroom, feeling the familiarity of each step, recognising the curve in the stairway, feeling suddenly fourteen again and set for an evening of watching *Four Weddings* and eating crisps. Nothing much had changed in the house, except that everything looked somehow smaller and felt almost surreal. It was almost like travelling back in time to the early noughties when life was laid out like a map with short-term goals and lots of free time around the edges. Only they hadn't appreciated it then, of course.

Along the road was the house *she*'d grown up in; the one she'd lived in until she'd left for uni. She'd been devastated when Mum had sold it. 'I can't stay here on my own, Rebecca!' But suddenly, now, she understood her mum's reaction a bit more. Sometimes a place absorbs memories that are hard to bear.

She almost laughed when she reached Amber's bedroom and saw the painted sign her parents had bought for her, aged twelve, a year before their divorce – cursive writing on a little piece of wood, the words 'Amber's Room' next to a picture of a little girl in a summer hat.

Then she stilled herself, tried to arrange her face into the position of someone who hadn't just thrown her life down the toilet (as her mum might term it) or embraced change (as perhaps Maud would) and knocked.

'Yeah?' Amber said from within.

Becky opened the door and peered around a crack. 'Time for a visitor?'

'Oh, thank God!' Amber sat up a little against the pillow. 'Mum keeps knocking to see if I want any more soup and honestly it's kind of her, but...'

'You hate soup?'

'You got it!' Amber nodded. 'But she'd forgotten – it's been so long since she's cooked for me. And I took a bowl just to be nice. Now I'm worried I'm going to have to have it every day.'

'Come back hospital food, all is forgiven?' suggested Becky with a grin.

'I wouldn't go that far,' said her friend darkly.

They both laughed then, as if they'd been choreographed,

and turned their eyes away from each other as the laughter died.

'How you feeling?' Becky asked.

'I'm OK. More scared than actually sick.'

'Scared?'

'Yeah. It's like in the hospital I had all these doctors and nurses to tell me whether I was OK or not. Now it's just me and Mum and every ache or twinge makes me panic.' Amber shrugged. 'Guess it's in the genes.'

'Come on, Amber. You're nothing like your mum. I mean, she's adorable. And she loves you. But you've always been more confident, less anxious than her.'

'Until now?'

'Nonsense.' Becky gave her arm a squeeze. 'It's a setback, that's all.'

'Do you know that Mum had a year when she could barely leave the house? That's why she didn't come to my graduation. I said she was ill, and everyone just assumed... physically. She's got better since then, but I never really understood how the outside world could be scary – until now.'

'Oh hon. You should have told me!'

Amber shrugged. 'What if that's me, now? What if I get so nervous I throw my life away?'

'Hey. I won't let you,' Becky promised. They smiled at each other and she gently rubbed her friend's arm. It was hard to see Amber in this state, weird to see her in this house. And heartbreaking to realise that for the foreseeable future, they wouldn't be living together any more.

'Promise?'

'If all else fails,' Becky said, keeping her face serious, 'I'll send *my* mum around to get you out of bed.'

Amber laughed properly now. 'I don't want you to go to extremes!'

They were silent for a moment, the sound of children playing in next door's garden reminding them both that it was summer, early evening, that brightness and light awaited them outside if they opted to choose them.

'Anyway,' Amber said, attempting to sit up a bit more. 'Tell me about your day. First day back. Were you nervous?'

'It was fine,' Becky lied. 'Let's not bog ourselves down with work talk. What about you? What do you think you're going to do this week?'

Amber grimaced. 'Look, I know I told you off for being self-obsessed. But right now? I don't want to talk about me. I need a distraction. Please tell me about your spreadsheets and your emails – I need a dose of normality.'

Becky made a face. 'Not sure you're going to get a dose of normality from me after today's complete disaster.'

'Come on, now you *have* to tell me,' Amber said, looking and sounding momentarily more like her old self.

'OK. Well, you know our favourite comfort film?'

'*Love Actually*?'

'No! *Jerry Maguire*.'

'Oh no.' Amber said, making a face.

'What? I haven't even told you yet.'

'But it doesn't bode well. Don't tell me you wrote a mission statement for your firm?'

'Not quite.'

'Someone made you promise to show them the money?'

'You're getting closer.'

'Your fiancé punched you in the face?'

'I wish. Not that I have a fiancé of course.'

'Insignificant detail.'

'OK, well, I flipped out in the office, stormed out. And oh

God, Amber, for a minute I thought about grabbing one of the fish.'

'You... what?'

'Yeah, I saw the tank and—'

'No, back up. You flipped out at work again?'

'Yeah, kind of.'

'On your first day back?' Amber's face was creased with concern. 'You didn't throw another—'

'Oh no! It wasn't like that. Not stress-related at all, really. No laptops or interns were harmed. I did a good day's work, more or less.'

'So, what happened?'

'Maurice wanted me to stay and I refused. Told him I had to see you. And he lost it!'

'So you quit? Tell me you didn't actually quit. Not for me. Oh, Becky!'

'I did quit. And not just for you. I need a job that allows me to have some sort of life. And I guess I was scared that if I agreed to stay, then it would be a slippery slope back to... well, back to the way I was living before. Because I wasn't happy. Not really.'

'Your mum is going to kill you.'

'I know.' Becky covered her mouth and looked at her friend's shocked face. Then, as was always customary in the past when they'd been sent out of class for talking, or got into trouble for sneaking sweets into lessons, or that one time when a bouncer denied a relatively sober Amber access to a club for being too drunk, they descended into giggles. Hysterical, disbelieving, life-affirming giggles.

'Oh my God. I can't believe you did that,' Amber gasped at last.

'Guess we're both unemployed.'

'And unemployable.' Amber's remark sobered them both up

for a moment. 'What are you going to do?' she asked. 'You could still retract it? Say you were stressed? You'd probably be able to speak to—'

'No.' Becky shook her head.

'It's worth a—'

'It's not,' she said. 'Yes, I could probably pull a few strings, do a bit of grovelling. Cite stress or bring up hormones – Maurice can't handle talk of hormones, he'd probably give me a promotion just to shut me up. But you know what? It felt right. It feels right still.'

'Storming out?'

'*Getting* out. Getting away. I... This is going to sound crazy but I feel like something's changed in me. I don't belong there any more.'

'Really?'

'Yeah. I mean, I probably should have done things more professionally, but...'

'That ship has sailed?'

'It's disappeared over the horizon for good.'

Amber looked at her hands as they rested on her duvet. 'Are you going to go back to France or something?'

'No, don't worry. I'll go and do the launch. Say goodbye to Maud properly. See the café for the last time. But I'm not going to stay there.'

'Are you sure?' Amber shifted slightly, her voice more animated. 'Because you know what I'd do if I were you? I'd get on that plane and not look back. You've got Pascal, you've got a business. Everything's opening up for you over there.'

'You would?'

Amber squeezed her hand. 'In a heartbeat. I mean. Look at me. I've lost all of it. Rufus really has it out for me—'

'We can take him down. Together. I'll help. We'll get a lawyer—'

'I don't know. We could. And probably should. But it will take ages and lots of energy that I don't have yet. Either way, for now, my career is... tarnished, to say the least. And I have no idea when I'll feel OK to work. Physically, I'm all right. They told me to start exercising, start getting on with life. But mentally I'm... stuck.'

'Oh Amber.'

'Yep. Do you know what I'd give to have options? That's what money gets you, you know. Options.'

Becky nodded.

'But look,' Amber said smiling. 'You quit your job for me. That's pretty amazing.'

'For you, *and* for me. And because I guess I've changed.'

'Or you've found who you really are. Who you already were. There was something right about seeing you in France.'

'Maybe.'

'So go back over,' Amber said firmly. 'Finish the job. See what you feel like. But, well... at least don't write off the possibility that you could stay. I know I would.'

Becky reached for Amber's hand. 'But what about you?'

'I'll be fine. You know for a fact I won't starve. There's always soup! And if you stayed because of some sort of loyalty to me, I'd hate that. I really would.'

'Oh.'

'I love you, chick. But I'm not responsible for you. I can't carry that as well,' Amber said firmly.

'OK, well, I guess I've got a lot to think about.'

'Looks like it.'

'Will you do one thing for me though?' Becky said softly.

'What?'

She grinned. 'Will you call my mum for me? Because honestly, I think she'll probably lock me in *my* bedroom if she gets wind of this.'

'Afraid you're on your own,' Amber grinned. 'One difficult mother is my maximum.'

They laughed. 'Ah, but they love us,' Becky said.

'That they do.'

Half an hour later, Becky left. Passing a slightly less hostile version of Amber's mother. And feeling, if not upbeat, then at least like someone with more of a sense of purpose than she'd entered the house with.

That was what best friends did, she realised. They held you up no matter what.

30

There was a crucial difference between herself and Jerry Maguire, of course, Becky thought as the plane taxied on the runway and slowed to a stop. When Jerry Maguire left his toxic workplace, he had had a plan for his future. He'd wanted to start a new company that would treat people with more respect. Whereas she'd stormed out of a pretty good job to half-heartedly go to France for a few days, then see what happened. Plus, where had Jerry's mother been in all of this? He hadn't had one single conversation with her for the entire film. His situation was definitely the more straightforward for it.

Still, she thought, looking out of the window onto the sun-dappled runway... At least, in her story, the sun was shining, and although she didn't have her future mapped out, the next few days were spoken for. She'd tried to lose herself in them and worry about what happened next... next.

Less than an hour later she was well on her way in a taxi, watching the semi-familiar views on either side of the route to Vaudrelle. Buildings she recognised, others she'd clearly missed on her previous journeys. Old stone houses and peach-coloured modern cottages. Sun-drenched orchards and children's play equipment. Swimming pools, restaurants and picnic areas.

The farther the taxi burrowed its way into the French countryside, the more relaxed she felt – like a hypnotherapy patient descending more deeply into her subconscious. And by the time they pulled up outside the café, she felt somehow lighter.

She'd spoken to Pascal last night after everything had sunk in – sobbing down the phone about whether she'd made a mistake; worried about references, her future. But he'd simply said: 'Come to Vaudrelle. Everything will be OK.' And somehow, at least in this moment, something in her felt calm, as if everything would be.

Pascal had clearly gone to town on the idea of a launch – he'd put paper up at the windows to hide the interior, and a giant sign informed would-be punters that the café was closed until the grand reopening tomorrow. She smiled, thinking of the type of do she'd put on for clients in London compared with their offering here. But somehow this was sweeter, more authentic.

She used her key to open the door then, closing it behind her, she walked across the strangely dark interior, bumping into one or two tables that had been rearranged in her absence. The air smelt of paint and paper and glue and, as she neared the counter, the unmistakable scent of freshly ground coffee beans. Reaching the door to the kitchen, she knocked – not wanting to burst in and surprise anyone on the other side.

There was the sound of a scraping chair in the wake of her knock and when she opened the door, she saw Pascal and Georges, the former sitting at the table, the latter standing, awkwardly clutching a sheaf of papers.

'*Bonjour!*' Pascal said, rather loudly, and stood up, arms outstretched, pulling Becky to him in a tight embrace.

Over her shoulder she watched Georges regarding them both impassively. When she pulled away, she grinned. 'So, what are you two up to then?'

'What do you mean?'

'I'm joking – you just looked so guilty when I walked in. I thought you might be planning some sort of illegal deal or something!' she laughed.

'Ah, I love this sense of humour!' Georges also said loudly, his words sounding a little false. He stuck his hand out for a shake, having finally sensed perhaps that Becky wasn't the biggest fan of the cheek-kissing he usually favoured. She took it gratefully. '*Non*, I was just having a look at your new interior. It is very smart.'

'And today I offered him some of our new drinks,' Pascal said, clearly proud of himself. 'I read the instructions and it was not too hard.'

'Yes, they are very nice,' nodded Georges.

'Right. Well, good!' she said. 'That's good.'

They all smiled at one another, none of them quite sure who would make the next move. 'Well, I must go now,' Georges said to Pascal. 'Remember what I said.'

Pascal's smile looked rather forced. 'Of course. But I do not think it's a good idea.'

'What was all that about?' Becky said when Georges had finally left.

'Oh, nothing. He likes to talk. He likes to think perhaps that he has to control everything in the *commune*,' said Pascal. 'It is not important.'

'Right.'

She was about to ask more when Pascal spoke again. 'Ah, it is nearly time!' he said, glancing at his watch.

'Time for…?'

'We must go and collect Maud. To show her the café!' he said. 'I told her I would do this tonight. I was not sure that you would be here so early, so it is perfect.'

'Oh. Great.' The last thing Becky felt like was getting in a car with Pascal and bumping down more French back roads. In fact, she'd been hoping for a bath – however cramped – and a bit of a lie-down before anything else. And at least a coffee or two. It was a café after all.

Then Pascal stepped forward and took her hands in his. 'It is very nice to see you,' he said, leaning forward and kissing her gently on the mouth.

She looked up at him. 'How long have we got?'

He grinned. 'Enough time for a proper reunion, if you'd like.'

* * *

When they arrived at the home two hours later, Maud was in the reception area sitting on a padded blue chair, dressed in a coat and hat, bag at her side. They helped her to the car and she sighed as she deposited herself on the back seat. 'Why on earth they forced me to wear my coat in this weather, I'll never know,' she said, pulling her arms from the sleeves.

They talked for a little while about Amber and Becky's stay in London – although Becky omitted her brief entrance and exit from the workplace – then fell into companionable silence. Glancing in the rear-view mirror, Becky saw that Maud's eyes were fixed on the scenes that played themselves out on the screen of the back door window – the familiar views that must seem like old friends to her aunt. When had she last been back to Vaudrelle?

'Do you miss it?' she said.

Maud looked at her. 'Vaudrelle?'

'Yes. It must be hard, coming back.'

'You have no idea,' she said, blinking rapidly. 'Seeing it again. I mean, I have visited occasionally. But it is hard.'

'But you're happy at the home, too? They're looking after you?'

She nodded. 'As well as can be expected.' She paused, thinking. 'The thing is, Becky, you'll find when you get older that the body ages much more quickly than the mind. My body needs the home – I can't do things for myself in the way I used to. But my spirit... It never really left.'

'Oh. I'm so sorry.'

Maud shrugged. 'I'm better off than lots of others my age. I'm alive, for starters.'

'Maud! I am sure you will live a very long life,' Pascal interjected.

'Yes, perhaps. But there are different levels of living. Not all of them are as wonderful as we'd like to think they are.' She shook herself. 'But listen to me, moaning on when you've given up your evening to show me all your wonderful changes. I'm grateful, I really am.'

After Pascal finished parking and Becky had offered thanks to the road gods for sparing their lives once again, they helped Maud across the road and into the café, where Pascal snapped on the light. Maud wasn't the only one to gasp. Becky had only seen shapes in the darkened room when she'd arrived, and although she knew Pascal had been working hard throughout the days she'd been away, the final result was stunning: the painting was all complete, as he'd said it would be, but he'd also polished the woodwork, installed a glass-fronted display for cakes and pastries. The new coffee maker gleamed and her new mugs, as well as a set of new smaller cups for espressos, were stacked neatly beside it.

But what really drew the eye were the photographs. Black and white stills of people, vibrant views of foreign streets, local snaps of light hitting water, a crumbling yet charming building. One or two Becky was sure she'd seen before. But not here. Somewhere else. 'Wow,' she said. 'It looks... it's even better than I... wow.'

She looked at Maud who was sitting on one of the yellow chairs at a new table, wiping the corner of her eye.

'Oh, what's wrong?' she said. 'I know it's different, but...'

Maud shook her head. 'It is different.' She paused. 'And when you said you'd made changes, I was worried. Worried I'd be... written out of the history of this place. But you've made it... it's even more *me* than it was before,' she said. 'Thank you. Thank you so much.'

'These are all yours?' Becky gestured towards the walls.

Maud shrugged. 'Just a few examples.'

'They're amazing. Mum said you'd been published in *The Times* quite frequently. I'm not surprised!'

'Once or twice.'

Pascal laughed. 'Your aunt is being too modest,' he said. 'She is quite famous in France as an artist. Her photographs are in many galleries in Paris.'

'Oh!' Becky glanced at Maud with renewed interest. 'Why didn't you say?'

'I suppose I prefer people to like me – or not, as the case may be – for who I am as a person, rather than for what I can do. I had enough of that, you see, in London. A top female lawyer, working my way to being a barrister. People always talked about what I did, and I felt...'

'You felt...?' Becky prompted after a moment.

'I felt like a thing rather than a person. What I was doing was unremarkable in its own way. I just wanted to be allowed to get on with it. Here, I don't know. I found a whole new me and I didn't want to tarnish that with the same problem. I am me, and I am also a photographer. But what I do isn't who I am. It's better to keep the two separate.'

Becky nodded. 'It makes sense. Do you photograph anything now, at the home?'

Maud shook her head. 'Too difficult. Unless I want to photograph my sparse little bedroom.' She saw the expression on Becky's face. 'Oh, don't pity me. I'm happy enough in my own right.'

'Well, we'll bring you over more often. You should be here; it's still your café, really.'

Pascal looked at her with surprise but didn't say anything.

'Thank you. Although this one is, of course, off to Paris soon!'

Pascal blushed. 'Not quite yet,' he said.

Later, when they'd eaten, Pascal had left to drop Maud back off at her home.

When he'd returned, she'd heard the door of the café open and shut behind him, his footsteps on the stairs.

Even so, when he knocked on her bedroom door, she started.

He opened the door a little and stepped inside, smiling.

'Was Maud OK?'

He nodded. 'A little sad to return to her home, I think. But very happy about the café.'

'I'm so glad.' Becky sat on the bed, then felt a bit awkward and stood up again. How could it be that they'd been so passionate a few hours before, and now everything felt a little bit forced?

'Tell me,' he said. 'You told Maud that you would bring her here more often. But I thought that you had decided to leave? To sell?'

She shook her head. 'I knew as soon as I said it... I shouldn't have mentioned anything. My life is in London still – I can't stay even if I wanted to. Only when I'm here, it's so easy to forget that – so easy to imagine that I could stay here for longer.'

He walked over to her. 'If you were to stay,' he whispered, 'it might change everything.'

She looked at his earnest eyes. 'Really?'

'For me, *oui*.' He leaned in for a kiss.

She leaned away. 'But what about your mother? You told her there was nothing here for you.'

He frowned. 'I did?'

'Yes, I heard you on the phone. Sorry. But you said...'

He laughed. '*Non, non*! You misunderstand. There are no publishers here, not many bookshops. Nothing for me in *that* sense. That's why I must go to Paris frequently. Because I need to become involved in the book world. But if you were in Vaudrelle...' He kissed her and this time, she let him. 'If you were here, then it would be everything.'

And even though she still wasn't sure what the future might hold, Becky closed her eyes and let herself get swept up in the fantasy of it all.

31

She awoke the next morning to find herself alone in Pascal's bed. It was seven, and the morning stretched ahead of her with nothing particularly to fill it. Everything necessary for the launch had been ticked off their 'to do' list and all she had to do was wait. Rather than that making her feel relaxed, though, she felt edgy and nervous – her fingers twitching for something to do.

She sat up in bed and texted Amber a good morning.

BECKY
How are you?

AMBER
I'm OK. You?

BECKY
Yeah. Pretty good.

AMBER
Called your mum yet?

BECKY

Told your mum about the soup?

AMBER

Good comeback!

She got up slowly, took her odd little bath, and pulled on some jeans and a T-shirt. Thoughts kept popping into her mind – work, her mother, Pascal, Amber, the café, Maud – but none of them formed anything coherent for her to hang on to.

A note informed her that Pascal had gone to pick up the fresh macarons and pastries they'd ordered; he wouldn't be back for a while.

To stop herself spiralling, she decided to go out herself and buy a gift for Maud. Something to brighten up her room at the home, perhaps. A little reminder of the café that she would get some pleasure from looking at. Only she had no idea what. Perhaps a mug? But then the café's mugs weren't particularly distinctive. Not something that would spark memories.

She could of course take a picture of the café, have it framed. Maybe get it printed in black and white to make it look a bit arty. But she remembered Maud's photographs now hanging in the café, and her newly acquired knowledge that her great-aunt was quite a celebrated photographer. A picture taken on her smartphone just wouldn't cut it.

Then it came to her. She could draw the café herself. Perhaps it wouldn't be frameable, but it would be personal. Besides, it would take a few hours to do and she really needed to have something to get her teeth into before she descended into anxiety.

She remembered seeing some thick, cream-coloured card down in Maud's studio, so made her way down into the cluttered space, clicking on the light as she went. Walking in, she felt a little trepidatious, as if she were entering somewhere she shouldn't. But she pushed on, found the card and a couple of fineliners and made her way back upstairs. She set herself up at the large kitchen table then took a breath and began to draw, using some pictures on her phone for reference.

* * *

'Becky?'

A voice at her ear made her jump. She looked up and felt her face get slightly hot, realising that not only was Pascal right next to her, grinning, but that he could see the picture she was working on. Which was both unfinished and looked – to her eye, at least – embarrassingly amateur.

'Oh! I didn't hear you come in!' she said, her heart still thundering. Pascal was close to her and she could smell his habitual scent of fresh air, coffee and the clean, soapy smell of his aftershave.

'Yes, I noticed.' Pascal was still smiling. 'I spoke to you two times before you heard me. What are you working on?' He leaned down.

'It's a drawing. Of the café.' She covered it instinctively with her hand.

Pascal laughed. 'Yes, I can see that,' he said. 'I mean what is it for? I wondered perhaps for the wall of the café?'

'This? Oh no!' she said, hastily. 'It's... I'd hate that. Sorry. It's just a picture I'm thinking of giving to Maud. If it turns out OK.'

'It looks very good to me,' Pascal said.

'Thank you.' She looked at it again. It didn't quite match the picture she'd hoped to create in her ambitious mind. But it was OK. With a bit more shading, a little dash of watercolour here and there, it might even be quite good.

'Anyway, I wanted to know if you wanted to come for lunch? I cannot cook today, so I am going to the restaurant.'

'Lunch?' she touched her phone to wake the screen up and saw to her surprise that it was 12.30 p.m. 'Oh my God, I hadn't realised! I've been doing this for, what, about three hours!' It didn't seem possible. 'It felt like about five minutes.'

Pascal nodded. 'This can happen.'

'Yeah?'

'*Oui*, they call it a creative trance,' he said. 'When we are fixed in our work, and our subconscious mind takes over.'

'Sorry, what?'

'It is a good thing. The feeling of losing ourselves in our art. I have experienced this too when writing. Although not as much as I would like. Sometimes, for me, writing can be almost painful!' he grimaced. 'You lost yourself for a little.'

'So that's a thing?'

'*Oui*, it is, as you say, "a thing",' he said with a smile. 'And you are good, *non*? When did you last draw?'

'Well, I did something back in England. Just a silly sketch really. Before that? Probably not since school,' she admitted.

'That is a shame. It feels good to create something.'

'Maybe.'

'I mean it. You have your aunt's talent perhaps? Her eye?'

'Oh no. Nothing like that.'

Pascal shrugged. 'I think you are too modest. But then I cannot draw.'

'But you can write, evidently,' she said. 'How are things going for your Paris plans? Have you heard from the publisher?'

He looked at her. 'Yes, it's good,' he said. 'I have told them now that I might not be in Paris all the time. It is fine of course; I am not Michel Houellebecq – the demand is still quite small. And I want to be here. With you.'

She felt a frisson of excitement at his words. The idea of staying longer, staying with him, was close enough to touch. Yet how could she? 'You'd really do that?'

He nodded. 'How could I not? So now you must decide to stay here and be with me.'

Her heart soared at the idea, then sank. Because the present here felt wonderful, but what would her future be like if she stayed? There would be no progression; no plan. Clearly, everything back home was going to change. But perhaps she could embrace that, but in a more structured, safe way. Maybe get some training. A different job in a different field.

'Oh Pascal,' she said. 'You know I'd love to stay. For as long as I could. But... I just don't know. I'm not sure I have it in me.'

'But why not? It is simple, surely?' He crouched down next to her, his beautiful eyes fixed on her face.

'I just... I'm not like that. A month ago I had it all laid out. The plan I'd been working towards for years! And now... I've left my job. But I can't just drift around doing nothing. Everyone I know is starting to put down roots, settle down, they're getting promoted, doing well at work. Thriving.' She thought of Amber, but pushed the image away.

'What people?'

'Old colleagues, classmates. I'm on a business profile site and you get updates... Pascal, I spent so much time being ahead, doing better than everyone else. And now... I've left my job but I've got nothing to update anyone with. I've got no direction.'

He put his hand gently on hers. 'If you have no direction, perhaps the answer is to stay still?'

'But I can't live my whole life running a café. It's lovely. It's great. But it's not enough. Even for you, it was a stopgap, not your whole life. I just...'

'But why does it have to be your whole life?' he said softly, looking at her with steady eyes. 'What about a year, or perhaps two?'

'Because I'd get stuck! Once you get off the corporate ladder, you get left behind.'

Pascal regarded her. She looked away. 'But why do you want to be on this ladder? What is at the top?'

'Success!' she said. 'Money! Status!' She was beginning to sound like her mum, she realised.

'And these things are important to you?'

'Yes. No. I don't know.' She put her head in her hands. 'They were. Maybe they are. Oh God, it's so complicated.'

'But it doesn't have to be. Nobody is asking you to live here forever. But take a breath. Take a year, two maybe. Find out what you want. Explore your art, try new things. Maud didn't run the café all the time. It was there for her when she wanted, but she had people to help her. The café runs itself, in essence. The café gave her the freedom to be whoever she wanted.'

She looked at Pascal. 'But I'm not like her.'

'Perhaps you are. Perhaps not. Perhaps you do not yet know who you are. And it's OK. Because I don't think anyone really does. That's what my book is about. People who are taking journeys. And are scared because the destination is unknown. But that is what makes it magical too.'

'I'm thirty, Pascal.'

'*Oh, mon Dieu*! You are so very old!' Pascal's eyes widened, then he laughed. 'You are a *bébé* in that case. Why not give yourself time to work out who you are. You talk about this ladder, but there are other ways to find status and success if that is what you truly want. There are *ascenseurs*! Lifts, I mean. And those moving stairs... And... and helicopters!'

It was impossible not to smile at his enthusiasm.

'So you're saying, if I stay, I could always get a helicopter to put me at the top of the ladder in a couple of years' time.' She grinned.

'Why not? But I think you might find that you do not want the ladder at all. Why climb a ladder when you can relax and find your own way to success, or happiness – whatever is important.'

She lay her head on the table momentarily and groaned theatrically. 'Argh. I just don't know, Pascal. I don't know.'

'*Exactement*. And that is your gift. The not knowing. It means that you are open to possibilities. You have time. You have space. You have the café. You have life to live and explore and find out. Becky, you are very lucky.'

She thought about Amber then. Amber who'd said something similar – not everyone could sidestep life, give up a job without fear of destitution and have somewhere rather wonderful to work out their next steps. She remembered the words *I would, in a heartbeat*.

'I'll think about it,' she said at last.

'*Bon*. I will take that,' Pascal said. 'But now there are important matters to address.'

'There are?'

'*Mais oui*! If we are not quick, we will miss the *plat du jour* at the restaurant. And it is *moules* – mussels. My favourite. We must get there urgently.'

'Oh no! Sounds serious!'

'I am French. Many things are serious. But lunch, it is sacrosanct.'

32

At three, they brought Maud to the café again. The paper had been removed from the windows, revealing the interior, and already there were one or two would-be patrons in the street, waiting for the three-thirty launch.

When Maud was installed at a table near the counter, her stick leaning up behind her, Becky handed her a paper package, with a blush.

'For me?' Maud said. 'You shouldn't have, honestly.'

'Wait till you open it. It's nothing special.'

Maud carefully unwrapped the picture, her eyes sparkling as they alighted on the drawing in its new wooden frame. 'You did this?'

'Yes, but you don't have to put it up on the wall or anything,' she said, feeling quite embarrassed. 'I know it's quite... rudimentary.'

'That's so kind. And it's lovely.'

'It's... I mean, the colours aren't quite...'

'No,' Maud said. 'Don't apologise for your work. Be proud of it. It's good. Truly. And what makes it more beautiful is that you've painted the café the way you see it. Something only you can do.'

They smiled at each other for a minute and Becky felt herself glowing. It was a bit like when she'd been seven, showing her teacher a picture at school, or the times when she'd called Mum to tell her she'd been given a pay rise or promotion. A contented glow washed over her.

In reality, it didn't mean much. Maud would probably love her picture no matter what. But her approval fed into some sort of need in her, fed the part of her that was afraid to tell her mother that she'd quit her job. Was that it? Was it her need to please others – or impress Mum – that made her as driven as she'd been?

Maybe it was the same for everyone, she thought, considering Pascal's own situation. Maybe all of us are just children trying to make our parents proud.

But if our parents, in turn, are trying to fulfil the wishes or desires drummed into them by their own parents, then are any of us actually living the life we would choose? When does giving someone advice and direction turn into mapping out their life for them?

She had never told Mum what *she* thought, what *she* wanted. She'd never really had the space to find out what that might be. Mum had such confidence that her way was right, Becky had never really questioned it before this point. She was reliant on the guidance and structure she'd been given, she realised. If she stepped away, who would she be? Would she simply be lost?

But this was no time for introspection. 'Ready?' Pascal said, and unlocked the door, throwing it open to let people inside. There were twenty-four in all: young; old; couples with children;

people in their work clothes, sports gear, gardening overalls. They shuffled in and Pascal showed each to a table.

The next twenty minutes were a whirlwind – offering and making coffee, handing out madeleines and macarons. By the time everyone had been served, Becky felt hot and sweaty. She dabbed her skin with a disposable napkin and looked at Pascal, who nodded. It was time.

Feeling nervous, she struck a teaspoon against a coffee mug and all went quiet. Twenty-four faces were looking at her expectantly.

'*Bonjour*,' she said, glancing at Pascal then at the piece of paper in her hand, on which she'd written the translation of what she wanted to say. 'Welcome everyone to *La Petite Pause*. Your local café, with a new look.' It was all the French she could manage and she knew her accent was off. But she'd wanted to show that she was trying.

Pascal then took over, speaking in rapid French. And at the end, Maud said a few words. There was silence. Then applause.

They milled around afterwards, collecting plates and cups, being congratulated. People dropped in and out, exclaiming, conversing together. Noting the art on the walls and the softness of the chairs. The newly painted decor and the new beverages and snacks on offer.

Sitting at the corner table with Maud, Becky sipped her latte and felt a warm, contented feeling come over her. They'd done it. They really had. And if she wanted, there was a beautiful life here for her. Even if it wasn't forever. Even if it was just for a heartbeat.

When the café was closed and the final cup washed, she turned to Pascal and sank into his arms. He wrapped her in a tight embrace. 'You did it,' he said. 'It was marvellous.'

'*We* did it,' she said. 'And yes, it really was.'

The Village Café in the Loire

He kissed her softly.

'Is there something I should know?' came a voice, as Maud brought her cup rather unsteadily to the sink and looked from one to the other.

They laughed. 'Perhaps,' Becky said. 'We'll see.'

'And in the meantime, we should eat,' Pascal said.

* * *

In her bedroom, working out which outfit to wear for dinner, she messaged Amber.

BECKY
How are you today?

AMBER
Yeah. OK. Kind of.

BECKY
Wish I'd stayed.

AMBER
No, you don't. And it's fine. Miss you though.

BECKY
Me too. We complete each other!

AMBER
Yes we do. Although it's OK if you decide to move on, you know.

BECKY
I'll never move on from you! Are you OK really? Emotionally?

AMBER
Not really. But I will be. Love you.

She felt something sink inside. She should be there. If she was any sort of friend, she'd be there.

Feeling sick, Becky made her way down to the kitchen to get a glass of water and found Maud sitting there at the table, the local newspaper open on a small article about the launch. 'Hi,' she said.

'Hello again!'

She sat down with her glass and took a sip. Then sighed.

'Are you all right, love?' Maud said softly.

She looked up and saw Maud's intelligent blue eyes watching her.

'Yes,' she said. 'Just thinking.'

'What about? Maybe I can help?'

'I've quit my job,' she said. 'Not necessarily to come here. But... well, I might. For a bit.'

'Well, that's wonderful news! I did wonder when you said about my coming over more often, but...'

'But it's so complicated. Complicated to stay and complicated to leave.'

'How so?'

'Mum?' Becky said, raising an eyebrow.

She expected Maud to say something derogatory – perhaps that her mother had to learn a bit of humility, or not to take her into account. But she didn't. 'Yes,' she said instead. 'Poor Cynthia. She probably would take it hard.'

'So you think it's a bad idea?'

'No,' Maud said, shaking her head. 'Not at all. As long as you accept that the consequences may not be as you'd like.'

'What do you mean?'

'Well, initially of course she might be hurt, angry. But hopefully she'll come around. And maybe visit. Perhaps even start to enjoy spending time here again. After all, she's done very well for herself, the financial pressure on her isn't what it was in the past.'

'Yes, hopefully.'

'But she might not. She might dig her heels in and decide to resent you for it. And that could be difficult.' Maud reached out a hand, covered Becky's. Her palm was soft and cool. 'But you mustn't let that sway your decision. Because if you bend to your mother's will, you'll end up resenting *her*. Just as painful, but with more regrets from your side.'

Becky nodded. 'Yes. I can see that.'

'Don't be swayed by me either, of course!' Maud said. 'I know, perhaps I... well I hoped to encourage you over. But I'm not here to manipulate you. I just wanted to... show you what was possible, I suppose. Because you were never much like Cynthia, yet I saw that you were living a similar life – the sort of life she would choose for you. It made me worry.'

'Thank you,' Becky said, resting her head on her hand, keeping the other tucked under Maud's. 'It's Amber too,' she admitted. 'My best friend. I feel bad about abandoning her. She... she really helped me in the past and I feel like I should be there for her too. She's not well at the moment.'

'Oh yes. The girl with the heart problem? Pascal told me. Poor kid.'

'Yes. I think... she's going to be fine. Health-wise. But she needs me right now.' Becky shook herself. 'But listen to me! I'm thirty. It's normal that Amber and I should move apart, not be in each other's lives so much at this age.'

'Do you think so?' Maud looked at her intently. 'Really?'

'Yes. I mean, it's natural that we would... move apart as we get older.'

Maud's eyes were fixed on hers. 'Why is that, Becky? What makes it natural?'

'Well... it's what people say...' Becky shrugged. 'It's most people's experience, I suppose. People grow up, have families. Time gets stretched and friends fall by the wayside. Sooner or later Amber or I will meet someone and we'll move apart from each other anyway. Maybe I'm putting too much stock into holding on to something that's... well, kind of doomed, long term.'

'Yes. People do say that. And it's true of most friendships I suppose. But it's not a given. Nothing is. Just because things have happened before to other people doesn't mean that our lives are made inevitable. Everyone, everything, every situation is different. When I stepped off the kind of... carousel of work that I'd created for myself, the world didn't fall apart as I'd thought. And I was able to live differently, on the edge of it all. It made me realise—'

'What?' Becky prompted gently.

'That all the things we take for granted – the life recipes we're given – the benchmarks we're expected to hit... Education, work, relationships, children. Someone at some point made them up. And if measuring ourselves against them makes us unhappy, well then there's something wrong.'

'So you're saying I should choose Amber? Try to stay close to her?'

'Being with Amber... it makes you happy, doesn't it?'

'I never had a sibling,' Becky said with a shrug. 'She's it, I suppose.'

'Then why do you let other people's assumptions affect you? People only grow apart if they neglect their friendships. It's not necessarily the path you have to take.'

'But it's hard. Because I can't have it all, can I?'

'None of us can,' Maud said softly. 'But perhaps you can have more than you think.'

A moment later, Pascal entered the kitchen. He'd changed into a powder blue shirt, black jeans. His hair was gelled. 'Are we ready, ladies?' he said jovially. Then his smile disappeared as he saw the expressions on each of their faces.

Standing up, Becky shook her head. 'I can't,' she said. 'I'm sorry, Pascal. I know what I said. But I just can't.'

33

Of course it was raining. It might be June, it might have been dry for the past week. But if Becky was going to do something like this, then fate dictated that it would rain. She'd watched enough movies to know that.

Her lightweight coat was soon saturated. Her hair hung against her face in thick wet strands and she understood perhaps for the first time why people tended to call them 'rat-tails.' She thought of the café; now closed for the night, how well the launch had gone and how, for a moment there, she really thought she'd found her niche. Part of her wished she was there, ready to climb the stairs to her room and fall into bed.

Instead, she had decided to rush here. Soaked to the bone and completely alone. On a mission that might well end in tears.

It was dark, and she'd felt vulnerable walking the last hundred metres or so. Nobody was about, but the street that looked so welcoming in the daytime had taken on a more menacing air in the blackness; the lights gave out little halos but didn't share much brightness with the street below. The rain made things even more impossible, hammering on her head,

The Village Café in the Loire

running into her eyes. She was bedraggled, freezing, and would give her right arm now to be tucked up in her bed above the French café.

But she was here. And it was important, she reminded herself. It was one of the most important things she'd ever done.

She opened the gate and crept along the side passage, hoping that there weren't any security lights to spring to life and alert those sleeping above to her presence. Luckily, everything stayed dark.

Feeling a little shaky, she stood on the darkened patio and looked up at the window. There were no lights on in the house; clearly everyone was asleep. Was she being completely insane? Could this not wait until morning, when she could return in dry clothes with an umbrella? She checked her watch; it was 3 a.m.

But for some reason she felt it had to be now.

Taking a deep breath, she selected a stone – one with enough weight to make it possible to project and aim it, but not so much that it would cause any damage, hopefully – and threw it at the window. It bounced on the sill and landed back next to her with a gentle click.

Annoyed, she picked up another. This one struck its target, making a little clink against the glass. She held her breath. But nothing.

This time she picked up a handful of smaller stones and flung them with all of her might. They sprinkled the window, making a tiny clatter. She was bending down to pick up another stone, wondering whether to risk a bigger one, and feeling the rain drip down her back from her wet hair, when there was a voice from above.

'What the fuck do you think you're doing? I'll call the police!'

She straightened, looked up, allowed her face to be seen in the light now emanating from the window.

'Fuck's sake. Becky! What are you doing here?' Amber's voice was softer now. If anything, concerned. 'Has something happened?'

'Kind of,' she said.

'Why aren't you in France?'

'Well, I was. I was at the launch. And it went wonderfully.'

'That's great. But—'

'But then I realised something. I realised I'd made a terrible mistake.'

'And you couldn't tell me, say, in a text message? Or call around in the morning? You had to tell me standing out there in the driving rain?'

'Is it raining? I didn't notice!' Becky said, putting on an American accent and doing a pretty good impression of Andie MacDowell.

Amber smiled. 'Idiot.'

'Guilty as charged.'

'So you're back? You're going to stay in London?'

She shook her head. 'Going to France wasn't the terrible mistake,' she clarified. 'You were right. I ought to take the opportunity. Try things out for a while. I'm lucky. I have the option.'

'OK? Don't take this the wrong way, Becky, but have you been drinking?'

Becky let out a bark of laughter. 'No! Only rainwater, and that's been accidental.'

Amber leaned on the window. 'You know I'm always glad to see you right? But you've totally lost me.'

Becky sighed, wiped a strand of hair from her eye, looked up again at her friend. 'I came here tonight because I realised I wanted to spend the rest of my life with someone. And I wanted that to start right now!' she said.

'Hang on, isn't that from *When Harry Met Sally?*'

Becky thought. 'Well, not a direct quote. But maybe,' she admitted. 'I knew it sounded good in my head.'

'But seriously, what are you saying? Because I love you, hon, you know that. But not... well, not romantically! Not like *that*.'

Becky laughed again, looking, no doubt, completely insane in the driving rain, soaked to the skin in the dark garden. 'I'm not propositioning you!' she said. 'At least, not romantically.'

'Then what do you mean?'

'I mean, I don't work without you, Amber. I never have. And just because we don't love each other like that, in a physical way, doesn't mean our love isn't important.'

'Of course.'

'I started thinking about it. I've had a lot of time to think over the past little while. Lots of dull plane journeys and quiet moments. And I realised. You're the most important relationship I've ever had. You're my missing piece.'

'Oh Becky.' Amber smiled at her fondly.

'Well, it's true!'

'Well, you're that person for me too. But I understand you've got to do this thing right now. I'm OK with it. I'll still be here for you.'

Becky shook her head. 'It's not enough.'

'What?'

'Amber. I'm asking you to come with me.'

'What? Are you insane?'

'Never been saner. Come with me! Help run the café for a bit! I've thought about it. I'm crap at accounts. You're an accounting genius. I need you, not just because you're my best friend but because you're a math whizz. We can work together, work things out together.'

Amber looked at her. 'Seriously?'

'Seriously.'

'It's not a pity offer is it, because...'

Becky shook her head, rat-tails flying, slapping at her skin. 'No! Of course not. I came because I realised that whatever's happening with Pascal is wonderful. But there's only one person I've ever truly loved. And it wasn't the person waiting for me in the café. It was the one here, watching me from her bedroom window.'

Amber rubbed a hand underneath her eye. 'You, Becky Thorne, are completely crazy. But I love you too.'

'And I don't see why I should have to give up the love of my life just because my life has changed.'

'You know I'll be OK, don't you? That I would love to spend time – have an adventure – with you. But I'm not... I don't *need* to. I'm... I'll figure it out,' Amber said.

'Definitely. Look. The only needy one here is me. Because I need you. For fuck's sake. You and me. We complete each other.' She looked up again, grimacing.

Amber was silent. Her face, serious. 'You think that could work?'

'Yes. Why not? Why not try at least?'

'Well, I *am* unemployed.'

A silence. Becky could feel water begin to pool in her shoes. She shivered. 'Any chance I could come in for a minute?'

'Oh God. Sorry. Yes, I'll open the door.' Amber began to turn from the window.

'No! Wait. You have to answer first. Are you coming? Are you going to try this crazy adventure with me?'

Amber looked at her and she looked back. Their eyes locked and they were there again. The playground, Amber helping Becky up after a fall. Doing homework together and swapping answers. The moment when Becky took the blame for a note that Amber had sent whizzing across the classroom. Weekends spent at each other's uni accommodation, drinking, dancing, putting the world to rights. When Amber moved in after Becky's dad had died. Becky rushing home when she heard Amber was sick. The thread that connected them was strong, reinforced over the years by their shared experiences. And in that moment, they both realised – no matter their future relationships – that there might never be a person who knew and loved them so well.

'Becky,' Amber said.

'Yes?' Becky looked up, still nervous despite Amber's grinning face that her friend might, after all, turn her down. That she might have to turn back and go to France without her found family. The silence between them was almost painful; then finally Amber leaned forward a little and called down into the wet garden.

'OK. Let's do it.'

'Really?'

'Yes. You had me at *bonjour*, Becky. You had me at *bonjour*.'

34

Cynthia walked into the smart London restaurant wearing her habitual dark trouser suit, bright blouse, steely expression. Her hair was, as always, perfect. She scanned the dining room for a moment until she saw Becky. If she was surprised that Amber was there too, she didn't show it.

'Hello, girls!' she said, sliding into her chair. 'Well, isn't this a lovely surprise! Amber, how are you feeling?'

'Yeah. Not too bad, thanks,' Amber replied. She glanced at Becky, whose expression looked rather frozen, her jaw, tense.

'So,' Cynthia said. 'I suspect I know what this is all about.' She gave a knowing smile that sent a chill down both their spines.

'You do?' Becky asked. It wouldn't be the first time that her mother had seen right through her. She'd wondered, on occasion, whether Cynthia might have some sort of psychic powers. But she'd never dare suggest it.

In the week since she'd returned to the UK, she and Amber had been planning, packing. They'd bought a car to make the trip in – opting to take it slowly rather than rushing. They'd visited the doctor and made sure everything was in order. They'd checked out their rights and applied for visas. Not everything was finalised, but they were almost ready to go.

Cynthia was their last hurdle.

'Of course. Lunch at my favourite restaurant? I expect we're talking flats, aren't we?' She looked at them both expectantly. 'Deposits?'

'Oh. No. Actually, I cancelled the reservation,' Becky admitted.

'Oh? Why's that?' Her mum's tone was suddenly sharper. 'Second thoughts?'

'Something like that.' Becky glanced at Amber, who was studying the menu intently. Under the table, her leg was pressed into her best friend's. Now and again, one would give the other a nudge of solidarity. They would get through this together.

Amber's mother hadn't been thrilled at the prospect of Amber leaving so soon to go to France with Becky. But Amber had promised to register with a GP as soon as she got to Vaudrelle, to call her every day. Promised she would fly back and visit, and encouraged her mother to look up flights for a visit to France herself. In the end, she'd acquiesced. 'Perhaps the change of scene will be good for you,' she'd admitted. 'But you know...'

'I know. You'll worry,' Amber had said fondly. 'But Mum, I'll be OK. I'll have Becky. And I'm only going to be an hour and a half's flight away.'

'You will visit me, won't you?'

'Just try to stop me!'

Cynthia's blessing, Becky suspected, would be a little harder to obtain.

'What it is, Mum,' Becky said hesitantly, 'is that I've decided to spend, uh, a little more time in France.'

Cynthia's eyes narrowed. 'A little more time? What, a week? Two?'

'Maybe... maybe a year or two?' Becky hated the way her statement came out as a question, as if she were still, at thirty, seeking her mum's permission.

'Rebecca! A year! Two!' Her mum was shaking her head rapidly. 'No. No. This is twaddle. You are not thinking straight, darling.'

'I am. I am thinking straight. I've done... well, so much thinking recently.' Becky tried to put her hand on her mother's arm, but her mum whipped it away as if she were inflicting a blow.

'Maud's got into your head. I knew she would! I knew it!' Two spots of colour appeared on Cynthia's cheeks. A vein on her temple began to swell. 'You can't listen to her, you can't. She's... a lovely lady but she doesn't know you. Doesn't know what's right for you!'

'It's not Maud. I mean, obviously she's the reason I went to France in the first place. But... this is all me, Mum. I promise.'

'So you're seriously telling me you think that owning a café in a tiny town somewhere irrelevant in France is going to make you happy? Come on now, Rebecca. This isn't you. This won't be what you're looking for, I can promise you.'

The waiter arrived, stood with his pad, sensed the mood and muttered, 'I'll give you a moment,' disappearing quickly across the restaurant to another table.

None of them moved.

'No,' Becky said. 'I don't think that owning a café is going to make me happy. I don't think I'm going to want to work my whole life as a barista.'

'Well, exactly. Darling, you are so much more than that. Listen, if you're worried about references after that... unfortunate incident at work, well! You needn't. I have several openings at my place. You could even take over the marketing department, with your skills. And I really need—'

'No, Mum.'

'I'm sorry?'

Becky shook her head. 'No, Mum. It's so nice of you to want to help me... like that. But my mind's made up. I'm not going to change it.' Her voice shook a little. 'I'm going to France. Setting off tomorrow, actually.'

'And what do you think of this, Amber?' Cynthia turned to Amber, eyes sharp. 'I hope you've tried to talk her out of it!'

Amber paled a little under the intensity of Cynthia's gaze. 'Actually,' she said quietly, 'I'm going with her.'

'I'm sorry, *what*?'

'I'm going to do the business stuff. The paperwork. Accounts,' Amber said.

Cynthia took a deep breath. 'Now, Rebecca, I see what this is. You two... you're a couple? Because if that's it, you really don't have to hide it.'

Becky laughed gently. 'No, Mum. It's not like that. We're friends. Best friends. Nothing romantic. We just – well, I've got the chance to work with my best friend. Do something together, figure things out together. Why not? It sounds brilliant to me.'

The waiter came back, looked at Cynthia's horrified expression, and walked away again.

Cynthia laid down her menu decisively. 'Rebecca,' she said. 'I want you to think long and hard about this. In two years' time, maybe three, you were going to end up running a division. Maybe you'd even be starting your own firm. I know things have been tough, physically, for you but trust me, this is temporary. You can't throw it all away on some... flight of fancy! What kind of future will you have out there?'

'I have absolutely no idea!'

'Well, clearly!'

'But that's the beauty of it, Mum, don't you see?'

'I'm sorry?'

'I don't know what's going to happen. Maybe I'll end up staying forever. Maybe I'll be back in advertising, working freelance or remotely. Maybe I'll take a course, start another sort of business. Become... well, work on my drawing. I don't know. And Mum, that's what I'm saying. I don't know, and that's OK.'

'I don't follow.'

'Mum,' she reached out a hand and this time her mother didn't move away. 'All my life I've had a plan. A fixed plan. Targets. Sometimes from school, society. And from you too. Five-year plans, ten-year plans. My life mapped out in bite-size chunks. And I know that's helped me get where I am today. I'm not ungrateful. I'm really not.'

Cynthia hmphed.

'But Mum, I had to step back. And when I did, it was the first time I'd ever had the time to... look at it all. I'm not sure if the life I've built makes me happy. If it's what I would have chosen myself. I have no idea. I've never taken the time to think. To look about me. To think about who I am. What I want.'

'Oh Rebecca. Are you sure you've thought this through?' said her mother, shaking her head. 'I know things are different with you millennials, or whatever you call yourselves, than they were in my day. All this self-examination, all these emotions. Being triggered. Your *feelings*. But it's very self-indulgent.'

'But Mum, why shouldn't I indulge myself? I've worked hard, I've got qualifications to fall back on. I've been given this... opportunity. At worst, even if I decide I want to come back... resume things, I won't have missed much. And it could be... it could be wonderful.'

'*What* could be?'

'Having absolutely no plan at all.'

Because when she was trying to decide whether to choose her life in London or her life in France, she'd realised what she wanted more than anything.

And it was absolutely nothing.

She didn't want to make a choice between two different lives. She didn't want to think about where her choices would lead her. She didn't want to sign on a dotted line, or shake on a deal, or commit herself to anything.

She wanted to have the space not to know.

And wanted that not to matter, if only for a little while.

'It sounds,' Cynthia said, 'as if you might be having a breakdown after all. Look, I wasn't going to say, but my friend knows a really good doctor. Fantastic chap. I could...'

'Mum. I'm OK. I'm just saying I want to try a few things. Take a break.'

'A break? Hogwash! You're thirty, you have to keep the momentum up if you want to achieve what you've set your sights on.'

'And what is it that I've set my sights on, Mother?'

'Rebecca! Don't cheek me. Success, of course. Self-sufficiency, independence.'

'I don't think I have.'

'Rubbish! Everyone wants to be successful, Rebecca.'

'Well, maybe. But Mum, I've been thinking... and I'm not 100 per cent sure what success actually means for me.'

'Of course you do... It's...'

'No, Mum. I know what you wanted. I can even see now what Maud wanted, when she made her move and changed her life. And you have done amazing things. Both of you. But I don't know what success looks like for *me*.'

'Now Rebecca, I think it's important that you don't do anything hasty...'

'I couldn't agree more! That's what I'm saying. I'm going to take a bit of time... get to know myself. And while I'm doing that, I'm going to do something worthwhile. Run the café, learn a little French, experience life.'

'You've already experienced life!'

'OK, experience *living*. I haven't lived, Mum. Not really. Haven't found out who I am.'

'Claptrap. You already know yourself, Rebecca. And if you don't, well, I can tell you exactly who you are. Who you could be with a little work.'

'Mum, you don't even seem to know my name. I'm Becky. Not Rebecca. And yes, I am good at marketing, advertising. But I don't know if it makes me happy. And working the way I've been working made me bad at everything else. Being a good friend. Even being a good daughter. I found my work niche, but lost everything else.'

'But you—'

'And I'm just not sure if that's a price I'm willing to pay.'

* * *

Over by the kitchen, their waiter was talking to his colleague, Steve. 'I'll give you ten pounds to wait that table for me,' he said.

Steve looked over. 'Those three? They look all right.'

'So you'll do it?'

'Go on then.'

As he walked over, clutching his pad, the original waiter leaned against the wall. Thank God for that.

35

Becky revved the engine of the soft-topped MG and she and Amber looked at each other. The day was warm, the top was rolled back and Amber had even put on sunglasses and a head-scarf. 'Well,' she said. 'This is all very Bridget Jones.'

They looked at each other and started to giggle. 'Can you actually believe we're doing this?'

'I know.'

After Becky had bought the car on a second-hand selling site five days ago, they'd mapped out a slow route through France, staying at B & Bs on the way before arriving at *La Petite Pause*. Pascal had agreed on the agenda – he had to leave for Paris a few days later, but would be back after a short break.

Becky put her hand on the gear stick, and Amber covered it with her own. 'Let's do this,' she said.

It had taken a while to settle into driving on the wrong side of the road when they'd exited the ferry three days ago but eventually, away from the main route, it felt easier, more natural. Once in a while, Amber would say 'Get over!' when another vehicle approached and she'd realised she was drifting left a little. But most of the time it was a comfortable ride.

'It really is beautiful here,' Amber said, watching the buildings and grassed areas and woodland and open skies play out through the passenger window. 'I could get used to this.'

'You'd better.' Becky reached over and gave Amber's knee a squeeze.

Now on the last leg of their journey, with just sixty kilometres to go, she could hardly wait to get to the café, to see Pascal again. To settle into her room and even take a bath in the odd, tiny bathtub. She couldn't wait to start this new life she'd chosen.

They switched on the radio, where a French song with a beautiful melody was playing. Occasionally, as they caught one or two words in the chorus, they tried to sing along. The result was hilarious rather than musical.

Then, as they passed a sign reading *'Vaudrelle 4 km'*, Becky suddenly signalled and turned right.

'Um, what are you doing?' Amber asked.

'Just a little side mission,' Becky said. 'You'll see.'

'And it's a secret because…?'

'Because I'm terrified it's all going to go wrong.'

Amber looked at her but didn't probe further. They passed through a small village with several stone farmhouse-like properties, a small bar in what had clearly once been a barn, and a little *boulangerie*. Then out again into the countryside. Eventually Becky signalled and turned into a car park near a sign that read *'Maison du Bonheur'*.

'Oh!' Amber said. 'I'm getting to meet Maud!'

'Yes, you are.'

'Hang on. Do I have to win her approval or something?'

Becky laughed. 'No. Not that she won't love you of course. But... well, it's something else.'

Out of the car, the sunlight on their skin, the smell of flowers and foliage in the air from the well-stocked front garden, they made their way to the entrance. Now familiar with the layout, Becky signed them in, then 'Come on,' she said, leading Amber to the room where Maud would likely be at this time of day.

And she was. Sitting in her habitual chair, with its garden view. Amber could see the back of Maud's head, her grey hair pulled into its usual bun. What she didn't expect to see was a man sitting on a wooden chair, pulled so closely it was almost touching Maud's cushioned one, holding a sheaf of papers.

'Oh!' she said, stopping so abruptly that Amber bumped into her.

'What is it?'

'It's Georges.'

'The mayor?'

'Yeah. I mean, I know he visits Maud but...' She looked over. Something seemed odd in his demeanour. He looked purposeful. Businesslike. He was showing her a document and talking earnestly.

As Becky debated whether to cut and run, Georges turned, saw her – a look of surprise flitting over his face before he quickly replaced it with a wide smile. He stood up. '*Madame Becky!*' he said warmly.

Maud turned her head a little and saw her too. Becky had no choice but to walk over there. Amber stayed back, uncertain of what to do.

'Hi,' Becky said, ignoring Georges's proffered hand and leaning in instead to hug Maud. The old lady's arms wrapped around her, pulling her close. She smelt of lilies; perhaps a new eau de toilette. 'Just thought I'd pop in on my way back to Vaudrelle.'

There was an awkward silence, none of them quite knowing what to say. In the end, it was Becky who broke it. 'So, Georges, what's all this? Are you writing a book or something?' She'd already seen enough of the layout on the paper to see that it was a legal document, but feigning ignorance made it easier to ask the question.

'This?' Georges flushed slightly and lifted the hand holding the papers as if he'd quite forgotten they were there. 'Oh, it is nothing.'

Maud looked at him. 'I don't think it needs to be a secret, Georges?'

Georges smiled awkwardly. 'Perhaps not.'

Maud looked at Becky. 'Georges here would like to buy the café for the *commune*,' she said. 'He wanted to see what I thought first, before contacting you.'

'Yes, forgive me.' Georges made a little bow. 'I did not realise you were going to come back.'

'Well, I did. So, I guess that's your answer!' Becky looked at the papers pointedly.

'*Oui*, I suppose. But I would like to speak to you, in any case.' He glanced at Maud who nodded.

'I want you to think carefully. Because it is wonderful that you want to take on Maud's legacy. My worry is that you are new here. You do not speak very much French. And perhaps you have already come to love Vaudrelle, but you do not know the place. You do not know what people need, maybe.'

'Pascal has already...'

'But Pascal is leaving, soon, *non*? His future is also not in the café.'

'Well, he's going to be back. True, he won't be working there any more, but—'

'And so you will be alone, perhaps with your English friend,' he nodded at Amber. 'But I worry that this will not work. That you will change your mind again and the village will suffer.'

Maud was looking at Becky. 'What do you think? I mean, I'm thrilled you want to run the place. But is it truly what you want? Because if it isn't, this is a chance to... make another choice.'

'I—' Becky began.

'With Maud,' Georges interrupted, 'she came to the village and knew nobody. And I am not sure of her level of French.'

'Awful,' Maud interjected.

Georges smiled. 'OK, so she too had the awful French,' he said. 'And I think the local people, when she opened the café, were not sure about it. But she since spent so many years here. And now people see her as part of the community. But it took a long time.'

Becky nodded. 'I understand, but I am hoping that won't be an issue,' she said. 'I'm going to get lessons, work hard. But there's something else.' She moved forward and crouched in front of Maud. 'Maud,' she said, 'the reason that I'm here is to ask you a question.'

Maud sat forward slightly. 'Do stand up though, won't you? My legs are aching just looking at you in that position.'

Becky laughed, moved her legs so that she was kneeling, which was admittedly slightly more comfortable. 'Maud,' she said. 'I want to look after the café. But I also want to look after *you.*'

'What do you mean?'

'Come back,' she said. 'We can make adjustments to the living space. We can convert the sitting room into a room for you, downstairs – I've got a little money saved and we can get a loan if we need to. We can hire some help, and Amber and I, we can help too.'

'But—'

'You said yourself that there's nothing wrong with your mind. And that's completely obvious,' Becky continued. 'And you were right, perhaps you are no longer well enough to run the café. But with the right support, you could live there, *be* there. Still be a part of it. And spend time with me too. We've lost more than twenty years. I don't want to lose any more.'

'Oh,' Georges said into the silence. 'But that would be wonderful—' Maud held up a finger and he stopped talking.

'My dear girl,' she said. 'What a wonderful offer. But I'm... things are not easy for me. I do need an embarrassing amount of help.'

'I know. And it's OK. I want to do it. We can get someone to help. But Maud, you belong in the café. That's what made it what it is. Not the decor, nor the fact that you can speak French. It's *you*.'

Maud's eyes filled. 'Oh Becky. That is such a kind offer. It really is. But I can't let you do that. You're young, you ought to be free. You don't want to be encumbered with an old woman like me.'

'I won't be encumbered, Maud! If anything, you will.'

'What do you mean?'

'I mean,' she said, leaning and lightly brushing a tear from Maud's cheek, 'I'm going to do my best to fill your shoes, but I can't do it without your help.'

'Really?' said Maud. 'You really need me?'

'Come home,' Becky said. 'Come home, Maud. Please.'

36

Becky rested the paintbrush in the tray and stood back to admire her work. Maud's new bedroom, a repurposing of the downstairs sitting room that Becky had only ever used once since coming, looked immaculate. Some more of her photographs were displayed in wooden frames on the walls, as well as some more ordinary photos found in albums. Maud as a child, Maud with her parents. Maud accepting her law degree. An unfathomably young Maud wearing a long floral dress, standing outside what was to become the café. Becky had added a picture of herself as a child with Maud, sent over by her mother, and a picture of them drinking from the new mugs in a recent café visit.

She'd hoped that Cynthia might come over, see the place for herself. But Mum wasn't ready yet. Still, she was softening, and Becky was convinced it wouldn't be long.

On the side table, Pascal had forced Becky to display her drawing of the café too, in a little ornate frame. She'd been embarrassed at the idea, but had eventually acquiesced. Now that it was *in situ*, she could see it had been the right decision.

Amber poked her head around the door. 'Do you guys want coffee?' she asked.

'Ah, do you mind?' Becky said.

They'd employed a young girl from the village to help in the café while they spent time organising Maud's living space and getting it just right. They'd had occupational therapists in to assess her needs, bought relevant equipment. But tried, too, to keep it looking like a room rather than a medical facility.

An arm wrapped around her waist and Pascal pulled her close. 'I think what you are doing is amazing,' he said.

She turned, kissed him lightly. 'Thank you. Although I meant what I said. It wouldn't be the same without Maud here too.'

It had taken six weeks to get everything ready, longer than she'd expected. But she'd learned not to be in such a hurry about it all. It had taken some time to organise the seemingly endless paperwork for Maud's release. And to get the rest of the place ready. With her blessing, Becky had repurposed Maud's upstairs bedroom for herself and Pascal had kept his room; although they usually spent nights together, it was important to have their own spaces for now. He travelled by train to Paris when needed, then squirrelled himself away to write his next book. 'Vaudrelle is perfect,' he'd told her. 'I don't think I could have written so well in Paris. It is too noisy!'

'I'm sure you could have.'

'Well, maybe. But there are other reasons to love Vaudrelle too.'

Amber, six weeks into her new life in France, was looking well too. Becky kept a watchful eye on her friend, but could easily see how relaxed she now was. They were learning to get there together – to slow down their pace and take time to live as well as work. And it was good.

Becky had invested in an easel and sketchbook and now spent some of her time drawing almost every day. So far, most of her drawings ended up as balled paper in the trash. But she knew she was improving. And, what amazed her, is that she felt she'd still be drawing even if she wasn't getting better at it. 'It's the journey, not the destination,' she'd remarked to Amber last night as they'd sat after closing time sipping red wine. 'Who said that?'

'Pretty sure it came from *Jerry Maguire*,' Amber had replied, rapidly looking it up on her phone. 'Oh. No. it was actually some sort of American philosopher called Ralph.'

They'd both laughed.

Romcom night was still on every Thursday and Pascal had sometimes joined them, back early from his Paris digs and seemingly as amused by watching them mouth the famous quotes in each film as he was by the films themselves. 'How many times have you watched this?' he'd asked, when they slipped a familiar DVD out of a rather battered case.

'Believe me, you don't want to know,' Becky had said.

'It's just our thing.' Amber had shrugged.

'I can think of worse addictions,' Pascal had replied, shaking his head and laughing.

Amber returned with the coffees and they made their way out of Maud's new space, shutting the door softly behind them.

In a few hours, Maud would arrive and they'd get her settled in, ready for her new adventure. And although she didn't have – or want – a fixed plan for her future, Becky had the sense that the next chapter of her life was going to be a happy one.

'Who are you writing to?' Pascal asked her as she started scrolling on her phone.

'Just sending some pictures to Mum,' she said with a wink.

He gave a small smile in return. Becky had been sending her

mother regular updates. Not revisiting old hurts but hopefully, by sharing her life, showing Cynthia that she still wanted her to be part of it. Once in a while she'd get a thumbs up or even a small heart in return. 'Your Mum is very set in her ways, in her thoughts,' Maud had said recently. 'It's a kind of self-protection, I think. But she'll come around, mark my words.'

'I hope it isn't stressing you out?' Pascal asked.

'No. It's just a few photos. I know I have to play the long game.'

'Are you sure? Just your eye... It was twitching again?'

She laughed. 'Actually, this time it was a proper wink.' She touched her eye, realising that somewhere over the last few weeks it must have stopped its habitual twitch.

The end of an era. Thank God.

A moment later, a message pinged on her phone:

MUM
Looks nice, well done.

BECKY
Come and see for yourself.

MUM
Maybe. Soon. x

It wasn't the end destination, but it was a step on the way. The cogs of life were turning again, and this time in the right direction.

'I think in the long term this might be great for Mum too. For me and Mum. Who we are to each other,' Becky said, showing Pascal the message. '"Problems are part of the journey to transformation."'

'That's a beautiful quote,' Pascal said. 'Is it Sartre?'

'No.'

Pascal frowned. 'I am sure I have heard this before. Perhaps the philosopher Camus?'

'Not... quite.' Becky's smile became so wide that it almost made her mouth ache.

Pascal looked at her. 'Becky. Is it the celebrated philosopher Jerry Maguire?'

She grinned. 'Maybe.'

The light had begun to fade by the time Maud's taxi pulled up outside. The three of them were in the now-closed café, sipping glasses of chilled, sparkling wine in anticipation of the celebration ahead.

'She's here!' Amber said, standing up.

They all went and helped Maud – Pascal carrying her bags, one of the girls on each side holding an arm. 'Don't make a fuss!' Maud said. 'One pair of extra hands is probably enough.'

'Ah, but we want to,' Becky said, and saw the older woman smile.

They stepped into the café and Maud stopped for a moment and breathed deeply. Becky, whose nose was now accustomed to the café's particular scent – coffee beans, polished wood, the ghost of this morning's now long consumed pastries, and the occasional whiff of fresh decor that still remained. But she knew that Maud was experiencing that sense of home that only comes when you're somewhere familiar – the type you experience with all the senses. And with your heart.

She squeezed her arm. 'Welcome home, Maud.'

Maud looked at her. 'This really does feel like home. And not just because I lived here for so long. But because of you. And you,' she added looking at Amber and Pascal. 'Home is more than bricks and mortar, it's where you are loved.' She put her arm around Becky properly.

'The perfect happy ending!' said Amber.

'Oh no. As the saying goes: "I don't believe in happily ever after. I believe in happy beginnings",' Maud said.

'Foucault?' asked Pascal.

'Not quite.'

'Oh no! Is it Jerry Maguire?'

'Jerry who?' Maud looked confused.

Pascal blushed. 'I am sorry, I think I have spent too much time with these two.' He grinned. 'Maud, what philosopher did you quote?'

'Pretty sure that was Cher,' Maud said firmly.

* * *

Passing outside the closed doors of the café, a couple on their evening walk paused. 'Can you hear laughing?' said one.

'*Oui*,' said the other. 'Perhaps it is a party.'

They shrugged. Smiled. And continued their walk.

* * *

MORE FROM GILLIAN HARVEY

Another book from Gillian Harvey, *Midnight in Paris*, is available to order now here:

https://mybook.to/MidnightParisBackAd

ACKNOWLEDGEMENTS

As always, I have so many people to thank. The wonderful team at Boldwood books who work so hard and support me brilliantly. In particular my editor, Isobel, who always makes me feel valued; Debra and Christina who help to polish the final draft; the publicity and marketing team, including Nia, Jenna, Wendy and Issy; and of course Caroline Ridding who always has her finger on the pulse!

My agent, Ger, who has become a great friend over the years. I truly appreciate your unwavering positivity through the ups and downs of this journey and am really excited about the future. Also, thanks for all the chocolate (brain fuel).

To the authors who have read and championed my work, the reviewers who participate in book tours, and those in the book community whose support of myself and other authors is truly invaluable.

To the online community of readers and bloggers who not only help my novels to find readers, but help me to find novels for my *own* reading pleasure – often ones I might have missed otherwise.

ABOUT THE AUTHOR

Gillian Harvey is an author and freelance writer who lives in Norfolk. Her novels, including the bestselling *A Year at the French Farmhouse* and *The Bordeaux Book Club* are often set in France, where she lived for 14 years.

Sign up to Gillian Harvey's mailing list for news, competitions and updates on future books.

Visit Gillian's website: www.gillianharvey.com

Follow Gillian on social media here:

- facebook.com/gharveyauthor
- x.com/GillPlusFive
- instagram.com/gillplusfive
- bookbub.com/profile/gillian-harvey

ALSO BY GILLIAN HARVEY

A Year at the French Farmhouse

One French Summer

A Month in Provence

The French Chateau Escape

The Bordeaux Book Club

The Riviera House Swap

The Little Provence Bookshop

Midnight in Paris

The Village Café in the Loire

BECOME A MEMBER OF

THE SHELF CARE CLUB

The home of Boldwood's book club reads.

Find uplifting reads, sunny escapes, cosy romances, family dramas and more!

Sign up to the newsletter
https://bit.ly/theshelfcareclub

Boldwood

Boldwood Books is an award-winning fiction publishing company seeking out the best stories from around the world.

Find out more at www.boldwoodbooks.com

Join our reader community for brilliant books, competitions and offers!

Follow us
@BoldwoodBooks
@TheBoldBookClub

Sign up to our weekly deals newsletter

https://bit.ly/BoldwoodBNewsletter

Printed in Dunstable, United Kingdom